Aleksander Granger

For Mary Elizabeth Jane West.

My first,
and possibly most terrifying, friend.

Author's Note

For parents notice: if you have so far succeeded in keeping your child's vocabulary clean, and wish to continue doing so, you may wish to go through and remove the occasional word with a permanent black marker.

Other than that, I can only say read on, and I hope you enjoy reading it as much as I enjoyed writing it, and more than I enjoyed editing it!

70689AD

70689AD

First published in 2007
By William van Niekerk

Copyrighted to William van Niekerk 2007.

Cover illustration by William van Niekerk,
All texts by Aleksander Granger.

ISBN: 978-0-9556779-1-5

Printed by Lulu

Watch out for other works by Aleksander Granger, coming soon to either lulu or somewhere else:
Murder, Myth and Tea – the sequel to 70689AD, expected to be completed by March 2008.
Seventeen – A collection of short stories concerning the survivors of the Wellsworth Massacre, some instalments available by 2008, complete collection to be compiled by June 2010.
Places – a book of landscapes as the first part of the home/here series of photographs, currently available from lulu.

About the Author:

Aleksander Granger is not my real name. My real name is mine, and thus the book is not allowed to have it. Nevertheless, I shall tell you a little bit about me before you finally commit yourself to reading this book.

I was born in late January in the year 1990. I don't specify a date because it took three – I was so determined, from the very start, to be right, that I decided to satisfy my mother's prediction and the doctor's prediction all at once, and so I did.

I met Mary Elizabeth Jane West after we moved to West Sussex in the early nineties. We had a turbulent relationship, which involved a combination of trying to kill each other and Mary coming back for me in the egg and spoon race when I was so completely fascinated by something that was behind me that I hadn't actually started the race until she had nearly finished. We also took up horse riding – I fell off immediately, and so her mother banned her from going again.

It wasn't long after that that my mother and father decided to move me and my older sister to Zambia, in south-central Africa. I resented this at first, but by the time they decided to bring me back to England, I had grown to like it enough to resent being moved back. I was determined not to be happy, and went through a very angry phase. My "artwork" gained me a reputation as a psychopath, which I am still trying to discard. This reputation was not helped by all the biting I had done in my primary school years, which I no longer remembered, but everyone else seemed to.

I was, foolishly, determined not to make friends, and so I managed in my own very special way to generally upset people enough for them to never want to talk to me again. This was difficult, and if it wasn't so ridiculous, I would be almost proud, as English people are uncannily friendly. In fact, the only way I found that really managed to put them off was to be unkind about the very country I had been saying was the absolute best in the world for the past eleven years. As they say, the grass is always greener on the other side, but in those first few months I was far too blind to realise that England was that other side, and now I have to pretend that I don't know that, between England and Zambia, England is the only one I could really live in.

And now I've said it.

Before you read:
These are the things I have always wanted to say, and so now I am going to. And there's nothing you can do about it.

There are some things in life you just can't change, but that doesn't mean you shouldn't try.

If you have never seen a steak on someone else's plate stand up and moo at you, just try to imagine how it feels.

The greatest loss for Britain occurred during the American Revolution, when someone decided to blame British injustice on an innocent shipload of tea.

Communism is a brilliant idea. People just don't fit it very well.

Tea and coffee need not be in competition with each other – drink tea throughout the day, with occasional coffee breaks.

Fur is murder. I feel very strongly about this. A certain large-bottomed Latin American singer turned actress whose name sounds like an American conserve continues to fail to grasp the fact that her bum will look big no matter how many animals' heads she puts on it.

I never get answers wrong. The question may be wrong, but the answer is not.

If you can't bear to know what you're eating, you probably shouldn't be eating it. This goes for artificial additives as much as it goes for pigs, cows, sheep and their various bits and pieces.

If you're talking to someone who doesn't understand your language, raising your voice isn't going to make them.

I am not opposed to any race of humans. I am opposed to many things some races do. I shall not go into these at length, but killing whales is plain wrong, it's pronounced tom-mar-toes, and seahorses are a really stupid cure for the common cold.

If you eat fish, chicken, shellfish or any other animal, you are not a vegetarian.

And finally, while chocolate is necessary to reduce all the problems of the world, only one thing can truly overcome them:

TEA

Aleksander Granger

70689AD

Chapter 1 - Begin

My name is Jack. The year is 70689, the year of our lord.

Does that surprise you, that we're still using the birth of Christ to name each year? Do you still use it, wherever you are, or is it just us "beasts" here on earth?

I suppose you expect us to have forgotten all about those days, don't you? But you're wrong. Not all of us that were there then are gone.

I know of at least three of us that were here before the ice – not that we expect you to know about the ice. Perhaps I should explain. The ice came because of your species, not mine. Those of you arrogant enough to call us monsters – just because we were different – were also fools enough to send a perfect planet into a deeper ice age. That's right, an ice age. Three quarters of the earth are covered in ice – lots of ice. Perhaps there are records of your beloved cities somewhere. They are all, apart from a few in the tropics, gone.

You're surprised by the ice age, I suppose? You don't have to answer that, just think about it the next time your king is defrosted. He was one of the ones responsible for this.

You don't know what they did? Surely you must have heard about how they left?

They moved the Earth. They moved it away from the sun just to get your ancestors away from the boiling planet they'd created – and froze it. They used Jupiter's gravity to move us about thirty kilometres away from sun – don't ask me how – and that did something that sent you all flying into space. Sixty-eight thousand, six hundred years ago today.

I suppose you wonder why I'm so bitter? You'll just have to work it out for yourself. When your people were still here, my name was Jack Parkinson Hanov Himmerden. Look me up. They'll probably refer to me as a murderer in their stories. They tend to forget who I was being paid by. She may even be your Queen. Alice Kerrow. Yes, you're surprised, aren't you? She's always been so sweet, kind – she would never have hired a werewolf and an immortal, would she?

Don't believe a second of it. If you really research her, you'll find out what she is. She's a witch, and her husband – you know him, of course – he's one of us.

Don't misunderstand me. Alice Kerrow isn't a bad person. No, she was one of those who tried to go against the laws against us. She even tried to get some of us to stow away on her ship – managed with her husband, I suppose.

But she did hire us. And it wasn't just her idea. The government was all over us; the media loved us – the only people who didn't were the murderers. Especially those who had seen what I did when I was younger. Not that they noticed any difference in my age – the only one who notices it is me, and that's only in rare moments, when I remember that two of my children have died of old age.

One of them's still alive, somewhere. My favourite, I can tell you now, because the other two can't hear me. I occasionally hear from her, though. She came to Emily's funeral, too. They both went to Sam's funeral, but that was when they both lived on earth.

She isn't like me, or like Kathleen. She's a normal human – not a civilian, true, otherwise she wouldn't be alive still. She is a member of an independent organisation on Europa, working to improve relationships between us and humans. Not likely to happen, but it's nice that someone's trying. Shows that we're not alone – still, she is my daughter, so it isn't much of a surprise that she wants a better atmosphere.

She has managed to surprise me – last time she came out of the ice, she managed to get a human ambassador from somewhere in the Andromeda galaxy to attempt to set up a life on Earth. You'll have heard of him. It'll be in all your history books, the bold ambassador slaughtered by the monsters down on earth. What they won't tell you is how many of us he shot before I killed him.

Yes, that's right. Your people refer to me as the leader. Earth, though, has no leader. Certainly not in a human form – any sort of human. Earth follows no-one, and nothing. We're just along for the ride.

Kathleen helps, in her way – although sometimes I feel that there would be far more of us alive if she had got on one of your ships when she could still have reasonably been normal. Kathleen is still very naïve in that way – black and white are very separate.

But she cannot help it – nor can I, if I'm to be truthful – any more than most of the others can help what they become at every full moon. We are still only young, even if we have been alive for longer than any of your people. It isn't just appearances that stopped maturing.

Kathleen has just walked in – dragging what was once someone behind her. In only one piece this time – an improvement.

"She's still breathing, Jack. Help me here."

"What did she do to deserve this?" The woman's abdomen has been torn open, and blood pours over the icy floor.

"Goodness knows," Kathleen shrugs. I cannot help but frown – Kathleen would not mutilate a young woman like this for no reason, "I didn't see who did it," she adds, and I let out a sigh of relief. Even after all these millennia, you can never be entirely sure around Kathleen.

"Why didn't you heal her out there?" I demand, as she touches the oozing wounds gingerly.

"I tried. Nothing happened," she snaps.

"Someone did this with silver," I am surprised to see the edge to the wound is still sharp – no wound with anything other than silver would stay like that for more than a few seconds.

"If it wasn't, it would be gone by now," Kathleen rolls her eyes, "find some bandages."

"We don't have any. No-one's needed one for a hundred years.

"The ambassador must have had some."

"Three thousand miles away."

"You can get it very quickly," she sighs, "stop pretending."

Magic feels wrong by now. It was condemned just as much by most of us as by the humans – if not more. Humans no longer burnt witches – in the south, some of our kind – my kind – still did. Nevertheless, magic is often necessary. I concentrated a moment, and handed Kathleen the bandages.

"Is that it?" she begins to wrap it around the young woman.

"I'll try for some more."

"No need, it's enough." Kathleen seals the end of the bandage down with a quiet mutter, and the woman's eyes flutter slightly.

"When was the last time something like this happened?" I demand.

"The ambassador," Kathleen shrugs.

"Something this brutal," I persist.

"Probably when you ate the ambassador," she confirms. I did eat the ambassador, but food is scarce here, and he had eaten roasted wolf a few nights earlier. In a clear symbol of his power.

"When was the last time someone attacked one of our kind like this?" I almost shout.

"Probably those radicals back in the sixty thousands," she answers eventually, as the woman groans.

Kathleen begins to stand up, but hesitates.

"Jack," she whispers, "Jack, her blood," she touches the crimson liquid and, standing up, holds it at her eye level. Considering that she's quite a lot shorter than me, it's not the easiest height for me to see something at.

"She's not one of yours," Kathleen says eventually, "There's no silver in her blood."

She wipes her finger on the floor and returns her attention to the woman.

"There is an old hospital somewhere below us," I suggest, "We could restart some of the life support machines."

"There's nothing medicine can do for her that I can't," Kathleen snaps.

"Your magic could have run out," I suggest, and she is clearly very annoyed by this suggestion.

"Magic doesn't run out, Jack." She puts her hand on the icy floor, and we both watch as it swiftly melts away beneath her fingers, leaving a small spinning globe of ice in midair.

"Who's going to break their ankle in that first?" I mutter. She freezes it over again before returning her attention to the woman.

You're probably a little confused by all this. After all, a first name is hardly enough to tell you who I am talking about, so it is most understandable that you would not understand.

A description could help, as I don't think anyone on Earth knows what her surname is. We could dig up her gravestone, but that would take years to find – and we can't move attached objects by magic, or ourselves. Not that far, at least. Her hair, the only thing that kept growing after we stopped getting older, is thick and black, and trails perhaps a metre behind her on the ground. It was longer until we cut it ten years ago – long enough to be woven into rugs, which we sold to the humans on Europa and Ganymede. We even had a few buyers from a village on Adrastea.

She has darker skin than most of us northern werewolves, and is just over five feet tall. She is one of three or four permanent inhabitants of Earth that aren't werewolves – and she is the only one of those who comes to the ceremonies. The images you have seen of her probably involved heads on sticks and lots of blood. Until about seventeen millennia ago, that was how Kathleen behaved. She was the one who killed those who committed capital crimes – yes, we have those too – and you might have thought she enjoyed it. I'm not entirely sure she didn't, but at the moment, she refuses to even attend an execution. These days, the only blood you'll see her covered in is that of those she heals, for she is a witch - like me, like almost a quarter of all of us here. Her particular powers lie in healing and divination.

So now you remember. The history books' prime example of a witch. No doubt you are even more nervous of me, now, with this evil immortal as my companion.

We, however, are not the ones you should be nervous of. The real evil is in your own world, believe me. Everything they tell you is seeded with lies – at least everything about the separate races. I don't know if your colony had anything to do with the destruction of the Estranchant people, but they had never harmed any of you. Some high up members of your species assumed they were a threat because they were surrounding the earth, and some had followed your colonies to wherever you settled.

They were what we once called angels. They used to speak to us – those that are left live in isolation from us now, and only come out to bring messages – which they will only deliver from a distance.

But I can't blame you for that – chances are, there are still thousands of them on your planet. You might even know some of them. All I can say is that that is just one example out of several thousand races your species suddenly developed an irrational fear of, and tried to destroy.

Back in the present, Kathleen is peering into the woman's wound, which she has uncovered, and is blinking frequently. Not the normal Kathleen.

"What now?" I demand. Kathleen grips my arm with a bloodied hand, and drags me closer.

"Look at this," she whispers, and pokes at what should be the woman's liver. Like a matt of hair, it parts as her finger touches it. For several minutes, we both stare in silence, and then, as a low humming fills the air, we both jump as if we've been stung.

"What's that noise?" I whisper, but we both know. An almost inaudible rumble, so very different from the helicopters that first spied on us in the years before people left. A quertinak.

"Hide her," Kathleen orders, "the human media."

"Propaganda," I hiss, hastily wrapping the bandages back around the woman's body, and, with no time to think of anything else, close her in the cupboard, and seal the door closed.

We walk outside, expecting the bullets that thunder down around us. They're silver, but of no real harm – Kathleen has closed a spell of safety over us, and even humans aren't heartless enough to kill the horses. The house, though, crumbles as the burning hot metal thuds into it. Ice wasn't built to withstand that many bullets.

And that, of course, was their intention. As the ice turns to steam, she is clearly visible to the cameras – as is the long trail of blood leading to the ruins of our home.

"Come down," Kathleen shouts, gathering her hair around her to seem more human, "we've found someone of yours."

They weren't expecting that. It is against our law to allow human reporters to touch the ground, and they know it. They forget, though, that Kathleen isn't a werewolf.

The cameras are switched off, and the quertinaks come down to the ground. Even now, I can't help feeling a little bit in awe of the design – if you've never seen one, they're oval shaped from below, and the tail end folds upwards and through the body of the plane. Except, of course, it doesn't go through.

The pointed tip of the tail unfolds to form a three-legged support, and a man and a woman come down the stairs.

"What do we do now, Karst?" the woman demands. I can't help sniggering – Karst is their version of Chris. What makes me laugh is that their laws state that they must use earthly names. They think it is. Just as they think that Karstophri is how Christopher is pronounced. These must be those legendary inhabitants of one of Alpha Centauri's seven planets. Idiots, the lot of them.

"I don't know, Phlorde," he whispers in return. That anyone could name their child that is very amusing to Kathleen and I. We believe that it once meant Maude.

"We found a woman," Kathleen calls, "she's in a bad way. Human, too. Can't heal her."

They hesitate on the step above the ice.

"We've got our cameras off," the man calls, "we're not trying to steal your souls or nothing."

"Whatever happened to the English language?" I hiss to Kathleen, "They've murdered it."

"Yeah, you can take your natural forms," the woman adds, "We won't shoot you."

I ignore her, and pick up the 'woman' that Kathleen found.

"You weren't expecting this reaction, were you?" Kathleen laughs, as they take that final, petrifying step onto the ground, "We won't hurt you."

"Camera, Karst," whispers Phlorde, and I bring the woman closer.

"You can't really use this against us," Kathleen almost seems surprised by their lack of morals, "this was never alive. Your audience will see that."

"Take her away," I tell them, crushing the camera and replacing it with the fibrous body. The man, if you can call him that, almost collapses under its weight – which is little more than twenty kilograms, a lot lighter than when Kathleen dragged it in, and is spread between both his arms.

"Now go," I growl as they just stand there watching the fibrous model falling apart.

"Go!" I snarl, and they seem rather surprised to be beset by a wolf where what looked human had been. I snarl again, and make a mock lunge, and they scurry away, back into the glowing warmth of their quertinak, which swiftly closes and, with the rest of the fleet, vanishes into the sky.

"Well, that was a pushover," Kathleen considers as I return to human form, and we walk towards the stables.

"That was just a tiny beginning," I guess, "why else would they have fifty ships?"

She glances up into the sky, and I follow her gaze. From between the summer clouds, small, dark grey ovals are emerging, and growing larger.

"Far more than fifty," she swallows. "I think, Jack –" she pauses, and I take the opportunity to say what we are both thinking.

"Furriers."

"I think so."

"Why would they be bringing reporters with them?" I can't help but wonder.

"I'm sure we'll find out soon enough," she sighs.

"That's easy for you to say," I snort, "you can't even feel pain. Some of us do."

"Jack, how many bullets shot at you have actually hit you? In the past sixty thousand years?"

I count – it isn't a large number. Somewhere in the region of seventeen. Out of quite possibly several million that were shot at me.

"That many?" she raises an eyebrow, and I glare. Kathleen has an unpleasant habit of reading your mind to find the answers to her questions. One of a few things I can't do.

"Let's just hope they don't land here," I say eventually, as we contemplate the ruins of our home, and the seven or eight neighbours beginning to gather around.

Neighbours, as always, are something of a nuisance. We would take perhaps two hours, at most, to rebuild the house on our own. However, our neighbours don't really know about magic – even if they wouldn't burn us, they might well become rather vicious, and there is an old silver mine not twenty miles to the east – a short run for one of them. And guns certainly aren't extinct – although whether anyone other than Kathleen or I knows that is another question.

"You'll need help," calls the oldest neighbour – a rather dull character who has recently taken a wife – poor girl's about twenty years younger than him. Still, he seems to love her, and she looks forward to having children. Whether they're his children or not, I can't say, but she is certainly three months pregnant.

"Can't hold the ceremony in a place like this," agrees a more likeable neighbour, Astrid. Nobody has surnames here – at least, none that they could recall without first looking up their name in the book of children, which will only be dug up at the naming of the next child.

I had forgotten the ceremony completely.

"Me too," Kathleen smiles understandingly.

"Stop that," I hiss, and I know she has withdrawn. Fortunately, Kathleen has grown out of her sulking age – which lasted until she was about six thousand years old, if you care to know.

Fortunately, there are still three days until the ceremony, and we should be able to get plenty of work done while everyone else is off howling at the moon.

Perhaps I should explain. There are three main types of werewolves – there are those who change every night – who are rare, it must be said. They tend to die out because they cannot have children. Then there are those who only change under the full moon – unlike those who change every night, there are two divisions here, those who are conscious, and those who aren't. Nowadays, most are conscious.

Then there is the third and smallest group. As far as I know, there have only been two or three of us (humanoid ones at least) in all of history. I am the only one alive today; that is certain. We only change when we want to, and that can be at any time of day. Of course, emotional peaks can cause a partial change, but that doesn't happen much. Over seventy thousand years, I have had plenty of time to learn to control my emotions. Well, most of the time.

Our neighbours were all of the second sort – those of the first sort haven't been seen in the north for at least a thousand years. In fact, I don't think that the people here are aware of the differences there can be within our kind.

On the first night of the full moon, it is one of these modern werewolves' strange traditions to be sociable – everyone in the "village" changes together. Our village extends about forty miles across the middle, so it can be quite a trek for those who live in the suburbs.

We are not in the suburbs, fortunately, so I didn't have to go far. In fact, it is only about two or three miles to the town hall, and then it all begins. I have to pretend to be normal while Kathleen pretends not to be using magic to restore the house – she can always say it must be a blessing in the foundations or something.

I stay with the pack for a few minutes, towards the back as they howl pointlessly at the moon. While they are all staring, I slip away quietly and return home

The village is much more peaceful on nights like this. Tomorrow night, when they all go off to hunt, there will be much more noise at this time – those who are disgusted by blood will be moaning, those who love fresh meat will be rushing about with their tails wagging – it can be very amusing to see the priest wagging his tail.

I return to human form as I come to the house, and see the horses milling about. The unicorns, clearly, had gone to join the hunt.

"Is that all the grass you could manage?" I ask Kathleen, avoiding some of her sickles as they whiz past. She has a nasty habit of using silver ones.

"There's some more over there," she points to the back of the house, and I look to see about thirty sickles whizzing through another patch of grass – which the horses have wisely evacuated.

"What are we going to tell them tomorrow?" I ask, glaring at the valuable glass of the window until it re-assembles itself and leaps into midair, waiting for the walls to be filled in around it.

"How do you do that?" she demands. Kathleen never has much luck with glass.

"By concentrating," I retort. Kathleen snorts, and snaps her fingers at the crumbled ice still covering the furniture, which swirls into the air and, faster than I've seen it work before, leaps into place, making the walls slowly spiral up to a rounded top.

"You forgot the door," I remind her.

"Can't we just use one of the windows?" she moans. I glare, and the ice where the door should be swirls into the air, and she reassembles it as a wind-cock on top of the building. One of the handiest things about temperatures that don't rise above minus ten degrees Celsius is that the ice-sculptures don't melt. Ever.

We do have a summer, I think – summer is the time of year when the temperatures reach their highest. By my judgement, the warmest we've had in recent years was when it reached minus nine (according to the thermometer I salvaged from the ambassadors helicopter – very primitive) in the summer of 70601. Most of the year, though, it stays at around minus thirty. Kathleen, lucky for her, can't feel the cold at all, although I can hardly complain of being sensitive to temperature.

Attempting, and failing, to outdo her, I rebuild the other seven windows at once. Because she is unable to make glass obey her, this seems to her to be a lot more impressive than it is. So she turns her attention to the stables.

"Nothing too fancy," I warn, as sculptures of angels appear in the air, and, nodding, she turns the angels into a soft white snow.

By the time we have finished rearranging – and in some cases improving the furniture, which certainly needs it after thirty years with very little repair, the howls of the hunters are beginning to come closer. Most of our furniture is salvaged from crashed spacecraft or given to us by our children – her son Billy married my daughter Cat when they were in their mid twenties. They visit every two hundred years or so – in between meetings.

We quickly clear away the grass, and as the other werewolves appear, some of them growling in confusion, we smile and lie that we just found it the same way as they did.

It's a lie we've told at least eighty times before, and so it comes off our tongues rather easily – despite not having been used in over a thousand years, it still works just as well. Even if it is in a slightly different accent.

The next two days pass uneventfully, apart from the witchdoctor digging in the snow around us, trying to protect us from the magic that is threatening to infringe on our lives. We let him, and summon a fire lizard to chase him away. He emigrates before the ceremony.

Finally, the day I've been dreading. There are three children in the village – out of about a hundred – that are coming of age today. By law it must be a Sunday, after prayers. With the witchdoctor gone, no one utters false curses as we all walk to church, threatening us with mumps or other pathetic human diseases if we do not forsake our God. I've seen his crucifix, though – and I've seen him going to confessions, begging for forgiveness for denouncing God. Foolish man.

I don't know why it is always me that has to be the conductor of the ceremony – I had hoped that that particular idea would die with the bishop, but sadly it didn't. They all know there's something different about me, but they think it makes me special. Blessed, perhaps, to live so long. And they seem to hope that will be passed on to their children. They never seem to remember that they were the children once, and they have aged.

Mass drags by slowly, very slowly, but I wish it would go even slower. All too soon, it is over, and we all leave the church, the three children slowly shedding layers of thick coats as old as I am as they come towards the moment that truly decides what they will be for the rest of their lives.

There are two girls and a boy – the boy's mother has never married, and, although he wouldn't know, there is a possibility that he is my son. If he is, I can only hope he does not follow in the footsteps of the last ten thousand, three hundred and sixty-seven children who have been asked to decide.

Kathleen slips away silently halfway to the house, and when we get there, she is sitting above the door. This door, and the room behind it, has stayed standing every time the humans have bombed it. It is almost sacred, even to me, perhaps just because of the number of years it has been here. That it is three thousand years younger than me seems irrelevant.

Kathleen, her hair falling over the door like a curtain, sits up as the first child – the boy – is pushed forwards, now clothed in nothing more than the Sunday best that is warm enough for a werewolf. He is almost going blue with cold.

It is easy enough to slip through the door as Kathleen gazes down sternly upon him, and I turn and watch through the thickest of the cracks in the wood. There is an unnatural silence hanging around the people, and their faces are all the same expressionless grey.

"Charles, son of Imogen," she says eventually, and I can hear her distaste as she pauses where she would normally say the father's name. She knows very well that he is quite possibly mine. I'm sure if I asked her, she could tell me his father's name, but she won't search that deep into his mind if I don't, "Are you ready to make your choice?"

He controls his shivering, and, as every child does, tries to look her in the face as he answers. I don't even have to look to know that his gaze drops instantly.

"I am," he whispers, ashamed. Almost every child answers in the same way, ashamed that they can't look someone they have known since the day they were born – who in all probability was present at their birth – straight in the eye and say the five simple words.

"How have you chosen?" she asks, more gently, almost pityingly. She already knows.

"I," he glances back over his shoulder for his mother's reassurance, and she puts a hand on his shoulder. Through the crack in the door I can see that his eyes flicker first to his mother's unscarred neck, and then towards the door. For all his sixteen years, he is as afraid as he would have been if this were his second, "I want to stay here. With my family."

Kathleen nods, and my heart sinks. Ten thousand, three hundred and sixty-eight.

I withdraw into the shadows as Kathleen hands his mother the knife. The knife – almost as old as this disgusting tradition – is to show the children that they still have a choice, and when they are out of sight of their parents, they can still decide their fate – it generally shows as a sudden, sharp pain between my ribs if they don't really want to go through with it.

"If you are sure of your choice," Kathleen says, the practised words rolling easily off her tongue, "you must prove it to us all."

If it was me there, I would throw the knife at someone. The same thought is going through his mind – unfortunately, though, the knife isn't silver. All he would gain would be a painful death.

He takes the knife from his mother, and walks slowly, petrified, towards the door.

The door creaks open, and, not shivering because of the cold anymore, he holds the knife out to me, as if he can see me. The door creaks shut below him, and I can see him jump.

"You don't have to do this," I remind him. It is not my place to say this, but his eyes are too similar to my own for me to not care.

He looks at me, petrified, but refusing to give in, and forces the words out of his mouth.

"You don't have to worry. You're not my father."

His mother told him to say that.

I have already said too much, so I wait for him to hold out his wrist, and hold it gently, knowing that he is still human. Easily broken.

He breathes in deeply as he feels his wrist lifted to my mouth. And, like almost every child that has been through here, he utters a shill scream – almost too shrill for his age – as my teeth cut into an artery. The blood sprays over my face for a split second, before my teeth pour the silver into his blood. His scream dies as the wrist heals over, and the cold starts to fade.

"Tell your mother not to lie to me," I mutter. Everybody knows she has no idea who is or isn't the father of her child. He nods, and hurries back out into the hall.

The next child doesn't shiver. She is a bright, rosy cheeked girl who has never really paid much attention to the temperature and, lucky creature, has never been ill. Her choice is given before Kathleen even asks for it, and she laughs as she takes the knife. As the sun is beginning to set, a few of the less controlled adults and older teenagers begin to filter outside.

"Aren't you going to bite me?" she demands, as the door closes behind her.

She bares her neck, where she knows the women get bitten.

"You might as well get on with it. I won't scream," she laughs. She, a fool in many ways, no matter how quick she is at school, knows almost nothing of pain. I say nothing, but try not to cut into her skin too fast. She screams as soon as the skin is stretched inwards, and by the noise she makes when my teeth reach into her flesh it sounds as if I'm murdering her.

As I begin to pull back, she thrusts the knife into my chest. Not expecting it, I hear the hiss of air as my lung empties itself the wrong way, and then heals.

"I don't mean," she gasps, touching the diminishing wound, "I don't mean I didn't want to stay…" she pushes the door open, sees her blood dripping off my face. She moans, and hurries into the crowd.

The last child smells strongly of Kathleen's magic, and there is something about her that marks her out from the rest of the crowd. I know her story – she had leukaemia. At her baptism, her leukaemia was miraculously cured – not a coincidence that Kathleen had helped to prepare the little girl for the ceremony. By the official village doctor's reckoning, she would have died within six months. That much magic will stay around her until the day she dies.

She stands up in front of Kathleen and I see what it was that was odd about her. She isn't afraid. Everyone here was afraid when this was their day – for as long as I can remember, they have always been afraid.

"I don't want to stay here," she says, as soon Kathleen has asked if she is ready to choose.

Everyone falls silent. At that moment, I could rush out and hug her, but the silence is almost too sacred. All that moves in the room in front of me is the curtain of hair as Kathleen stands up and drops to the ground.

"Jack," she says quietly, "clean yourself up and get out here."

I blink, and the blood falls away. For the satisfaction of the silent audience, I splash the basin of water next to the door with my hand as I pass.

"Polly," Kathleen says at last, and the girl looks at her through bright red hair, "come with us."

Polly scurries after her, avoiding her trailing hair, and I walk slowly behind as Kathleen leads her into the kitchen, and out into the open air.

It's snowing now – snow is a fine white dust that is frozen water. Only here, it is not just a dust. Great plates of snow float down from the sky like tiny parachutes, and the girl, clothed only in an ancient dress, shivers violently in the cold.

"Two hundred years, Jack," says Kathleen pulling open the door next to the oldest unicorn's stable. This door hasn't been opened in that long – nobody here may know about it. It's too dangerous. This door keeps our people safe from all the horrors of the past, and from central heating.

70689AD

A wave of heat rolls out, and Polly stops shivering.

"Do they still keep the line open?" I can't help but wondering, "With Cat asleep –"

"Cat isn't the only human who cares," Kathleen reminds me, putting her hand on the concrete floor.

Polly, who, while only being alive due to magic, has never actually seen it, gives a cry of surprise. Anyone else here would combine disgust with that cry, but there is no hint of that in her voice, only awe, as the floor, solid, hard-cured concrete, melts away beneath Kathleen's hand, and the trapdoor becomes visible.

"You first," Kathleen opens the lock with a touch of her finger, and Polly climbs inside.

We follow her in, and watch her staring around at the room. The walls are covered with plastic – something almost unknown to this world – and steel. Polly shies away from a light that blinks, and a screen suspended from the ceiling – about as thick as a sheet of paper – that crackles with static as we get closer to it. Kathleen touches it, and the static settles down. A frozen face appears before us, and Polly's eyes widen in surprise.

"It's a window," she exclaims, "Why's she frozen?" She taps on the screen with her fist, and peers behind it.

"But she isn't there!" she protests, recoiling and hiding behind Kathleen's hair.

"Wait, Polly," Kathleen puts her arm around the panicked mortal, and sits her down on the warm, carpeted floor – another thing that Polly has never seen before: fitted carpets. She traces it all the way to the edge of the room, and, bending down, puts her hand on a button.

"Jack!" Kathleen yelps, "The heating!"

I leap to the board, and deactivate the heater before it thaws the whole building.

"Hello?" calls a sleepy voice.

"Lena," Kathleen smiles at the face on the screen, "how are you?"

"Wonderful, thank you. What year is it?"

"70689," Kathleen replies. Lena blinks.

"Two hundred," Lena breathes, "that's a record. Where's the child?"

"Polly," Kathleen beckons, and I steer the confounded girl towards the screen.

"Polly," I tell her, "daughter of…"

"Sorry," Lena yawns, "we can't put her parents' names on her papers."

"What?"

"I've a message here, for you, for when you next called. The federation rulers have the names of every werewolf alive on earth. They check every child to make sure that they do not come from a werewolf family."

"Why would they care what we are called and who our parents are?" I demand.

"I have no idea," Lena yawns again, "you should ask your daughter. Polly, now, be a good girl and walk outside. Three steps straight out of the door, okay? And turn your face to the sky."

"I'll get her parents," Kathleen murmurs.

Her parents, though, refuse to come. She is no longer their daughter.

You sometimes get families like this. They want their children to do what they did, to make the same decisions they made. In a few years, they will come to accept that Polly is an individual. If she doesn't like any of the human worlds, she may well come back and change her mind. And then they'll disown her again for not sticking to her decisions.

So there are only two of us there to say goodbye to Polly – me and Kathleen. The girl shivers and stares up at the sky.

"Goodbye, Polly," Kathleen smiles, "We'll see you again, one day."

"Will we?" I murmur, as a beam of while light shines down through the night, and Polly vanishes.

"She's going to be frozen a few times, I reckon," Kathleen shrugs, as we make our way back to the screen.

"She's just outside," Lena stands up, and peers over the camera. Kathleen kicks me as she notices the direction of my gaze, "now, I've got leave to go on. They're just defrosting my family."

"Humans," I sigh as the screen fades into static and goes dead. "Why would they freeze an entire family?"

"Why were you looking at her breasts?" Kathleen comes straight out with it.

"Why shouldn't I be?"

"Because she's married." Kathleen hesitates, "Oh yes, some of the others were, too, weren't they?"

I hang my head, and then realise that I don't have to take this.

"I'm not the only one," I point out, "unless I'm very much mistaken, you've been with some married men."

Kathleen holds her head high, "that was twenty thousand years ago."

As we get back into the house, everyone is leaving. The last two or three to go are losing control as they walk out, and we can hear their howls receding into the distance.

Then another sound, quiet at first, but growing louder.

"Outside," Kathleen exclaims, "I think –"

As we step outside, the sound grows louder. It is an unusual sound, a long, low, wailing, but somehow beautiful, and we both realise what it is at once. It's so long since we heard their voices that we had forgotten they existed.

"I hadn't realised," Kathleen breathes, "I hadn't realised there were so many of them left."

"There weren't," I whisper, "They do have children. Why are they making that sound?"

It doesn't occur to us at first that they are bringing bad news. There is a sudden flurry of wings and one of them – a woman, robed in white, silky material – lands, and our attention is drawn away from the shimmering thousands in the sky.

"We are sorry that we only emerge now, in this time of sorrow," cries the angel, in a voice that echoes around the sky, but is almost silent at the same time.

"There is no sorrow," I frown.

"They have come for the fur," the angel shakes with sorrow, and possibly fear; "they come with many people."

"Here?" I stare at the angel, and wonder at her pale power. They are breathtaking every time I see them.

"They will kill all they find," she nods, "You must save all you can." And she vanishes.

"How you manage to talk to them, I do not know," sighs Kathleen, searching the sky with worried eyes, "where did they go?"

"They have as much reason to be afraid as our people do," I murmur, "the humans know how to kill them."

"How do we get the others back here?" Kathleen demands.

"We must chase them," I say eventually. There is no point calling them. When they hunt, all their concentration is on their prey – poor animal.

Kathleen nods, and turns to the stables. Two doors fall open, and a horse and a unicorn come out.

The horse is nearly as old as us – born around the year two thousand. The unicorn is much younger, but one of the finest we've raised. It's the same red as Polly's hair, the same red as the blood I spilt today.

Kathleen is on the unicorn before I can blink, and receding into the distance. She has gone east, and so I must go west. I won't be needing magic.

Lycanthropy – that is the name of the fine mare that has lived so long – launches off the ground, spreads black, leathery wings across the night sky, and plunges towards a distant howl.

But we are not the only ones in the sky. From up here, the northern lights outline the silhouettes of quertinaks zipping in all directions. A ring of them spreading out like hunters, cornering their prey.

There truly isn't much time.

I seize one wolf around the neck, and, with all the power she can muster, Lycanthropy heads home. Kathleen is also returning, with two young wolves – the children who chose today – in tow.

Then the howls stop, one by one, and are replaced by the hum of speeding quertinaks. We rush back out towards the wolves, but humans are too fast. All that is left of the people we shared this age with are bloody patches on the ground, and occasional skinned corpses.

Having searched all of the eastern and southern quarters of our territory, Lycanthropy and I fly back home, slowly, shamefully.

Kathleen has had more luck. Three wolves – one woman, two men, are standing outside our home.

"They had no skin," she tells me eventually, as we board the six in, "I was only just in time."

"I can only hope," I say, as we scan the now empty skies, "that there are some who weren't... satisfactory."

Kathleen nods, and we open the stables to let the horses out onto the snow. All of them.

"Take them south," I whisper in the ear of the oldest unicorn, Primal Fear, as we let the unicorns out as well.

There are not many animals here that were there when we were still children. Five, I would guess – Primal Fear, Lycanthropy, Werewolf – Lycanthropy's mother, Aphrodite, who was born in my sister's care, and, finally, the largest horse ever to live – Adrastea. Nobody expected her to live this long. Nobody knows why she has, but she still lives, and mothers yet another unicorn foal every year. She, though a horse, is the favourite of the only full unicorn we own.

Kathleen glances south, and throws up her hands. A ribbon of thick, green grass unrolls out of the air, with small rodents scurrying amongst the blades, and most of the horses and unicorns begin to follow this ribbon, the pure horses between the horse-wolves and the unicorns, supported by their warmth.

We only keep three animals with us. Lycanthropy, Adrastea, and the blood-red unicorn. Adrastea can carry anyone safely, for however far they need to go. The fact that she's pregnant is almost irrelevant.

We know where the furriers go, from previous encounters – although none of them so sudden and brutal. Normally, it is only one or two thugs that get caught, when out looking for a fight. They go to the far north, to Svalbard, and there, what we find is always different.

It won't take long to get there. The unicorn and Adrastea are both unnaturally fast animals, and Lycanthropy, in the sky, can keep up with anyone. This unicorn, Bloodloss, is the fastest we've had, with a top speed that we have estimated at around one hundred miles per hour. Adrastea, when galloping against a horse, couldn't go that fast, but is seems that no matter how fast Bloodloss goes, she keeps up.

It takes only two days to get to Svalbard, and we pass through many almost deserted villages on the way, occasionally seeing fearful eyes in the homes, clusters of human children around the one or two surviving werewolves, receiving bites to keep them from dying of cold or hunger.

Nobody talks to us, though. The redder the unicorn, by legend, the greater it appetite, and nobody is sure of how safe they are.

I see Svalbard first – no longer an island with sheer edges, now just a mountain in the snow.

"We're here," I call, as we come to a field of hovering quertinaks, and another vessel, shaped like three overlapping rings, presumably with similar qualities to quertinaks. Beyond the field, is a door in the side of the ice-mountain, with two human guards stationed outside.

"Halt," one of them cries out, and as Lycanthropy slowly lowers herself to the ground, I slip off her back and land beside Kathleen.

"What are they doing here," mutters the other, a woman, "what do werewolves want with furriers? Wolves aren't their prey. It says in the books, they don't eat…"

I glance at Kathleen, who frowns.

"Stop, or I'll shoot," warns the first, a man. He fires a round off at us instantly, and the two horses and I both cry out with pain.

"That was very stupid," Kathleen grips Adrastea's withers, and the bullets fall out of her knees. I yelp in pain as I stand up, and wave a hand at Lycanthropy. Kathleen looks concerned, but obeys, going to Lycanthropy before coming to stand behind me, her hand on my shoulder repairing the damage done by the silver.

"Who's in charge here?" I demand, as the female guard fidgets uncomfortably.

"What's it to you?" This time, the horses have the sense to bolt out of range, but I am not expecting such inhumane treatment. Three or four bullets thud into my chest, and I find myself knocked over by the force. Standing up again, hardly noticing when the pain stops and the bullets fall to the ground, I pull away from Kathleen and walk up to the man.

"That was a very stupid thing to do," I echo Kathleen, when I am close enough to lunge forwards and rip his throat out with my teeth, and the gun is pointed straight at my heart, "Now, if you would kindly tell me who is in charge, and where they are, or do I have to skin you alive?"

He doesn't understand.

"But the wolves aren't your concern," he frowns, "surely they're taking away your food…"

I narrow my eyes, and he falls unconscious to the ice.

"We're not going to get anywhere asking them," says Kathleen as I consider the woman, and get the feeling that she is considering me, "they know hardly anything of the operation."

"Dumb muscle," I say at last, and resist the temptation to bite the unconscious man. It will be dark soon, and he would become the victim of his employers then. Sadly, he is not the one who we came to punish.

"Why is there suddenly such an interest in fur?" Kathleen wonders as we walk away, "and why yours?"

"Humans are disgusting," I shrug, "there are probably surveys on the populations of other animals on earth. We're not cared about so much."

"And skin won't change back, either," Kathleen nods, "so no-one will know."

We sleep under the stars – we still need to sleep – while the horses and unicorn graze and, in the latter case, hunt, in the meadow that Kathleen provides. Sleep is good for a lot of things. Working out what to do about genocidal maniacs might well be one of them.

"Jack," Kathleen grips my hand, long before the moon sets, "Jack, they didn't kill them all."

I blink. Just because I don't die easily doesn't mean I enjoy being woken up.

"I know they didn't kill them all," I grumble, and push closer to the warmth of the horse breathing gently behind me.

"Jack, I don't mean the ones we found."

I sit up grumpily and glare at her.

"What on earth do you mean?"

"You saw the bodies. About ten we saw coming north. In your territory –"

"Yours too," I point out. Just because the rest of us occasionally display dog-like behaviour to establish our boundaries doesn't mean she doesn't live there too.

"The point is, I didn't see as many as two hundred in the Eastern quarter. In your territory, and with your nose, we should have seen or smelled at least fifty if we went in a straight line.

"We do hunt in packs." I remind her, unsure of what is coming next, and therefore uncomfortable.

"Not when you're attacked. Everyone knows the rules are to split up and run. And every body we saw was alone."

I hesitate. This could be leading somewhere.

"So you reckon they've taken them alive?"

"For experiments. Their laws – and ours, last time I read them – prohibit the use of humans in experiments."

"They prohibit the use of *Homo sapiens*. That includes us."

She rolls her eyes.

"You can't seriously have expected them to keep that up? Jack, nine hundred and ninety-nine million, nine hundred and ninety-nine thousand, nine hundred and ninety-nine in every billion despise your people. I shouldn't be surprised if you're classified below bacteria in their new genetic groupings."

"Humans listen to science. That's why they hate us. Because they can't explain us. They wouldn't have us reclassified without any evidence."

She doesn't even have to reply. I can see her thoughts as clearly as she can see mine. Propaganda is as alive as it has always been, and there is no more successful lie than that which people want to believe.

"We have to get inside their base," she decides eventually. "See what we can do."

This is unusual for Kathleen. She doesn't like coming into close contact with humans anymore. In fact, I think that the guards today were the first, other than our little family tree on Europa, since humans began to hate our kind.

"We can't," I sigh, "the guards won't be so pathetic next time."

"An interesting point," she agrees, "I wonder what will happen to those two we met yesterday?"

I stand up slowly, and stare up at the ice-mountain.

"They can't keep many people ignorant of the whole operation," I say at last, "they're probably at a different door, nothing more."

"We could always kidnap someone." This is probably one of the strangest things I have ever heard Kathleen say – aside from when she last asked me to cut her hair. It had been her pride and joy, and in dire situations, a handy length of rope. That was when it was at its longest – I was personally surprised that she wasn't always tripping over it, and have to say I still suspect she uses magic to control it.

"I should be saying that," I retort, when I recover from the shock. It may not have been true about forty-seven thousand, three hundred and forty years ago, but it is now. That has been my solution to most human-based problems in recent years.

Three hours later, we and our mounts are hidden in a miniature snowstorm. Mine, I am proud to inform you. I'm not always just following Kathleen. If the guards hadn't just been knocked out by Kathleen's magic, I'm fairly certain they would protest as the storm tears into the building.

"Damn," says Kathleen, as the snow settles about twenty metres down the corridor.

"It was a bit conspicuous," I console her. She nods, and glances around.

"Pity the guards are so disposable," she sighs. We had considered kidnapping the two that we met here today, but they were clones. They had a very limited lifespan anyway. Perhaps six months after maturation. Which is ridiculous, considering how long they were in the making – probably over ten years.

"I'm fairly sure those two yesterday weren't clones," Kathleen considers. I have to agree – anyone cloned to be a guard – particularly of something like this – doesn't ask questions, just shoots with silver.

"Someone's coming," I hiss as the air starts to hum.

"Darn computer," Kathleen glances at the minute little console on the wall, and the humming stops as it melts.

But I know it's too late. The clones won't have been the only guards on duty. Sure enough, a sudden pain in my back reminds me that I'm not immortal, as everything fades to black.

Annoyingly, I am now awake. I would guess that we have left Earth by now, and entered some other system – about three minutes ago, there was a terrific shaking, presumably what woke me up.

What is most annoying is that, despite the fact that I am awake, I have been frozen. And right now – due to some inhumane dose of a silver-based tranquilliser – I'm not able to summon up even a bit of warmth, so I just relax and ignore the cold. I can see there are other shapes in the ice, some halfway between human and wolf, and I know that Kathleen was right.

I'm beginning to feel a little better, and I think I'll risk a little magic.

The ice around me vanishes with a hiss, and I watch a tunnel of it melt away before me. It's supposed to be taking me to Kathleen, but it seems – judging by the rush of air, to be leading me out of the ice.

I begin to walk down the tunnel, just to check, and knock my head on something solid. Upon closer inspection, it proves to be eight – no, four, red legs, with black hooves at the ends, all tied together.

"Humans," I spit, and the ice crumbles to let the unicorn out. He shakes his head angrily, and digs his claws into the ice as he starts to slip away.

Perhaps I should explain a bit about unicorns. I'm sure you'll have heard of them, but, like us, humans don't seem to like them much. So I wouldn't be surprised if you had only heard of the creamy white unicorns that come out and dance in the dusk, and carry the good girls where they want to go.

I'm sorry to kill your fairy-tale, but that's about as likely as a chimera surviving in Athens.

The only true things you're likely to have heard about them are that they're very long lived, and related to horses. They are very rarely creamy white. They tend to be a shade of red – although we do have a few blue specimens, and one black. They eat meat, and the reason they were considered a myth until post World War Three was that they tended to eat most of people who saw them. Then someone who got eaten had a camera, and after that there was a whole expedition to Peru to find them, which ended up being more dinner than discovery, as far as these ancient predators were concerned.

Unicorns aren't magical. That might seem surprising to you, but it's true. Unicorns do live forever, and are most common in a space out of space (purgatory). But they have no magical powers. A wonderful array of senses, true, enough to find one soul in amongst trillions, and a strange ability to understand humans, but they are no more magic than your average neutron bomb. Deadly, but not magical.

One of the most disgusting lies is that they are dainty animals. They aren't – their blood is as thick and red as ours, their bodies are, if anything, sturdier than horses, and their hooves – well, their hooves aren't exactly one-toed. They have five thick, retractable claws with razor-sharp edges which can interlock and become like a horse's hoof – without the frog, though. They need bigger hearts to compensate for this.

Finally, their horn. It is not a short, pretty, spiral. It is a lethal eight-foot – more in adults over a thousand years old, less in juveniles – weapon. It has back-barbed spines which will not come out without gutting their victim, and is curved slightly upwards towards the tip – very useful when they want to puncture a brain.

Unicorns have one natural predator, which hasn't been seen on earth for millions of years. It is a spirit-monster, and even it does not succeed in killing the unicorn permanently. Not even in the same limited way that humans can.

So know you know how it has claws, and why it isn't going to fit with the fairy tale.

The rope turns to a fine black dust that quickly vanishes into the air.

We reach the edge of the ice, and I find myself holding back. There is no barrier, but something tells me that something is wrong. I can see Kathleen, though, and the horses. They aren't in ice, but do seem to be held in some sort of suspended animation.

I can get to them.

I close my eyes, and step out of the ice. At first, nothing happens. I breathe a sigh of relief as the unicorn follows, and smash the glass window in between me and Kathleen.

She blinks, and yawns.

"I was dreaming," she mutters, and steps gingerly over the shattered glass.

She looks at me, oddly, an expression of worry on her face. The unicorn snorts uneasily, and shakes its skin.

"You look unwell," she frowns, and the unicorn, shaking a fine whitish dust from its coat, sniffs me.

I glance at my reflection in the glass below our feet, and, before Adrastea's massive black foot crumbles the reflection to nothing, I see a sight that I have never seen before, and not one that I had ever wanted to see.

My skin is flaking off, crumbling away like dust. My teeth fall out of my mouth, becoming nothing before they even hit the ground. I feel myself falling, and as I fall, everything that is me disintegrates, only moments too late for me to be spared the sounding of the alarm.

You can rest insecure in the knowledge that I am not dead. I do have a soul. If I were dead, I would be seeing the dim lights of purgatory – probably one of the lower levels. As it is, I see nothing. Now, in my mind, that is confirmation that I am not dead.

I also suspect that the dust has re-gathered swiftly.

Well, I am alive. I can't move, and I haven't a clue where I am. My heart isn't beating, my innards aren't moving, and I can't see anything.

I can't even do magic. I'm actually rather surprised that I am able to think – it seems that every other part of me is inactive, so I can hardly see why my brain isn't.

I haven't a clue what's happened to Kathleen. I hope, but seriously doubt, that she is nearby – in a situation better than mine.

I hear a crack, and something has plunged through my skin. Not a very big thing, I would guess, but enough to hurt.

Probably a scalpel. Ah well. No harm done.

But I don't feel my skin closing over, even if I haven't felt the bitter touch of silver. Instead, it all seems to be crumbling away – air is stinging what should be wounds.

"Extraordinary," someone whispers, and my senses begin to return to me – I can hear the low rumble of voices, and the metallic tinkling of laboratory tools.

"Their guts are so normal," comments a female voice with an accent that could be American, but could be Scottish.

"Perfectly preserved," says another, similar voice, "amazing."

"Yes," says the first, "most singular for the waste to regroup like this."

I feel a little life returning to my flesh other than my nerves, and force my eyes open.

The ceiling is a very boring colour. A sort of vomit-brown. Somewhere between beige and wine. The humans don't seem to notice that my eyes are open, and I don't really feel like alerting them to the fact. It is not a large room – perhaps twenty feet by fifteen – and I am on a silver table. Not made of silver, but probably plated in it. There are three people standing around me in red coats. They don't show up blood so well, I'm told.

One of the people is poking around in my chest. It isn't a pleasant feeling, but what comes next is worse.

"The heart," he proclaims, holding up a chunk of shrivelled, dried meat. I had always imagined my heart to be a little bigger than that.

"Why's it so small?" the woman asks, as the man puts it to one side.

"Remember, they have been travelling through space unprotected," the man who took my heart out reminds her, "every second is amplified millions of times when that happens. This body has been dead millions of years."

Space travel has always confused me. I think – but I wouldn't swear by it – that the way quertinaks and the like move causes time to be stretched out exponentially. That's why they have giant freezers on board – so that although they lose two thousand years to the second, they are unaffected.

I'm just about to sit up, when he pulls something else out – from lower in my chest this time.

"What is that?" the younger male – who up till now has been almost silent – stares incredulously.

It's a small snake. To cut a long story short, I was possessed – a very long time ago – by the spirit of a monster the Aztecs worshipped. A creature made entirely of snakes (although the Aztecs prayed to a female version who had bits of jaguar in her, too). If I ever find it useful, I am able to take the form again. Clearly, there has been a trace of it in me the whole time.

The snake is a coral snake. Being human, you may not have come across one of these. Well, in case you ever do, they're highly poisonous. Unless you want to die, don't prod one.

It bites the man, who drops it, and as it falls back into my chest cavity, I sit up.

They scream. Not surprising. I would too if I could see me, I should think.

As they huddle to the other corner of the room, I consider my autopsy.

There is a dried out crust of skin on the table. Unpleasant.

I snarl at the dissectors, and they shriek painfully.

"What's happened?" I demand, pointing one dry, cracking finger at them as blood starts to ooze through my arteries again.

They seem to be too petrified to speak, so I sit down on the table as I shove my shrivelled little heart back into my chest.

"I asked you a question," I remind them, watching as the desiccated lump of muscle squeezes between two empty lungs, and disappears behind healing flesh and bone.

"Start by telling me what you were doing with me," I sigh eventually.

The young man seems to recover, and announces:

"As a freak of science, you are not permitted to speak," he bursts out, "you are to be dissected and stored for future reference."

He isn't joking. Well, Kathleen was right. They have reclassified us. Freaks of science.

He seems to grow in confidence, and approaches with what I would guess to be silver-laden morphine. He tries to stab it into my arm – but, unfortunately for him, he expects me to abide by their laws.

I kick out with one foot, and as he falls forwards, I catch him by the neck, with my teeth.

I regret it instantly. He tastes of salt and grease – and his blood is the most disgusting that I have ever been unfortunate enough to taste. It leaves a bitter aftertaste in my mouth, and a slimy feeling on my tongue.

"Werewolf," stammers the older man. The woman has fled – locking the door behind her. Sensible creature.

"I've been dead a few million years," I remind the man, "I've missed a lot of meals."

He tries to flee, and I watch him struggling with a ventilation shaft as the younger man, already healed, collapses to the floor.

Not waiting for my skin to fully reappear, I walk to the door, and step through. See how long it is before they realise that the werewolf in there isn't the one they left there.

I am annoyed to find that we're still in the ship – quertinak, when my memory recovers – and these sloppy humans haven't tidied up the mess I left.

In real time – not travelling time – it can only be about six days since I turned to dust, and I can still smell Kathleen.

Pricking my ears, I can even hear her pulse.

"Kathleen," I call. I cast my gaze in the direction of her pulse, and hear her faint breathing. Typical Kathleen. Asleep while I'm being dissected.

Moving towards the sounds, I can see nothing. All that's there is a thin screen – perhaps two inches thick. I step around it, and see nothing.

The sound is behind me, now. I turn to the screen, and consider it. It is about six metres long. Three high, and, something I hadn't seen before, it has a metal door built into it.

It's locked, but that means nothing to me. The door swings open, and I find a room very different from the one I should be seeing.

Of course. Above total utilisation of space. Big human thing.

"What took you so long?" Kathleen demands, rolling off a shelf.

"I was being dissected. Sorry."

The horses snort, as if not believing me, as they clatter out of the shadows.

"So where are we?" I ask, as Kathleen brushes dust of her shirt.

"A quarantining moon," Kathleen peers out of a window, "The stairs are there."

"They won't have left the door unlocked."

"Jack, humans are stupid. Never expect any sense from them. A little blonde woman just ran past and went out. Too much of a panic to switch it off."

"You're one to call her little," I point out, as we begin the long walk down the stairs.

"I was bored," she shrugs, "can you blame me?"

I never realised Kathleen's touchiness about her height went as far as shrinking people. Still, she's had a few million years with only herself as company, so what can I expect?

"It was very dull."

"Stop that."

"I was only awake a little while," she admits, "a hundred years or so. We slept most of the time."

"Kathleen, you reek of lies." She doesn't, actually, but I can now see the lining of the door. This is one of the areas where the space moving past has no effect.

"Know it all."

The steps beneath the door have been torn off – presumably in an attempt to contain me – but a ten foot drop is no deterrent, not even to Adrastea, the most delicate of us all.

"Where's the unicorn?" I ask eventually. Kathleen shrugs.

"Followed the blonde woman out."

She glances back beneath the quertinak, and we see the remains. The unicorn glances up from its bloody feast, and we both shudder.

"Ow," Kathleen comments.

"So what now?" I ask, "Do we fly the quertinak back to earth?"

"No unauthorised take-off," Kathleen informs me, "the moon is man-made. A coded magnet, I think."

"How can you code a magnet?"

"An electromagnet, then. Lots of them.

"We could destroy them."

"If we had a hundred years. They're at the centre of the moon."

I glance at the ground – a dull, concrete grey. You'd think that after all this time someone would have come up with a more interesting – and less painful – floor, but no. You humans never do move forwards, really, do you? Only catch up with the place you were before your last laws.

"We have a lot longer than that," I remind her.

"The people in the ice don't," she glances around, "they'll be here, soon. The guards."

"They can't do anything, really."

"Jack, you can't really believe that there isn't silver in their guns?"

She has a point. While silver means nothing to her or Bloodloss, it makes quite a difference to Lycanthropy and me. And the real problem, I see as the floor starts to glow, is that there's nowhere to hide.

"There's everywhere to run," Kathleen is reading my mind again. I let it pass, and nod.

"They're watching us," I point out, "they'll find us soon. And when they do, it's not just me they'll want to dissect."

"We can't leave the others." She stares at me.

"I didn't think it."

Unfortunately, that seems to be the only thing we can do. After a few moments of thoughts, Kathleen turns to the quertinak and whispers something. It promptly vanishes.

"We have to leave," she talks as though agreeing with me, and as if I have the faintest clue what to do about that.

"How?"

"I have no way of doing it. You might."

I consider it. Her face drops, and I realise my smile isn't exactly as concealed as I hoped.

"What are you thinking?" she demands.

"The atmosphere here is very thin," I reply.

"That's not what you're thinking."

"They can't be posted up here. They're in there," I point at the ground, "and the authorities will have vehicles in there."

"So we steal one? And you don't think they'll notice two horses and a Unicorn trampling around?"

"Oh, the whole point is that they notice you. They're going to take you captive."

"And not you?"

"Remember, back in the twenty-first century, when I became a mass of snakes?"

"And in the twenty-third, you did it again. Yes, I remember."

"I think I could do that again."

She stares at me.

"How does that help?"

I don't answer. There is a humming noise, and some sort of shuttle zooms out of the ground. Kathleen blinks, and it crumbles to ash.

But a second and third appear, and, before she can react, she is frozen in a beam of blue light.

A second light catches the unicorn as it attempts to abandon its meal, and a third Adrastea. I hold a finger to my lips, and concentrate.

The change is almost instantaneous. In less than a second, I am a man made entirely of snakes – and, by relaxing, I become nothing but a tangled ball of snakes.

I quickly slither apart, and scatter.

A snake – even the two giant boas whose heads formed mine – is rather less conspicuous than a human or a horse, so as men in suits and respirators come out of the ship, it is only four beings they collect – and almost a hundred go free. All the pieces that make up me.

It does not take long to find cracks in the ground – a snake's belly is far more sensitive than a human's eyes. Down I go, in my many pieces – although some of me only find their way down about an hour later, on the other side of the moon.

The coral snake that holds the entire structure together is one of the first through, and I can feel the heat of people moving busily below – tourists zooming between shops, buying last curios of the planet this moon orbits. The heat generated by all their vehicles is phenomenal, and the smell of sulphur dioxide is thick in the air.

I avoid the centre of the paths, but soon find myself being picked up by a small child. I hiss, and show off my teeth. He drops me, and returns to his mother's side with a wail.

As a coral snake, I don't really have the most inconspicuous colouring, and it isn't long before more people notice me. As soon as someone realises that the animal they are all closing in on is a snake, there is panic. How did one get here? Are there others?

All over their miniature city, I find myself being spotted, and most of me slip quickly into the drains. The cobras that make up the bulk of my mass vanish a little slower, and the boas and the coral snake are caught out in the open.

A hand reaches out for me. I lung out to bite it – and I'm caught. The coral snake, at least. One of the boas, not far from the coral snake, shoots towards me, but I get to the coral snake too slowly – some machine has already "disposed" of it down a drain.

Human rubbish is disgusting, and the human rubbish and excrement of two millenniums is worse. While the snake in me wants to look for rats, and forget about the world that dumped me here, I feel like retching. Midduns under trees are so much less offensive.

I can see a dripping drain, and slip into it, feeling a sharp stab of pain as someone shoots off the tail of one of the boas. I wrap it around him, until he is as cold as the handle of his laser gun.

And then, I see Kathleen. One of the boas – not the killer – has been caught and rolls a few times as it is thrown into the police vehicle.

The vehicle moves off swiftly, and I smile to myself. I can see the vehicle passing by from the other boa.

I gather in a massive vat of drinking water – ignoring the smell of chlorine – and start to head towards the free boa.

The people around it don't know what's hit them. One moment, they are cornering a twenty-foot snake, the next, scores of others are seeping out of the drains, and gathering around the cornered snake.

I stand, and all the parts of me hiss as one at the crowds – who shriek and flee into the shops.

I stare around, and see the vehicle. Staring around from the strangely lethargic body of the other boa, I notice something odd – all the others are slumped on the floor, scarcely even breathing. I begin to find it harder to breathe with the body of the boa, and its vision fades to black.

Wonderful. Until it wakes up, I'm a man of snakes.

But now the rest of me can see the vehicle, and the two men in the front. A small black mamba – one of my toes – lunges forwards, and whisks through a badly closed door.

Two bites, and they collapse in agony. Snakes are something mankind hasn't seen anywhere but earth – they never took them with them. They left them to die on earth with us, and as a result, there is even less tolerance to their poison than there used to be.

They are both dead before they even see the rest of me.

Kathleen, the equines and the boa are all lying unconscious on the floor as I step into the vehicle, and goodness knows how I am going to get this craft into space.

I don't have long to think about it – a siren begins wailing, and, thinking that that they are chasing us, I start pressing buttons. As the vehicle begins to move off, I hear word blared out on speakers:

"Red Alert, Red Alert. A dangerous creature has escaped from lab conditions. This is not a drill. Please proceed to the nearest shelter. Do not attempt to make contact with the creature. This is not a drill." It drones on as the vehicle gains speed, "scientists are taking all necessary precautions to prevent further escapes."

I don't even have to think about what these precautions are – the floor opens, and as we shoot into space, the empty space where Kathleen hid the quertinak explodes into a giant green fireball.

I think I'm passing out, or perhaps the craft's going too fast for me to see anything, but now, we're hurtling through an atmosphere, slowing down as the vehicle tries not to fall to pieces.

And we crash.

The craft shatters, and I tumble onto a burning surface. My skin hisses in the heat, and I stand up unsteadily.

The human sedative must have worn off, because I'm whole again, as close to human as I can be, and Kathleen is getting to her feet, some fifty yards away.

I look around for the horses, and see only Lycanthropy, standing with an expression of unease in the opposite direction to Kathleen.

And then I see something that just increases my complete lack of understanding of Adrastea.

She is broken on the white earth, a dirty red smear on the land, only recognisable by the remains of a black pelt, but as we move towards these remains, they seem to stir, and shattered crumbs of bone slowly begin to build themselves up into a skeleton, hardly visible before blood, muscle and fat spread over it, covered within moments by the fur.

If seventy thousand years hadn't already proved it, I would say there was something odd about that horse.

As for the unicorn, it takes longer to appear. In fact, we are all beginning to see straight by the time it trots over what could well be a hill with a large, ratlike creature in its mouth.

"This must be a human colony," I say as it swallows the last of the unfortunate creature.

"Must be," Kathleen agrees, "how did we get here?"

"I tried to fly."

I hold up the nearest piece of wreckage – a small light bulb.

Nobody needs to say anything more on that subject.

"We have to get back to that moon," is the next thing Kathleen says, as we all begin to walk towards the unicorn's hill.

"Kathleen," I begin, but I can't say it. Can I even be sure of what I saw? Perhaps I had already passed out. Perhaps it didn't kill them – it might have just been a nice, normal fireball.

"What?" she prompts.

"Nothing."

I feel sick straight away, but I cannot undo what I have said. I cannot ruin the relief we both feel as we see the massive expanse of water on the other side of the hill.

"Water," Kathleen screams – tearing at full speed down the hill, across the white sand and into the rippling water.

I follow at a more leisurely pace. I haven't drunk anything in so long that I hardly feel the thirst any more. It does help that the animals are hanging back uneasily.

Kathleen yelps, and explodes from the water to tumble to a halt at my feet. She looks up at me, and then back at the water.

"Sharks, probably," I inform her. We were both surprised when humans took shark embryos with them – but then, it was a delicacy, which was getting increasingly popular, to eat sharks' brains. I never really understood why people liked it.

"It wasn't a shark," she allows me a fleeting glimpse of her torn side as the blood is pulled back inside.

"What was it?"

"Nothing I've seen before."

Nothing like it ever reached our shores, when we lived near the pack ice, that's certain. The cuts were all wrong to be anything I'd seen – they weren't like knives had stuck in, it was more like a stamp had been shoved through the flesh.

"It wasn't even that big," Kathleen considers, "I thought it was a dog or something at first, but…" she trails off, and we watch as the thing crawls from the water.

It is vaguely dog shaped, but only at a glance. A second glance shows its fifth leg – a blunt-toed, coiled arm, perhaps three times the length of the animal itself, and the strange nature of its skin.

Or perhaps the strange absence better describes it. It's not an oozing lump of bone and muscle, but there is clearly no skin – there are no lips, no eyelids, no ears, no webs, just a purplish-blue net of blood vessels surrounding the body like a fitted sack.

It seems quite concerned by our presence, and I am allowed a closer look at the fifth limb. It is thicker than the others, and doesn't contain the usual number of bones before the wrist – at least sixteen joints are curled up around the central fist, which shoots out and snaps closed around my neck.

There is a quick spurt of blood as I feel it squash my jugular veins, and my teeth stab into the nearest of its veins. It withdraws with a yelp, and vanishes into the water.

I stop bleeding almost instantly, and I glare after the creature for the insult.

Perhaps you deserve an explanation at this point. Werewolves, unicorns and immortals, along with various other groups that don't officially exist, can be done no lasting harm except by certain elements, and some can't be permanently harmed at all – at least, not without divine intervention. In a battle or a fight, you will rarely see any werewolf blood spilled; even to be drawn back into the body, without the use of silver, because the creature will be expecting the attack. Immortals have the same qualities – although quite often, one will not be able to temporarily harm even a sleeping immortal.

So there is a reason behind me sometimes being unaffected, and sometimes bleeding for a few seconds. It isn't completely random. Unlike angels, werewolves do have to follow these rules of the body.

Unicorns, as I've already said, can easily be temporarily harmed – but nothing can cause permanent harm (not even being digested). Mandrakes, contrary to popular belief, are completely mortal – they are in fact just a subspecies of normal humans, which split off in the early stages of evolution to become nocturnal.

That's another point – mandrakes are not plants. That arose from their delight with causing horror to humans in the fourteenth century.

Enough of that. Even if you are human, I won't make you suffer all the gory details of mandrake culture. It has been known to make even some modern mandrakes sick. And mandrakes find it surprisingly difficult to throw up.

I, being a werewolf, don't. The very strange taste of the water creature's blood isn't only unpleasant in my mouth, but by gut doesn't like it either when it gets there. I retch, and taste, in amongst blood and silver, the remains of my last meal. As I haven't eaten in at least a decade, it is enough to make me retch again, but now there is nothing to bring up.

A relief, almost, now that I know that it's not rotting inside me. I see the parasites that can harm you humans so in disgusting detail as they squirm in the black lumps in the red stew I have left on this shore.

"We should leave," Kathleen points out, as the horses begin to get impatient.

"Head inland," I agree, with a last look at the worms before they shrivel to pale twigs in the heat.

We do, but it takes ten days for the landscape to look like anything other than a beach. Then it starts to look like a desert. A sandy desert.

It takes six days – and three hundred and seventeen ominous rumbles from Adrastea's belly – before anything else moves in this sandy world. It starts with dawn – the giant, red sun awakens something in the earth. It's more than the dunes moving in the wind – Lycanthropy takes to the air, and Adrastea begins to get jittery. Unicorns are far too similar in mind to humans to have a sixth sense, but I'm sure if it was to bother to sniff inside the soil, it would sense something. As the day wears on, a wind dragon – not a common sight, but one you learn to recognise after sixty-eight thousand years – begins to come towards us, and vanishes. While it is not unusual for dragons, on the rare occasions that they actually happen, to change into quite ordinary objects, or to seep away into the ground, it is extremely rare for them to just vanish.

As Lycanthropy lifts higher into the air, becoming nothing but a speck in the azure sky, the dune in front of us moves slightly, against the wind, and another moves beside it, and for a split second I think I see an eye open, only for the illusion to disappear into the sand.

And then? A short drag, and a giant trap snaps shut around me before I realise that I have been dragged.

Everything is dark in here. I almost laugh, except what I assume to be the tongue has crushed all air out of me. Some foolish animal has taken it upon itself to eat me. I feel the slipperiness of its throat, and suck in the foul air. The stench of putrid flesh hits me. Unpleasant at the best of times, but worst when you're contemplating whether to destroy a quite fantastic animal, or wait to be passed in its faeces.

I've never been particularly patient, and the fact that I can feel bones snapping beneath my feet, corrupted by the alkali in this animal's stomach, doesn't help.

I cut a hole in its stomach with my mind, and a dark green fluid – its blood, presumably, pours in, glistening in the light let through by its rough skin. It seals the hole before it has cut through to the outside, and solidifies like plastic around me.

I taste the sticky surface with the tongue of a wolf. Not as foul as the water-animal's blood, but disgusting nonetheless. I glare at it, and it crumbles to dust. I cut the hole open again, and the same happens – except that this time I am out of the way of the liquid when it clots. I crawl along the ceiling of the stomach, towards the vanishing light, and rip the cover of the hole away with my teeth, before burning through the rest of the flesh.

The creature expires with a loud rumble as I scramble out through the sand, and the wind soon covers any remains.

I glance around, and see that Lycanthropy is landing. The unicorn materialises a few metres off – presumably having been digested. Adrastea and Kathleen clearly chose a much less unpleasant method – I can see the horse, with a rider, being pursued over the dunes about half a mile away. The animal chasing them, similar to the ones that ate the unicorn and I, moves in short leaps on tiny frog-like legs.

They return soon enough, and by that time they have just enough distance for Kathleen to turn and freeze it.

It looks remarkably like a toad, really, despite its fifth leg beneath its belly. As we move within snapping distance, I recall an earth creature similar – you may have seen one: a frog fish. I only saw them before your kind cast me out, but the entire process of opening their mouth and closing it with an animal inside takes so little time we cannot see it happening. They're hideous animals, with lumpy, bumpy skin that makes them blend in perfectly with their environment, and oddly placed fins more like webbed feet.

37

Take away a few of the fins, and make it the size of a boulder, and you have this animal. Oh, and add a spring-like leg in the middle of its chest.

"Is it dead?" I touch the steaming animal, and find that it's cold.

"Just frozen," Kathleen shakes her head, "where were you?"

I choose not to answer that.

Chapter 2 – Digestion

We leave before it frees itself from its icy prison, and we are fortunate enough to see no more life in the desert. This does, however, make the next seventeen days somewhat duller.

One thing we do see a lot of is human waste. At first it's only food packets being blown about – the usual rubbish. Then I get hit by a flying window. Over the next few days we see deserted buildings – being revealed momentarily between the dunes before being buried again.

As the ground becomes firmer, they become more visible, and more intact. The wind still tears at them, but we risk going inside one.

It's huge, but there is no life in it, not even rats. There is thatch in it, though, so the horses eat that without even checking for poisons. Fortunately, they're still walking (and on occasion flying) an hour later, so all seems well as we come into sight of a forest.

Before the forest, there is a small pool, filled with clear water. I walk tentatively to the edge, and as I'm pulled in I wonder why I ever dare to hope. I boil the water, killing my attacker, which floats up to the surface with me. I scramble onto land, and turn to the corpse

Once again, it has five limbs. It looks fairly similar to a boto, but it has no fins on its tail, and three where a river dolphin's pectoral fins would be, and two further back, at the base of its tail. Two identical creature's surface as the water cools, and watch as the unicorn devours the animal. Its blood, I notice, is a rich, deep purple, and doesn't seem to be stopped in its spreading. It moves first in narrow rivulets, which radiate in all directions, until they touch something. Like ants, they swarm towards it, and become a purple mass, crawling all over it.

Needless to say, I am the something. I jump back from the streams as they approach, and land in another, and within moments my legs will not move. Give it a second, and I am borne to my knees, the thick purple mess sucking my arms to my sides. Kathleen is screaming most unhelpfully, and it finds its way into my mouth, and down my throat.

I can see.

That's about it.

My eyes move.

I hate magical animals.

In fact, I hate magic almost as much as the werewolves back on earth used to.

My eyes have moved to the sides of my head, not that it's much of a head anymore. My biology is changing, and the brain is gone. The bones are gone. I have fins, and I feel Kathleen's hands on me. Why exactly she thinks rolling me back into the water is helpful I do not know.

Although it does make it easier to breathe. I move the fins – I'm calling them that because they feel like it. I can't see them due to the ridiculously long beak in front of my face, and the inflexibility of this stupid body.

If I was to list to you the number of times "magical" animals have taken it upon themselves to do this sort of thing – there were dragons (which was, apart from the first time, my fault, because I did break the barrier between normal earth and their space), unicorns (as an act of respect, apparently), feathered snakes, werewolves (well, hippowolves), hell-bats and goodness knows what else. I couldn't list them. I can't remember them all. Let alone name them.

The worst thing is, no matter how magical these animals are, they aren't immortal, and so suffer from that annoying feature called hunger.

I watch the other two, and wonder, in my human mind, what is moving this body. I'm certainly not.

Although whatever foul animal it is that they have rotting in the cave there is tempting.

I mustn't eat it.

I really mustn't eat it.

I find myself moving closer. It's against my will, but it's not. I want to eat that – if only because of this ridiculous hunger.

I never realised rotten meat tasted so wonderful. I gape open these pathetic jaws and suck in more of it. More of it. More. More.

And suddenly, food is the only thought on my mind.

I blink, and stand up.

"You're a great help," I snort at Kathleen.

"I know," she agrees, "I am."

She is a great help, of course, but I seriously doubt that she realised it was one of those hell-bat sort of things. Uses your body to take a form, and then releases you. Unicorns do the same thing when they get eaten – although I can't say I remember seeing that. I was the one doing the eating then. It's a long story, and you do not need to hear it.

I hate magical animals.

Over the next month, I am a mercifully accident-free zone. We see a number of unpleasant animals, and absolutely no pleasant ones, but the only one they try to eat is Kathleen, and even they find her inedible. Then, after a month of being careful, my guard slips, and I trip – within an hour – over a clean, new piece of silver. It cuts deep into my calf, and all I can do is glare at it. Kathleen works it out of the soft soil, and examines it.

"It's a hoe."

I have been harmed for the first time in I don't know how long by a garden tool that died out on the twenty-first century. Wonderful.

"This ground been recently turned," Kathleen continues, "and this hoe's made for human hands."

"Except," I point out, "that humans wouldn't waste silver on a hoe."

She considers my wound as the blood trickles away into the soil, and heals it before continuing.

"It's a paranoia thing, probably. They hear horrid stories about your kind, and want to protect themselves. Anyway, there's probably a few planets around made of silver."

I poke the skin where she's healed me. It never ceases to amaze me, how normal magically healed flesh looks. It even has the filth on it that it had before.

"The point is," she says eventually, as I straighten my clothes and stand up, "there are humans nearby."

I'm not sure why she sounds so pleased. She knows this.

"Humans have ways off this planet, Jack."

"And we're just going to ask them for help?" Somehow I think a unicorn and a flying horse will put them off us before they find out we're from earth. Even if we do tell them that she's not always a flying horse.

"They must be used to unicorns by now," Kathleen snorts.

"They're not any more popular than us," I point out, "I hardly think they'll throw a feast in celebration."

"They might help us," Kathleen shrugs, "no harm in trying."

Not for her, perhaps, not for the unicorn – not even for Adrastea. But some of us can, and will, die if we're battered enough.

"Stop being such a coward."

"Stop reading my mind!"

"I'm not reading. I'm not even listening. You're broadcasting. I can't help hearing."

"Oh, shut up."

We glare at each other for a while – sixty-nine thousand years hasn't really done that much to mature us – before walking on. I amuse myself by standing on her hair and listening to her yelping.

It doesn't take long to find humans. They're not exactly the most inconspicuous of animals, and by the time they notice us, Lycanthropy is walking neatly along the ground, looking slightly out of place in this red-brown world.

"Mummy!" scowls a little boy who is attacking the ground with a small spade. I notice, to my displeasure, that it is silver.

I also notice that his mother crosses herself as she sees us. I think she was expecting us to vanish like smoke.

"You're not werewolves, then." It's not a question. It's a statement, coming with a sigh of relief. Before I can correct her, Kathleen saves us.

"No, thank goodness. Did you hear about those two that escaped from a scientific lab?"

"I can't say I did," the mother looks surprised, "still, no matter how foul the monsters are, I can't say I blame them. Wouldn't like to be under any of those scientist's needles."

She has one of the most amusing accents I have ever heard. It seems to move between Russian, American and Zambian, and when she asks us into her shiny, round home for "tig", I almost think she sounds cockney.

"Where're the pair of you from, then?" the woman asks later, over a cup of "tig". I can only assume that it's their way of saying tea.

I let Kathleen do the talking, and keep my ears on the conversation while my eyes wander over the room.

"We're on our honeymoon," Kathleen giggles sweetly, accepting a disgustingly sugary pastry, and some weird, purple triangle. There's a large painting of a burning witch above the door. The witch looks rather like my sister.

A crucifix dominates another picture, with a misty wolf silhouette dispersing in the background.

The conversation grabs my attention. The woman comments on the length of Kathleen's hair. Asks something about conditioner.

I would have expected them to have something more advanced by now.

"You have such lovely hair," the woman sighs longingly as Kathleen shakes dust and mud from the end, "must have taken centuries to grow it."

Don't jump, Jack, she's testing you.

"No," Kathleen grins stupidly, sweetly, "my hair just grows really fast. It was shoulder-length – when was it, James?"

Since when was my name James? She could have used something less depressing than her husband's name. They were just married when he got hacked up.

"Seven years?" I suggest, trying to make the pause sensible. The woman seems satisfied.

"So what are you doing here, Mrs...?" Kathleen pauses as she waits for the woman to supply her surname.

"Miss. Miss Yoners. We're on a cruise. More than my boyfriend can afford, but stuff 'im. Going round ten systems, and the kids too. I'm dumping him as soon as we get back to Alpha."

"Alpha?" I'm amazed at how well Kathleen does this, "I would have expected a slightly classier area, Miss Yoners."

"Oh, so where d'you live, then? Don't tell me Europa," the woman brandishes the cake-laser.

"That dump, no, of course not. Me and James live on Sweden Island, on Pthalo."

The woman looks surprised.

"You didn't look that wealthy. How'd you afford a place like that, then?"

I drift off again as they swap stories about work, and my eyes are caught by some of the moving paintings at the back of the room. I see a flicker of light from one, and my eyes peer closer. I pray to God she doesn't look at me – I know my pupils will be almost filling my eyes as I strain to see into the depths of the shadow.

A cross. I expected as much. On closer inspection, I see it is upside down. I stand up and walk towards it. This is odd.

Someone – a man – on the cross. Other people running away, their mouths opening and closing in screams. I peer in at the figure on the cross, and he seems familiar.

"He likes art, does he?"

The woman is watching me, so I have to control my reaction as I realise why the image is familiar.

It is me on the cross.

"I sell it occasionally," I lie, coming back down to sit. How could the humans create such a good likeness, in such a cheap, tacky resort?

"All this art is religious," the woman informs Kathleen, "has to be, doesn't it, what with all them stories you hear about werewolves. You have to make everywhere safe. That's why we came for this hotel. There was another, one of 'em fancy floating ones. Not a cross in it! Hardly a silver spoon to protect yourself with either. All ruddy platinum. What good is that, eh?"

"None, none at all…" I sink back into boredom as Kathleen replies, and watch as my figure on the cross turns into a wolf.

She is kind enough to lend us a room – although the horses have to be frozen, in what doesn't exactly look like the best facility for it. I sleep on the floor, with Kathleen's hair taking up the rest of the bed.

As she arranges it on the pillow, and kneel, and stare at her.

"Did you see the picture?"

"Which one? There's hundreds."

"The one in the dining room. The moving one with the cross."

"A cross? There's hundreds in the house.

I move closer, and lower my voice.

"An upside down cross."

"Probably one of their charms against the devil – draw him."

"I just hope she's short-sighted."

"Why? Should I make her be?"

"It isn't the devil on that cross."

"Who is it then?"

I look at her, broadcasting, as she calls it, and her eyes widen.

"Seriously?" I nod, and she crosses herself and bites her thumb, "she can't have recognised you."

I consider. There are ten children – the oldest fifteen – and two superstitious adults. The next ship to take anyone – including anyone from the other four houses on the complex – back to the space-station comes two weeks from now. At least one of them is bound to want to know the gory details of the picture. Their eldest daughter – fourteen – is studying religious art on school. She may even do a project on the picture while they're here. Her handheld teacher will tell her everything there is to know about it, and she will tell her mother. And her mother will slip in here one night and slit my throat with their (silver) breadknife. Even if life can be tiring, I don't want to die yet.

The next day passes with my heart thudding in my chest like a damaged record. The ten illegitimate children seem friendlier than they should, the boyfriend seems to flirt too little with Kathleen, and the mother seems too quick with the cakes.

But there are no glares, no glances at the picture, nothing incriminating, except from Immalyn. She looks at me almost admiringly through her thick make-up – and I'm fairly sure she didn't look twice at me yesterday. She does keep looking at the painting, touching it as she goes past, poking the moving figures. But only when none of her family can see, almost as if she knows the situation perfectly, and is sympathetic.

I find out in the evening how sympathetic she is. She slips into our room after the lights are off, and I can hear her parents screaming at each other – the father just proposed.

"Are you awake?" she whispers in my ear. I try not to move. "I know who you are," she continues, still hushed, "and I won't tell my mother."

The condition now.

"If you bite me. That's all I ask, a little nip, and make me one of your kind. I'll sell you my soul for this."

What does she think I am, the devil?

"Please?" Her blue eyes beg sickeningly.

This is a worrying dilemma. The very thought of biting her just to upset her mother is disturbing, as is the thought of being killed brutally and hung upside down off a cross.

I consider slowly. The girl's foul breath is making me nauseous – it would seem that brushing teeth is a thing of the past when you can just go to a healer to have them grown back. Or have werewolf ones from someone of a similar age implanted.

If I don't bite this child, she will definitely tell her mother what I am – at least after an ultimatum. I could always tell her mother myself, or get Kathleen to try to wipe their memories. But that doesn't always work (it depends on blood-group, or something), and sometimes it can make them more aware of whatever you want hidden. So telling the mother myself seems to be the best solution. I play out the situation in my mind.

I wince as the image ends with my head on a silver stick, with crucifixes shoved into my mouth.

Call me selfish, thoughtless, then. I am. And I know I will hate myself forever for what I am about to do.

The girl gasps as my teeth sink through her skin, and then sighs happily as the silver venom numbs the pain. The one mercy I can think of is that I haven't seen a moon on this planet – the synthetic one we landed on was of a neighbouring planet.

"Don't tell your mother what you are," I murmur, as the girl begins to get up.

She nods, and reaches for the door-handle with a satisfied smile.

Of course it couldn't be that simple, not with me. There is a click as her hand touches the door – at first I think Kathleen has sensed the intruder and locked the door, but it's not that kind of click. The claws on metal kind of click.

"Jack?" Kathleen sits up.

I don't answer. I can't. I'm watching my doom.

The girl is changing. And from her expression, I get the feeling that she isn't going to keep her personality as a wolf.

"Jack, what have you done now?" Kathleen demands, reaching for the light.

There is a crash, and the door shatters. The light goes on in time for Kathleen to see the wolf's back end.

"Jack," she stares at me, "tell me that you didn't bite anyone."

I hang my head in shame.

"Stop," she snaps. The falling shreds of the door freeze, and so do I.

"Jack," she comes over and kicks me, "Get up."

Her spell breaks on me, and I stand up.

"Who did you bite?"

"The oldest daughter."

"You fool," she hits me with the closest silver object, "you total and utter fool."

"She was blackmailing me!"

"Jack, her mother will find out that you're a werewolf anyway, now. She'll probably notice when she wakes up to find her daughter ripping the house to pieces with her teeth!"

"What do I do?"

"You should have thought about that first. There's nothing either of us can do now, except get out of the way. Get the daughter, and take her outside."

I meet her twenty minutes later, with the girl-wolf mid-bound, having pushed her through the air like a floating statue. Kathleen leads the horses out of the freezer, before locking the security doors on the outside of the house. She looks at the moon, sighs, and stamps her foot.

The wolf vanishes into the darkness almost instantly. It doesn't vanish into the darkness of my mind, hovering instead like a dying moth over my conscience, even as the buzz of life returns to the homes and the shadows catch up with everything we have moved.

The forest seems the most obvious place to hide. When we go in, not even Lycanthropy will talk to me. I trail behind Kathleen's stony silence, and it is at least another week before she starts to talk again.

It is surprising how patient she gets as time passes her by. Patient with her moods, that is. I remain, as always, the petulant child being told off. I have to accept that if it wasn't for her, I would have been killed at least a dozen times before humans cast us out.

In all fairness to me, it would be impossible to save her from death. There is no death for her.

The incident that gets her to talk is one of the most... educational we've had so far on this planet. The ground, still in the darkness of the forest, becomes crunchy underfoot.

"Jack?" Kathleen hisses, "stop moving."

It takes a while for this to sink in. in fact, I have become all but oblivious to her voice, and I have drawn alongside her before I realise that she's spoken. Her hand snatches my shoulder, and I stumble, and stop.

"Jack, can you see anything?"

"Light would help."

I don't have it in me to release the slightest bit of wolf.

"I don't want to disturb anything."

I consider it for a few seconds.

"Disturb what? The willow trees?"

The unicorn, a few metres in front, screams. This is, in case you are still unfamiliar with the ways of unicorns, is not good. Unicorns do not scream. Unicorns only scream when they are in gross danger of being eaten, and that should only happen in purgatory.

I blink, and my pupils fill my eyes to find whatever it is the unicorn is seeing. I see nothing – the unicorn has frozen, eyes rolling, under a cascade of willow-leaves.

I sigh, and start to move towards it. The ground snaps and crunches – but not so damply as the ground of any normal forest would. I glance down, and notice the odd colour of the ground – yellowish white, with sharp, stony edges sticking from it occasionally. I take another step, and reach forwards to push aside a curtain of leaves.

They're sticky. Very sticky. I pull my hand back, and they creak, but do not snap off as leaves should. Nor does my hand come free.

They are curling around it. Like many-jointed fingers, these leaves coil around my arm. My eyes slowly follow them up to the branch.

A crocodile's head peers down at me from the tree, and below it, a body suspended in the air, from which four six-fingered limbs dangle – each finger being serrated and green, and reaching down to just above the ground. .

I stare at it, and slowly see the fifth leg gripping the dead branch above it. My eyes travel from it, to the next tree, and see the creatures there, and on the next tree, and the next, and the next.

I glance back at the ones we have walked through. Even they have creatures dangling from them, but much smaller animals, with thinner fingers.

These larger ones we are tangled in seem to be producing silk. I had been distracted from my own situation. I snap my teeth closed around the leaf-like finger, and the fingers break off where my teeth touch. I glance at Kathleen – she and Adrastea look rather smug as the leaf-like fingers snap like streams of water on them. The Unicorn opts for my less effective solution. Lycanthropy has taken off again.

With a little work, the unicorn and I free ourselves, and began to move on. It isn't long before we begin to approach a new human settlement – only half built. The poor fools are building a campfire in between their tents, in a wide clearing on the outskirts of the "forest".

One of them says something about firewood, and stands up slowly. Two others – a girl and a young man, stand up and follow him into the forest, as do our eyes.

It isn't long before they scream. Two of the others follow them, and, before our very eyes, the "trees" launch their attack. It lasts perhaps five seconds, before all that is left is the dust of their bare skeletons. Small creatures drop from the pale, skeletal trees, and gather together even that, and drag it away in a weak, flopping manner. They wrap it in silk, spinning it around in their back limbs as their fingers ooze the liquid, and shape it into thin but perfectly balanced tree skeletons. They ooze large amounts of the liquid silk onto a spot on the ground, and move their new "tree" onto it. They scuttle up the branches, and dangle from their extra leg, looking once again like so many willow-leaves.

Lycanthropy lands behind us with a thump, followed closely by a dog-sized bat-like animal – with crocodile's jaws and a leg coming from the centre of its chest. Even the unicorn is slow to investigate, and Lycanthropy trots towards the safety of the fire as the thing stops moving.

Kathleen touches its grotesque head, and its eyes close peacefully.

"It'll be up in half an hour," she tells me, "I don't want to find out what it eats."

We need more people. Lycanthropy is already in their company, and they are patting her nose and stroking her coat as they wait slightly nervously for their five companions to come back out of the forest.

I decide perhaps now is the time to try honesty. I can see a silver knife beside one of the three remaining men, and a silver fork near the fire, so I can only hope this works.

"What are you doing, Jack?" Kathleen demands as I open my mouth to speak.

"I tried not telling anyone," I hiss, "look how that turned out!"

"It's your problem if they kill you," Kathleen retorts eventually. Her pause hasn't worked, sadly. I almost wish I wasn't about to do this.

"Hello?" I call. The nearest, one of the two women, sits up and looks towards us. Having been near the fire so long, she can't see me.

"Sygmom?"

"My name is Jack." I inform her, "I am a werewolf."

I have to say, they take it well. The man with the knife grabs it by the blade and cuts off two of his fingers. The nearest woman jumps up and her foot in the fire, and starts screaming, the other woman picks up a large gun, one of the men collapses, and the last hides behind a rock.

Aside from a few lead bullets, nothing hits me when I come into the firelight. Kathleen follows, with the unicorn just behind her, and heals the fingerless man with a touch to his bloodied hand. She grips the woman's shoulder, and the fire hisses and goes out, the toes exposed in the burnt shoe golden brown and unscarred.

"Son of Lucifer!" the woman with the gun screams. She hits me with it, and I sit down painfully on a silver fork.

"What are you doing here?" the man who has recently regained his fingers clutches at his hand as if refusing to believe that he has been healed, "isn't Earth enough for you?"

"It's plenty for us," I snap, throwing the fork into the forest (something yelps), "we don't appreciate being fur coats, though." They all stare.

I glance at the woman with the gun, and hold out my hand as Kathleen heals me. She point the gun at my head and shoots some more.

"The coat, you ass."

She hands it to me. I recognise the fur, by some sickening coincidence.

"This woman was born a human," I inform her. We all are, but Evelyn was a human that, at the age of twenty-three, came to Earth and asked to be a werewolf. "Her name was Evelyn Wilson."

"You're making it up. That's two thousand year old wolf fur."

"She was killed two thousand and three years, nine months and two days ago. Werewolf fur."

I return Evelyn's skin to the way it was when she stood in daylight. She was beautiful. Soft, clean skin, one of those who didn't know what they were doing when they were a wolf, but knew everything when she was awake.

"This woman," I hold her poor, beautiful skin out to them, "was engaged to be married when she was killed. Engaged to be married to me. She was already pregnant with my – my – child. And your people came and –"

I stop. I am holding what would have been my wife, if it wasn't for some rich, human bastard who wanted to buy this woman's great grandmother a fancy present.

"They made a fur coat out of her," Kathleen takes the horrible thing from my hands and drops it into the flames.

To reinforce my point, Kathleen waves a hand at the other people, and their coats become the skins they would have been at day. Their rug even has a face – though thankfully unfamiliar.

The gun is on the floor now. I pick it up slowly – their eyes widen, and without really thinking about it, I shoot every last bullet into my stomach. They fall to the ground in front of me, and Kathleen realises that I'm not going to be doing much more talking tonight.

"We don't want to hurt you," she informs them. I'm surprised that the knife isn't in my throat at those words, "but your fellows –"

"They're dead." I fill in for her, "Dead as dust. Dead, dead, dead. Dead as Evelyn."

"We didn't kill them," Kathleen protests as the man reaches for the knife again.

"What did, then, the forest?" he laughs sarcastically.

"There aren't any trees in this forest." She throws a ball of blue fire into the sky above the forest, and everyone can see one of the animals as it crawls pathetically along to ground, having been displaced from its stand, "and I'm fairly sure you don't want to go the same way as the others. So I suggest that you get off this planet as quickly as possible."

"Couldn't we just get away from the forest?"

I glance at Kathleen, to stop her from even considering this possibility.

"All they can cause us is inconvenience," Kathleen shrugs, "but if you feel like getting eaten, feel free to stay on this planet. But everywhere we've gone, Jack's been eaten."

They look a bit perplexed, but the man who hid runs into their craft and begins switching things on. His cowardice seems infectious, and the others carry things aboard – at one point shrieking as a swarm of five-legged rats storm out of the ground under one of the tents, and try and overcome one of the women. Kathleen freezes them, and blocks the hole. Within an hour, everything and everyone is inside, and a few tiny, five-legged lizards have been ousted back onto their planet.

As we take off, the sun is rising. It's a quite spectacular sight, surrounded by tiny, glittering moons (sadly, I hadn't noticed them before I bit the girl at the last place). The craft hurtles towards to sun for a while, giving me a chance to watch the ground go hurtling past below. I wretch at first, but my stomach is already empty. Once I am used to it, I begin to notice things. There are not hundreds, not thousands, not millions, but billions of deserted settlements, scattered all over the place, surrounded by various, five legged creatures, some as large as skyscrapers. Some even fly down beside us, and the unicorn, in compacted stasis, still manages to emit a very loud belly rumble. I glare at the tiny dark shape, and it almost seems to be moving. Who knows with unicorns?

"So, where are we going?" I ask, as we break through the ozone layer. The woman who shot me, co-piloting the craft, is the only one who answers.

"I don't know," she shrugs.

"Where do you live, then?"

"We don't. We travel."

I have always found this way of thought quite unnatural. Travelling generally gets me into horrible accidents.

She, however, has justification for it.

"We hunt vampires."

I laugh out loud.

"You actually believe in vampires?" I snort.

"We've never seen them, if that's what you mean. But we've been following their trails."

"What trails? There's nothing to follow."

"People go away to planets and completely disappear. That's the work of vampires."

I stare at her. I cannot be hearing this from the woman who quite sensibly tried to kill me a few hours ago.

"We have just left a planet where almost every single species was dependant on human migrants for food. Of course people disappear. They get eaten!"

"By vampires," she insists.

This is hopeless. Her red – extremely red – hair is clearly meant to be blond.

Something crashes into the side of the craft, releasing me from the pointless argument.

"What's that?" the coward shrieks from the cockpit.

"Why is he so petrified of everything?" I demand, as the craft turns to face the rammer.

"You'll have to forgive him," the man that chopped his fingers off twitches his left index finger twice in the air.

The man who collapsed explains from the pilot's seat.

"He's a eunuch."

That would explain the squeaky voice, too.

The redhead returns to the cockpit.

"She's a little random," the other woman informs me, "where's the girl?"

"I count as a woman," Kathleen appears behind her, "I have had a baby. I have been married. I have been faithful to my dead husband."

She directs a thought at me. Jade's image flares up in my head. She wouldn't mind that I'd let her go after a few dozen millennia, I'm sure.

"I need help with the weapons."

"They need crucifixes," the redhead calls, as the craft jerks back violently, "Ballsy!"

The eunuch scurries up to us with two crude crucifixes. I regard the little wooden things apprehensively. I doubt that they'll do much to protect us from whatever's out there, but you never know.

The finger-twitcher leads the way up the stairs, and to the weapons deck.

"This is a big ship for ten people," I realise.

"It was forty," the woman admits, "ten of them left not long after we started the expedition. The rest have been eaten by things. So now there's just me, Libby, Ballsy, Karl and Ollie here. Hunting vampires." I'm surprised at how normal the names are. Surprisingly similar to the names they started out as.

"You do realise they don't exist," I point out.

"Did your mother never tell you that werewolves didn't exist when you were human?"

"She died in childbirth."

The woman shrugs apologetically.

"So, if it's vampires you're after, why all the silver?"

She doesn't answer. She's concentrating on a dark patch in the sky.

"What is that?" Kathleen leans closer to the screen.

I look. It's a huge patch of absolute darkness, so I let my pupils fill my eyes. Still not the slightest edge of light coming off it.

"Kathleen," I consider, "do you remember anything called a black hole?"

"What are those?" asks the human woman.

"Black holes are basically squashed, dead, giant stars," Kathleen explains, "that even light can't escape from."

It appears that the humans' solution to this is to blow it up. They both fire their weapons, and blue streaks vanish into the black space.

It ripples like a liquid.

Very familiar, somehow. I search deep into my memories, my memories of the first few decades of my life, searching for the memory. Something about America, near one of the bombed cities.

A vertical pool of water. Darker than water though, and thicker. Pulls me inside.

And there?

What was there?
The memory won't come at first, and then –
Wings.
Bats wings, but bigger
Scales.
Claws.
It's coming back faster now –
Earth.
Air.
Fire.
Water.
"Dragons," I whisper, and the ship crashes into the darkness.

It takes a while for me to realise that I'm not dead. My eyes are just closed. I can't bear to open them for a while. Then Kathleen hits me with something. I open one eye and glare.

"Get up, you great lump."

I sit up begrudgingly.

"We are the first humans – well, nearly humans, inside a black hole, Jack, and all you've been doing is sleeping."

"Black hole, big deal," I mumble.

"Thirty-seven days asleep," she sighs, "who would have thought it of Jack Hanov Himmerden?"

"Since when did you remember anyone's surname?" I sit up.

"Everyone knows your surname off your planet," Libby shrugs, "does he normally do that when he's asleep?"

"Normally only when he's drunk." Kathleen frowns, and I glance around. Judging by the caked purple fluids on the wall, they dealt with whatever I dreamt up.

"So where are we, then?"

"Who knows? Looks like home, to me."

I stand up uneasily, and glance out of the screen.

"Earth," I confirm, "Not home."

Kathleen frowns.

"It's covered in ice," she points out.

"That isn't ice. It would be cold if that was ice."

"How do you know it's Earth, then?"

I don't, is the truth. I say nothing to avoid admitting this. It just feels like earth, you see. I block my mind so that Kathleen doesn't know that I'm going on a whim.

"If our computers have started working, they could tell you," Libby passes me a cup of something hot, "Georgie," she calls, "are you nearly done?"

"Almost. There."

The screens hum to life, and the locations and distances of the nearest stars appear on them, and, after about forty calculations flash before us, the wonderful word "EARTH" fills the screen.

"I've changed my mind," I say.

"You really hate evidence, don't you?" It's the first time I've heard Ballsy, or whatever his name is, speak – excluding, of course, shrieking in fright. He sounds very much like a child being strangled. Which is very disturbing.

"He's right, though," Kathleen backs me up, "show us the stars again."

Libby taps a screen as Georgie comes in.

"They don't look right at all," I insist.

"It could be the wrong hemisphere," offers Karl.

I give him a withering look.

"I lived in the Southern Hemisphere for ten thousand years. I think I'd know."

"I know what's wrong," Kathleen considers, "can you give us a mirror image of that?"

Georgie kicks one of the screens, and it spins around.

"That good enough?"

"That is exactly right," I stare. The sky that seemed so unfamiliar has suddenly become the very one I have stared at every night for nearly seventy thousand years.

"It doesn't look any different to me," Ollie frowns.

"You haven't spent very long looking at Earth's night sky," I shrug, "where's the moon?"

"Over there," Kathleen points out of the window. I glance up at it, hanging in the afternoon sky.

"It's full. If you want to stay human, we shouldn't stay out there long."

"Who said anything about going out there?" Libby demands.

"I'm going for a walk," I reply.

In the end, we all go, except Ballsy. Ballsy stays behind and hides somewhere. His loss. Libby opens a hatch to let a good bit of air in.

"It's dust," Kathleen whispers, as our feet touch the ground.

"Which part of earth are we on?" I demand. I cannot remember any deserts that existed after my sixteenth birthday.

"Somewhere near the – what's that word?" Libby hands a tiny computer screen to me.

"North Pole," I reply, "how can a navigator not know the word north?"

"Never heard of it," she frowns, as the two horses and the unicorn walk out of their compressed suspension pod.

"What have you done?" I demand, staring at the tiny creatures, and edging the unicorn onto the palm of my hand.

"You've never seen that before?" Libby laughs, as I try and pick my arm up. It is now pinned to the floor by a tonne of unicorn that is somehow only the size of a mouse, now the size of a rat, now a cat, now a dog – now a unicorn.

"I've seen it now," I pull by hand out from under its hoof, and glare at it, "and I think I deserve an apology."

"You're not saying it can talk?" Georgie stares.

"Not much, and definitely not English," I snort, as I get the mental obscenity the unicorn has sent my way. This animal is not our most polite unicorn, even if I still don't understand some of their swear-thoughts. I send a human one back at it.

"What does that mean?" Libby stares at the animal as we walk on.

"Something about being half human, I think," I shrug, "sorry, it's an insult from most large animals. Even werewolves aren't as despised."

It doesn't take long to reach a settlement, and I go up to the first door I see.

"Are you just going to barge in?" Karl demands.

"No, I'm going to knock."

I knock.

There's no answer.

I knock again, harder this time.

"Surely it isn't night yet?" someone – a woman – demands from inside.

"That's English," Libby grabs Karl, "they talk English."

"No," I call, "should it be?"

"Mary, mother of Jesus," the voice exclaims, "come inside, quickly!"

I open the door, and step inside. The others follow, and Kathleen closes the door once the unicorn has worked out how to get inside without breaking the building down.

"Goodness," the woman shuffles into everyone's view, "the clouds must have been thick."

"There were no clouds," I tell her.

"Is there an eclipse?" she demands.

"No," I'm getting confused, "why would there be?"

She stops and stares at me.

"You're not human, are you?"

"No," I shake my head, "they are, but I'm not. And she's not, and they're, well, they're obviously not."

"What on earth were you doing in daylight, then? No-one but humans walk in daylight."

"What, so the werewolves here can't survive in daylight?" I'm very concerned now.

"Werewolves? Don't be ridiculous," she laughs, "have a cup of tea. I've just made a pot."

"Why's he talking about werewolves, mammy?" a little boy, perhaps eight, looking sleepy, comes and stares up at the woman.

"He's just tired," she informs him, "you do know that werewolves are just stories, don't you?" she checks.

"Then what are you?" I demand.

She laughs.

"You're joking," she chuckles, "you had me for a while –" she stops. "You're not joking, are you?"

"No," seems most appropriate here. I have never been stared at for so long without anyone speaking.

"Libby, put that away," Ollie murmurs, "you could hurt Jack."

The hostess continues staring, but hands us tea.

"You're lucky you came here," a teenage girl walks into the room, wearing boldly coloured clothes, "nobody else puts up with humans but Mum. She doesn't mind your sort. More than I can say for your sort."

"Jack," Kathleen considered, "is it mildly possible that, just eensily, tinily possible that…"

She doesn't finish. She doesn't have to. I have finally noticed something that Libby must have noticed five minutes ago. The woman's upper canine teeth are almost as long as a wolf's, but sharper.

"Vampires," I whisper.

The girl raises an eyebrow.

"What are you, then?"

"Werewolf," Georgie replies for me, backing towards the door, "not to be rude or anything, but we really should be leaving now."

"Werewolves don't exist."

"Neither do vampires," Kathleen replies jovially, sitting down next to the mother vampire, "so, how old are you all, really?"

"Eight, seventeen, forty-seven. My husband's asleep – he's forty- six."

"Hundreds or thousands?"

"What? Oh, those are a human sweet, aren't they?"

"Cake decoration. I meant years."

"Hundreds of years? Someone's lived past a hundred years? Don't be ridiculous."

"I have," I volunteer, "and Kathleen has. And the horses have."

The oldest vampire faints.

We stare at her, and the humans stare. Even Libby is speechless.

"Vampires just aren't what they're cracked up to be," Georgie says eventually.

"What are we cracked up to be?" the seventeen-year-old laughs, "flyers?"

"Sexy blood-sucking babes?" suggests Karl. Libby stares at him.

"We do suck blood," the teenager shrugs.

Her little brother grimaces.

"Goats' blood." He sticks his tongue out.

"Some people have said I'm sexy, too," the girl flutters her eyelashes.

"He's taken," Libby snaps, and throws a silver crucifix at the girl.

"Ow!" she exclaims, picking it up, "what was that for?"

Libby stares.

"But you're meant to burn up! It's been blessed by a priest!"

"Why exactly would that make me burn up? What do you think we are, evil?"

"That is sort of the point of vampires," I point out, "in case you were wondering."

The mother vampire wakes up, and stares around.

"Where was I?" she asks, "who'd like some tea?"

We ignore her, and look at the teenager.

"Mum, they think we're evil."

"Don't be ridiculous, Filimel. Of course they don't. You were just dreaming."

The mother vampire goes red as she tries to remember what she was talking about.

"How old did you say you were?" she asks eventually, "I'm sure you said, I've just forgotten."

"I'm not sure we should tell you again," I consider, as she pours out eight cups of very ordinary looking tea, "you fainted last time."

"I wasn't dreaming, then," her shoulders sag. "Oh, no."

"What's wrong with that?" I want to know.

"If you've lived that long," she swallows, "it means you're definitely not vampires. If you're not vampires, they will – oh," she stops, looking very distraught, "not everyone's as... tolerant as us."

"She means they'll want to eat you."

"Do you have silver teeth?" I ask. The girl frowns.

"What's that to do with the price of milk?"

"Price of eggs," Kathleen corrects, "only silver can do us any harm. Well, only Jack can be hurt."

"Um," Ollie taps me on the shoulder, "have you forgotten anyone?"

"Oh," I consider. This is not good. I had forgotten about our little vampire slayers.

"I have a solution," the teenage vampire offers, "copper!"

"Copper?" I stare, "what's the use of copper?"

"It hurts more than anything else," she shrugs, "I think if you couldn't be bothered to wait a few years, that's how you'd kill one of us. That or letting them get us."

"Where do we get copper?"

"Don't you have any with you?"

She deserves an explanation.

"Listen, whatever your name is, they're humans. Never expect humans to do anything, anything at all, that could even possibly save their lives. Their sole aims in life are to die."

"Jack's quite good at dying, too," Kathleen adds.

"Shut up. That was once, and it was suicide. It doesn't count."

After a few more minutes of argument, the little boy starts to get hungry, so the girl takes him out of the room. A goat bleats in annoyance from the darkness. The mother occupies us with small talk, about what our names are, where we're from, and finally, most amusingly, what we do.

"We're vampire slayers," says Libby defiantly.

There's a patronising pause as the girl returns without her brother, and stares at us.

"Vampire slayers and no copper?" the girl snorts, "Good luck."

"We have silver, and wood, and crucifixes, and holy water," Libby retorts.

"Whatever you expect that to do," the teenage vampire snorts.

After a while, and several hours of staring at tealeaves, the two male vampires enter the room.

"Madeleine, I'm going out to work now," the father – a pot-bellied midget – says sleepily, "guests?"

"Just brought them in to get out of the sun," she smiles, and her ears go red in the darkness. It appears that vampires aren't as good at seeing in the dark as werewolves, because he makes no comment.

I wait until he's gone to question her on this.

"Why did you lie?"

"What?"

"Your ears went red," I tell her.

"Red? What's that?"

"The colour of blood," I stare at her, "you're not a very normal vampire, are you?"

She flushes.

"I didn't lie."

"Mum, why did you lie?" her daughter asks.

She keeps on denying it for the next few minutes, while Libby eases herself into a chair, and the unicorn lies on the floor and rolls.

Finally, the truth comes out. Slowly.

"He didn't need to know what you were."

"Why not, mum?"

"I just felt it would be better if perhaps…" she stops, "Which one of you's doing that?"

I glance at Kathleen. She looks away guiltily.

"Why did you lie, mum?"

"You weren't here last time," the woman sighs eventually, "the last time humans came."

"In your lifetime?" the girl frowns, "I thought you said they died out centuries ago."

"They were here," the woman chokes, "twenty-two years ago last month."

"What happened?"

She doesn't answer. She can't for a few minutes, as the door swings on its hinges, and an owl hoots. Even her daughter is silent, in rapture.

"Two thousand," she whispers eventually, "thought we could live hand in hand. They didn't believe all the dogma they'd heard about our kind. Young couples and rehabilitated youths mainly – a lot of past drug offenders. Looking for a new world.

"One of them gave birth. It was messy, blood everywhere," she blinks back tears, "the midwife devoured her. Once the smell of blood was out, all of our people were there, ripping, tearing, drinking. Even in the light of day. Not one human got away – down to the last baby, they were drained dry. Most of them didn't have enough blood to survive the change."

She looks up at us.

"These were people I'd grown up with. People I knew, just becoming monsters at the smell of blood. Seeing my husband tearing open children that played in our neighbour's garden every evening – it wasn't right. Now you just have to say the word human, and everything starts again."

"Why?" the girl demands.

"There's just something about their blood," the mother shrugs, "it sets our kind off. It's a craving they cannot resist."

"You did," Kathleen points out. The woman looks up, to see if Kathleen gleaned this from her mind, but we all knew it.

"I was the unluckiest of us all," she smiles sadly, "my mind doesn't work the way it's supposed to. The signals don't get the normal responses. I was a witness, too cowardly to go into the sun and try and stop any of the people I loved doing this to themselves."

"You'd better not start bleeding," the girl grins, and shows off long, gleaming canines.

"We should get off this planet," I suggest after a few minutes silence.

"We can't," Georgie looks at Ollie.

"We damaged the engines when we landed. It'll take Ballsy at least a week to fix it."

"We could use magic," I suggest, but Kathleen shakes her head.

"I tried. It's too over-complicated for magic."

"Surely you've landed that thing before?" I can't help thinking, "why couldn't you do it this time?"

"First, there's less people than ever before, and second, we were unconscious." Libby shrugs.

Well, I can't really say anything to that.

"They could stay here," the girl suggests.

"Your father would realise. He's not as stupid as you like to think, Filimel."

"We'll have to just blend in," Libby sighs, "Any advice?"

They can't think of anything, and soon enough their neighbours are popping in. As the sun is down, getting out of it can no longer be used as an excuse. Or she's just uncomfortable about what might happen to her children if one of the humans has an accident.

"They just look normal," says Karl as we walk away from the house.

"One minor detail they're unlikely to miss," Libby considers, "the teeth."

"No real problem," me and Kathleen both break in at the same time.

"Magic is a wonderful thing," Kathleen beams.

"Just a flick of a wrist," I sigh. Libby clutches her mouth in shock;

"Or a blink," Kathleen adds, and Ollie follows suit;

"And we're done."

Georgie bares her teeth at us as we finish this. Spectacular work, if I do say so myself.

"Time for food now," I add. The four humans follow dumbly, all poking at their teeth with their tongues, "Where would vampires go to eat?"

"Aren't you two going to do anything?"

"They can bite us all they like," I laugh, "we're not human."

I see a repulsive fluorescent sign blaring out the word "café", and all conversation stops as me and Kathleen make a beeline for it.

"Should we be doing this?" Libby demands of Karl as they follow us, "shouldn't we go back to Ballsy?"

"We'd just get in his way," Karl shrugs, "we might as well see the world while he's working."

"Why are there no windows?" I wonder, going inside the café. A few clearly drugged faces turn towards us as we come in, but otherwise, it's empty.

"Gut iffning," the attendant greets us, "Kan I bi ghettingh yhou anhythingh?"

"Tea?" whispers Kathleen.

"What do you have?" I ask.

"No ti. Onlhi eenstunt coghi ower hort shoclit. Ower wain iff yewl pai inuff."

"Foodwise?"

"Biskits. Sum Paystrees unt Pighs."

"Nothing for now," Kathleen has just seen the state of the pastries, "we'll wait a while."

We sit for a while, the humans talking about goodness knows what mortal nonsense. Eventually neither Kathleen nor I can bear to listen any longer, and we get up to wander around.

I spot the tank, and move towards it.

"It's empty," I complain. A woman in a smart uniform looks in.

"Nope, it's still hanging on in there. Boring as ever."

I step a bit closer, but still see nothing.

"I'm surprised it's still alive," she informs me, scrubbing dried vomit off a table, "I don't think it can ever get any food."

She switches on a light, and I peer more closely into the tank. She looks from the other side.

"He's looking quite good today, actually. Not seen this much movement before."

She lifts off the lid of the tank, and scoops some little animal out. I hadn't seen it before. It shimmers like moving glass in her hand.

"Very healthy," she nods, and puts him back in the tank, with a blue light on him to show him up better as more patrons enter.

The place quickly becomes filled with rowdy teenagers, and when we get back to the place we left the humans, we find, to our annoyance, that they have moved. Inconsiderate creatures.

It isn't difficult to spot Libby, mingling with a crowd of vampires, but looking rather uneasy. I squeeze through the crowds – the café is swiftly becoming more like a nightclub – and tap her on the shoulder.

"Where is everyone?"

"I don't know," she scowls, "they all just walked off and left me. I'm busy mingling. Go away now."

Redheads are hopeless. I would know. I was married to one.

By this time, Kathleen, thanks to her height, has just about disappeared. I'm lost.

I find my way to a corner near the bar, and looking into another tank – this one clearly not empty, with about four inches of earth on the bottom, and a tiny animal trundling about on it.

"You like dragons, then?" the waitress smiles at me as she sits down.

I hadn't realised that was what it was, but I nod.

"I'd guess you haven't seen many before. Am I right?"

"I've seen one or two," I'm not lying here, "but not this small."

"You've probably never seen earth dragons before, then," she grins, "they don't live as long as the others, normally. Only about three years."

"Why?"

"Well, for a start, there's nothing for them to eat. Even air dragons have something, but earth dragons just can't."

"I'm not sure I understand."

"I can't believe this," she laughs, "there are four types of dragon, right?"

"Earth, Air, Fire and Water?"

"Right. And they feed on the people of their element. Fire dragons eat fire people – us. Water dragons eat water people – humans. Air dragons eat witches. Earth dragons don't have anyone left to eat."

I look at the little thing. It's rather sweet now that I know it's harmless.

"What about when there's a human witch?"

"They're the only ones the air dragons eat. Our witches don't count as witches." She takes the earth dragon out of its tank, "would you like to hold him?"

I hold out my arms, and as Kathleen comes over, I feel the dragon cling to my fingers like a scaly winged mouse.

"Is that a dragon?" Kathleen peers in.

"An earth dragon," the vampire nods, "Don't tell me you've never seen one either?"

"So does nothing suggest what they'd eat?" I ask.

"Well, there were stories a long time ago, but nobody listens to them. Apparently, according to these silly old myths, they would eat –"

I yelp in pain. My hands feel raw – a feeling I am altogether unused to. The dragon has doubled in size, and is ripping off the flesh from the palm of my hand.

The waitress sweeps it away, and she and Kathleen stare for a while before:

"Werewolves," the waitress finishes. Kathleen glances up, snorts, and touches the raw flesh gingerly. The wounds vanish.

"Say that word again," Kathleen whispers, "and you will never say another."

"I don't think you need to threaten her," I hiss, and turn back to the girl, but she has fled.

She is replaced presently by Libby. Libby's face looks about as red as her hair – which is impressive.

"I cannot believe Karl," she moans, as Kathleen inspects the little dragon, clawing pathetically at the side of its cage.

"What's he done?"

"We've been engaged for five months, and he starts flirting with some vampire chick over there."

"Classic," Kathleen sighs, "Men are dreadful, aren't they."

I glance around the room for Karl. He is standing near the opposite wall, next to a rather gorgeous vampire. A waitress – not the one we were talking to, goes up to the vampire, and whispers something in her ear. She makes a face, and leaves hurriedly.

The waitress puts her tray down, and within minutes, she and Karl are kissing. I take my eyes off them for a while, and pretend to listen to Libby, but when I look back, they are heading, together, into the toilets.

I glance at Kathleen, and tell her silently. Her eyes widen, and she stands up.

"Libby, find Ollie and Georgie. We're leaving."

"The horses are waiting for you outside," I add, as me and Kathleen hurry towards the bathrooms.

There are crashes and bangs coming from a shower cubicle. Pieces of clothing fly over the door.

"Karl," Kathleen calls, "Karl, it's time to go."

He grunts, but doesn't open the door.

I look at Kathleen as the crashes begin to take on a rhythm.

"Karl, we have to leave," Kathleen calls. I wish I had managed to get a clearer picture of the woman's face. I could have used it to put a spell on her, but she is just a rocking foot now, and almost inhexable.

"I've never tasted a werewolf before," she whispers. The thumping stops, and Karl gurgles.

"Stop," I shout. The door flies open – courtesy of Kathleen. The vampire is completely naked, but makes no attempt to cover herself. She is too busy drinking the blood that is seeping unstoppably from the holes she has made in his neck.

I glance at her face, and she stops, unconscious.

"He has no pulse," Kathleen tells me, before she even touches him, "we should leave him."

"None of them do," I kick his corpse, "he'll wake up again."

I hear a scream, and the thundering of hooves. The vampires have realised that there is more than one human, and I can only hope the horses are fast enough.

"They'll be in here in a minute." Kathleen glances at the creaking door.

"They can't do anything to us."

"They can tear him apart."

True. Annoyingly true.

"Don't you have any spells for the occasion?"

"Jack, you do. You've just forgotten them."

"You've forgotten them too, then?"

She nods. We need a new spell, then, and fast.

"I don't want these walls," I snarl, mostly at the concrete walls, which fade a little but stay.

"Go, now," I snap at them, and, unwillingly, they crumble into nothing. I have about three seconds to enjoy the night air before vampires start to pour out of the alleys and streets, towards the smell of Karl's blood.

I drop to all fours as a wolf and make a mock charge. They stop, and some hurry away, realising themselves. The rest, however, keep on coming. I stand up again, and go back into the cubicle.

"Jack," Kathleen whispers, "do something!"

"You're the better witch," I hiss. Kathleen glares at me.

"I'm holding the body."

"Fine."

I throw myself at the crowd, landing as a pile of snakes at their feet. I press into the crowd, nipping all the ankles I see. This panics some of them, but the rest soon discover that the venom has no effect on them. I regroup, and stand up as tall as I can in the middle of them.

"Go now," I shout, going out on a limb, "or I will call a dragon to destroy you all!"

They laugh, and ignore me. Kathleen closes the wall with an icy window, but it breaks as they close in on her.

I start to say words I had never learnt, in some language your kind probably still speak on some remote planet in my universe. I think I started just to scare them, but the words keep coming even when I don't want them to.

Kathleen knows. She glances at me as she drags the body up onto the roof and melts the ladder she's made.

I stop, and realise that the vampires are staring at me silently. More specifically, staring at my left hand.

I look down at it. It glows weakly, and I open my fist in from of my face. A tiny egg, about the size of a grain of sand, sits glowing in my lifeline. I blow on it, not really knowing why, and it glows more fiercely.

After a few painfully long moment of silence, it cracks.

The tiniest dragon ever crawls out. It rears up on my hand and stretches its tiny wings. As it leaps into the air, there is a scream of a hundred voices from the vampires, and a searing wave of heat rolls out from the dragon, exploding out to a million times its size, until its wingtips brush against the buildings on opposite sides of the alley, and further, cracking the walls with its impossible heat.

It belches flames as large as itself, which tear through the wreckages of buildings, and destroy everything in their wake. It pours like liquid flame after the vampires, not seeming to do anything more than land on them before they vanish, and it swells yet bigger.

"Stop it, Jack," Kathleen screams, but I can do nothing. It turns, and comes towards me, mouth gaping, and I curl into a singed ball, but it stops in front of me. Any surviving vampires having fled, it curls up and becomes, once again, a tiny, glowing grain of sand.

"Leave it, Jack," Kathleen calls, dropping gently to the ground, still dragging the corpse.

I obey. I don't know why I had been bending down to pick up the grain – it's caused enough death as it is.

Neither of us are in any mood to use magic again tonight. We walk back to the ship. When we get there, the vampires are crawling over the ship like so many flies – normal people reduced to this, all thanks to one foolish human.

I see one the remains of one near the ship, a tiny thread of copper lodged in his neck, and know that the horses were fast enough.

"The daylight will be here soon," I realise.

"Try and convince them to go home," she nods, "I'll send as many as I can away."

I crawl on top of the ship, kicking aside cleaners, cooks, housewives and children. They are the lucky ones – hitting the ground seems to make them come to their senses.

"Vampires," I bellow, "your sun is rising."

This has a definite effect. About two thirds of the vampires glance towards me, and towards the tendrils of light clutching at the horizon. Along with most of those near Kathleen, they turn and flee towards their village.

"Go away!" I shout, "Before you all burn."

A few more leave, and the dent near Kathleen grows considerably. A small child bites hysterically at my leg, and knocks me off the ship.

I land on a bare patch of sandy earth, staring up at the light streaming across the sky.

It isn't only the light moving, though. Balls of fire seem to be hurtling overhead, some of them falling down towards the vampire crowds. The hull groans under the heat, and the vampires that were on it vanish into the flames. Some of the vampires on the ground flee, and those that are left continue to press almost desperately towards the craft, trampling me over and over again.

Then the daylight hits the earth. I notice its glow for the first time, and any that isn't shadowed by vampires quickly explodes into flames. These flames shape into dragons, tearing apart the remaining vampires, who only now break up and start running away, screaming as they are ripped into pieces and consumed by the fire.

Soon, they are gone, except for a smell of burning hair, and ash in the air. I lie on the bare earth for a few moments before I stand up.

"Kathleen?" I call, walking towards the ship.

There is no answer. I stare around. Surely the dragons couldn't have destroyed her as well?

There is no sign of her or Karl. My heart begins to pound within my chest, and I find myself turning around and around, scanning the burning horizons for any sign of her, but there is none.

I stop and reel as my brain catches up with the rest of me. The word tilts, and I feel my feet burning.

I glance down, to find that my feet have disappeared into the seething earth. I yelp, and run towards the ship, the ground seeming to draw me in as I go, but leaving the ship sitting firmly above it.

The ladder comes down, and Libby and Georgie shoot out to drag me up.

"I can walk," I snap. Georgie shrugs, and lets go.

I collapse on the floor. Brilliant.

"Would you explain what just happened?" Libby demands. I look at the falling tatters of skin.

"Your fiancé just caused the deaths of about thirty thousand people," I reply, "And could you explain what's happened to me?"

"Comparatively, you're fine," Georgie shrugs, "But you are messing up the floor."

I roll over onto my back, and lift my legs up. Blood oozes out of the bare flesh that used to be the middle of my calf. Fortunately, my jeans seem to be intact.

"I hate dragons."

"Little bastards," Kathleen's voice agrees. I breathe a mental sigh of relief, "I've locked Karl up in one of the bathrooms." She grips my knees, and my feet are restored, "what would you do without me, Jack?"

"Get a wheelchair, probably."

I stand up, and glance around.

"Are the horses alright?"

"Brilliant," Libby nods, throwing the tiny ball at me. I peer into the cold globe, and see that the horses are unharmed – if tiny, "I don't think I've ever moved so fast in my life."

I shrug.

"I'm sure they'll be glad to hear you enjoyed it." I hesitate, "And you do know that Karl will now be –"

"A vampire," Libby nods, "We're finished now, anyway."

I nod.

"How exactly," Ollie interrupted, stuffing his face on something greasy and foul-smelling, "how exactly are you planning to manage a werewolf, a witch, a vampire and four humans on board one ship?"

Kathleen smiles.

"Jack and I are going to have a little chat with Karl. A little chat about self control."

For the next three weeks, Karl does not move. Ballsy fixes the plane in less time than expected, and Kathleen and I find that we can be slightly useful with magic on a ship like this, summoning every tool that Ballsy complains that he's lost, or should have been provided with years ago. Libby, who normally would have been nipping in and out of the engine rooms to check that her baby was alright, instead spends her time staring in at Karl. We join her occasionally, if only perplexed by how she can still have any feelings for him.

After three weeks, he starts twitching, and his eyes flickering. By listening to his mind, we can hear some thoughts moving around, and soon enough his brain is working again.

He wakes up dead. I watch from a distance of a few metres as his eyes open, glassy and staring, and he sits up.

Slowly the clouds in his eyes clear. He touches his neck, and feels for a pulse.

It isn't coming. I say nothing, but Libby gasps quietly beside me.

"Quiet," Kathleen whispers.

Libby nods, and swallows. Karl stands up, and starts looking around.

"He hasn't changed yet," I murmur.

"No," Kathleen nods, "not yet."

Karl lets out a scream that sounds like he's dying – except, of course, he's already done that. His teeth are the first things to change – shorter and blunter than we made them look, but still a good deal longer than they were. His eyes, blue, flare red for a brief instant, and he rises off the floor.

"What's happening?" Libby squeaks. I am in a similar state of shock, but Kathleen has all the answers.

"He's changing from a water person to a fire person. All the water in his body is changing into steam."

Another scream, accompanied by an explosion of steam from his eyes, ears, nose and mouth. He sinks to the ground again, and collapses, dripping in the water that used to be two thirds of him.

"It's done," Kathleen murmurs, and the wall between us and Karl vanishes.

He glances up, his red pupils full of hate.

"What have you done to me?" he demands.

"You dare blame us for this?" Kathleen raises an eyebrow.

"You brought this upon yourself, Karl," Libby whispers.

The red glows almost white as he turns to her. His nostrils flare as he sucks in her scent, the scent of wet human blood, and he stands up slowly.

"Libby," he whispers, "I'm sorry for what happened, I really am," he moves towards her, and reaches out to touch her cheek.

"Karl, you can't do this anymore," Libby sniffs pathetically, "You're not –"

He lunges forwards. There is a metallic clang, and he collapses. Kathleen looks with satisfaction at the copper pole she had conjured.

"Safe," Libby finishes.

"I'm putting the wall back," Kathleen informs Libby, and Libby disappears behind a mirrored wall. Kathleen turns to Karl again.

"Karl," Kathleen smiles mirthlessly, "you have just caused a ridiculous number of deaths, of those who are now your kind. Did you know that?"

He looks up at her dully.

"I think there is perhaps a better way of putting it across," I offer, "I could just about open these blinds, and he could see for himself."

He yelps in fear as I pull the blinds and let the unfiltered sunlight in.

A dragon, somewhat out of place in the blackness of space, flares up against the window, trying to melt its way through the reinforced glass.

"Imagine, Karl," Kathleen lifts him off the ground and presses his face against the glass, where he can feel the searing heat of the dragon, "imagine the sky filled with that, and imagine people, ordinary people, like you, below that. People as far as the eye can see. Try to count those in your head, Karl, and then perhaps we won't have to let this at you."

Karl blinks silently, his pupils widening in fear, filling his eyes, and his face contorted in the pain the dragon's light is causing such wide pupils.

"You have a choice, Karl," I tell him, banishing Kathleen's wall, "You control yourself, or we won't have the luxury of choice."

Libby squeals as Karl pulls helplessly towards her – however, Kathleen is far heavier than him now, him having lost two thirds of his weight, and he cannot move.

"We're going to leave now, Karl," she tells him, almost apologetically, letting go. He drops to the floor for the umpteenth time today, and compulsively moves towards Libby, like a starved vulture stranded not ten feet from food, but unable to move to get there.

Kathleen glances down at him, flicks her hand, and walks out. Libby and I stay for a while, and watch the razor-sharp cage grow up, and the figure – an image of pale flesh, and the strong smell of life, within, chest rising and falling as if she were real, eyes fluttering, and moving around.

We close the door and bolt it on the way out, and go up to the next deck.

"Don't you think that's a bit dangerous?" Georgie asks me. I glance at the surveillance screen as she expands it to fill the wall.

"I think it's the best way for him to survive," I say eventually, not really sure if I mean it. Karl is pressed up against the cage, mouth gaping, blood trickling up his arms and face from the cuts the fine copper mesh leaves.

Over the next few days we get into a routine – every night, Libby and I go in there with Kathleen. Every night, Kathleen heals his cuts. As soon as he wakes, he drags himself towards the cage again, weaker every day, as close as he can get to the illusion, the image of blood.

After a month, we realise that he's starving. He eats the food me and Kathleen take to him, but no matter how much we give him, his health does not improve, falling instead into a steep decline.

Although he doesn't speak – I don't think he has the strength – Libby realises what he needs.

"Blood," she whispers, after a week of watching him get paler and paler, thinner and sicker, "He needs blood." She looks up at Kathleen from her cross-legged position on the floor, "I have to give him some."

"Don't," I snap, "I will."

"He might not drink werewolf blood," Libby protests.

"I'm not going to use my blood," I scoff. I take the empty bottle he has drained of wine just minutes ago, and squeeze my hand over it.

"What are you doing?" Libby asks. I don't actually know, so I shrug. At first I think nothing's happening, but then my hand becomes sticky with blood,

Libby gasps, and Ollie, coming in with a tray of fresh food for Libby, stops and has to sit down.

"You're taking our blood," Kathleen breathes, and puts her hand on Libby's shoulder. Libby relaxes, and as Kathleen heals her own blood as well, the blood tickles out of my hand into the neck of the bottle.

I know. I don't know why, or how, that happened – I had thought to create blood. Even my own blood is draining – I can feel a numbing near my heart.

The liquid spills over the top of the bottle, and I open my hand. A tiny streak of silver heads the downwards pull of the beautiful crimson as it drips off my hand.

"I'll take it to him," Kathleen stands up, looking the least drained of any of us, despite the fact that she has far less blood than any one of us in the first place. She picks up the bottle, the blood sloshing over the edge, and takes it in to Karl, bleeding by the cage.

"Karl," Kathleen whispers, opening the door. At first he doesn't react, but a drop of blood falls off the side of the bottle and hits the floor. His head snaps up so quickly that he scrapes half the skin off his face.

"Come here, Karl," Kathleen sits down. Karl tries to move, tries frantically, but his limbs won't work. Kathleen shuffles over to him, and puts the bottle in front of him. He can't even move enough to pick it up – his hand pushes along the ground, and knocks against it, but not even with enough power to make it wobble. Kathleen shuffles closer, picks up the bottle, and holds it to his mouth.

He swallows weakly, most of the blood pouring down his face, mingling with his own, and soaking his tattered clothes. Kathleen takes one hand off the bottle, and reaches for his, holding it to the bottle until he manages to hold on. As we watch, his fingers grow stronger, and he begins to sit up.

"Thank you," he whispers taking the bottle away from his mouth to breathe a spluttering breath. Kathleen smiles unwillingly. Libby sobs quietly behind me.

"More?" Kathleen glances at me through the wall she can only see as a mirror, and puts her finger to the empty bottle Karl hands back to her. From the tip of the finger, first a tiny beadlet of blood, and then a tiny crimson river, fall into the bottle. Karl takes it back, and drinks greedily.

Kathleen leaves him now, and as she comes out, she holds her head high to address me.

"That, Jack, is how you make blood."

I just glare silently.

Over the next few days, there is less damage for her to undo when she goes to see him every morning, and she fills two bottles with blood for him every day. Soon he has recovered from his sickness, and the illusion starts to fade as he ceases to pay it attention.

He grows less and less unpredictable – we start letting Ollie keep him company while he drinks (Ollie with six bottles of some strange alcohol, as opposed to two of blood). Soon, we feel that it's safe to let Ollie stay in there when we're not watching, and I (without error this time) replace the door's locks with a single latch.

We begin to reintroduce the others to him, and at first he does nothing inhuman. When the slip does come, it's hardly his fault – we let Libby, finally, go in with him again.

She bursts in, and flings her arms around his neck, apologising for everything we've done. He hugs her back at first, but after a while, he notices her neck.

Kathleen becomes agitated as he begins to trace his fingers over the veins, his hand moving with her pulse, and then, we feel, it's the right time for intervention.

We try and pull her away gently. Karl lets go, but Libby throws an instant tantrum. His eyes go slightly redder, and he lunges for her neck.

I yelp in pain. I don't know if he realised that I was trying to get in between them, but either way, he's bitten me. I turn and snarl as the blood trickles out of my shoulder, and he looks sheepish. I glance down at my shoulder – it stops this nonsense of bleeding, and the wound closes. I rub it tenderly.

"That hurt."

"You big baby," Kathleen pokes it, "tell me if you feel yourself dying."

I touch my neck to check – the pulse is still there. That's alright then.

"How long did it take for you to die?" I demand of Karl.

"I don't know," he stares, "I wasn't exactly timing it."

"No, you were having sex with a vampire, if I remember right," Kathleen agrees, "I'm fairly sure he was already gone when we went in, Jack."

I nod. A great relief, I must say.

"You mustn't do that again, Libby," I warn, moving away.

Apart from that first slip, there are no major incidents relating to his new species as Libby steers us madly through space. We do catch him licking up blood after Georgie missed a tomato she was chopping for supper, but he doesn't do anyone any harm.

Soon, he is even allowed to move back into his old sleeping quarters. We do make sure someone is awake nearby all the time, but he doesn't do anything but sleep at night. In fact, the next problem we have isn't related to him at all – Ballsy goes through puberty and starts becoming an overgrown sulky teenager after Kathleen heals him for a paper-cut, and gets angry with the Gravity Simulation Machine. He destroys it by kicking it when it refuses to hold Karl down as tightly as the rest of us.

"Right outside a black hole," Libby rages, "you lost our gravity right outside black hole."

She pushes him, and they shoot off on opposite directions. She squeals in exasperation, and pushes off the wall to slam into him again.

"You know, you're acting more childishly than him," Kathleen tells her sagely. Kathleen is floating primly above the kitchen sink. I snigger as a potato-peeler and some old peelings float slowly upwards to become entangled in her hair. She glares, and I take advantage of a passing bed to avoid the teaspoon she hurls my way.

"Can anyone feel something pulling them towards the control room?" Ollie asked.

"Yes," Kathleen nods, "It's the black hole. You'll probably all be torn through it now that there's no gravity."

Georgie looks up from trying to re-order the pages of her diary, and stares at Kathleen.

"Oh, don't worry about it," Kathleen snorts, "It'll turn out fine. Just like the Ficration."

"What on earth is a Ficration?" I demand.

"It's a ball of purple slime that feeds on bone-marrow," Libby grunts as she kicks Ballsy in the most unpleasant place to be kicked.

He crumples, and Kathleen grimaces.

"Sorry," Kathleen apologises, "that hurts a lot on men."

He agrees between gasps.

"You dreamt one up just after we woke up," Ollie bounces off the ceiling.

That explains the purple goo on the walls, then.

"Shouldn't we all try and deal with this gravity thing, though?" I query, pulling myself to the wall as a canary tears past, "where did that come from?"

"It was Sygmom's," Georgie apologises, "There's quite a few birds in his quarters. Surely you heard them before?"

"I can't say I did."

The canary zips into a cupboard facing the back of the plane, and floats there twittering. It is joined presently by three more canaries, seven parakeets, a fat macaw and two lovebirds pushing a nest.

"I wonder where the rest are," Libby stops pummelling Ballsy to consider. As if on cue, several dozen more birds – from two black swans to a small family of humming birds – slip into the kitchen and take refuge under the sink.

"This is ridiculous," I snap, and everyone drops to the ground. The fat macaw lands heavily on the hot water-tap. Ollie sits up, rubbing his head.

"Why didn't you do that earlier?"

"I didn't know I could," I shrug, "I just felt like it then."

"Mainly because we were all very close to the ceiling?" Georgie touches her back tenderly.

There is a deafening crash, and everything goes black.

Only, however, momentarily.

"I think we're through." Libby whispers as the lights come back on, and the cupboard closes on the birds.

"Good. Where are we going now?" I glance around.

"Where do you want to go?"

"We have to find some people," Kathleen shrugs, "there was a fake moon somewhere near where you found us."

I hold my breath.

"Kathleen," I say, when I get the courage, "they're not there anymore."

"What do you mean?"

"Just as we were leaving," I don't really know how to say this, "They took a security measure to stop a repeat of our escape. They blew the quertinak they were in up."

"What do you mean, you escaped?" Ollie demands. Neither of us answers. Kathleen is screaming at me inside my head, and is in no fit state to talk.

"What do you mean, you escaped?" Ollie repeats, a little louder. Kathleen withdraws.

"There was nothing you could have done," she whispers.

"What did you mean?" Ollie bellows. The fat macaw falls into the sink.

"We were taken for scientific experimenting," I snap, "most of the village was killed for fur, but a lot of us were taken for experiments. We got out while they were flying, and I think I may have killed someone."

"We're going back to Earth, then," Kathleen murmurs, "you?"

"I've never seen Earth," Libby nods, "it would be an adventure."

"Now there's no point hunting vampires," Georgie agrees, "we might as well go and meet werewolves."

"Those that are left," Kathleen stares at the floor listlessly.

"I'm sorry," I whisper.

"If we go back to Earth," Karl offers, "we could make sure they're prepared in case it ever happens again."

"I'll get us going," Libby rushes through to the cockpit, and Kathleen stands up.

"You're right," she looks up at Karl with more respect than before, and smiles, "We know what humans are capable of now, better than we did before. We can protect Jack's people."

"Our people," I correct her.

"Our people," she nods. Finally, a concession that she's more one of us than one of the people that hates us.

"Come on, I can't do this alone," Libby calls.

We follow through into the cockpit, and for the next five minutes, all seven of us are occupied with restarting the functions of the ship other than lights. The gravity simulator hisses and explodes as Libby tries once again to switch it back on. She shrugs, and turns her attention instead to the ventilators.

"Is the water up?" she asks, reaching towards a nozzle in a dent in the wall.

"Perfectly," Georgie nods.

Libby sighs happily as she drinks the water.

"Isn't that a satisfying hum?" she challenges us, switching on the control panel.

It whirrs, then settles into a quiet drone. Libby looks down at the instruments, cracks her fist down on them, and looks again.

"Somebody open the screens," she whispers.

I glance at them, and they retreat into their traps.

"There's nothing there," Libby stands up.

"It's probably just a dark bit of space," Kathleen dismisses her claim.

"No," Libby shakes her head, "even in a vacuum, there's something to read – in a vacuum, I'd be getting a low pressure reading, and probably some sort of tridit count. Here, there's just nothing."

"Not even photons?" Kathleen dredges up a word she learnt in secondary school all those years ago.

"What?"

"There's a star there."

Libby looks up at the light Kathleen is pointing at.

"It can't be," Libby shakes her head, "I'm sure it can't be."

She hits the instruments again, but still they give her the same output.

"I can't even move anything," her shoulders sag, "we need some sort of particles or pressures to move at all, and…"

There is an ear-shattering bang, and a blinding light so bright that everything not screwed down is hurled backwards. The ship turns over a few times, and Libby, blinking, hurls it forwards.

"It's air," she frowns, "it's just air now."

Then is a ripping sound as the air leaves us.

"What is that light?" I demand. Libby shrugs;

"A dying star? I don't know."

"I'm thirsty," Karl sits down.

"Here," Kathleen hands him an empty bottle from nowhere. He is about to complain when a drip of blood trickles out of the top.

"You're getting better at this," I comment. Kathleen smiles, the grievances of minutes ago long forgotten, and peers at the light.

"Go to it," Kathleen whispers. Libby frowns.

"I thought you wanted Earth."

"I want to see that light better."

Libby presses down on the accelerator, and we shoot forwards through space.

The light moves. I stare, and suddenly, we are on top of it.

Libby screams, there is a strange laugh, and the ship stops.

"You just ruined my creation," the voice that laughed said.

I turn around, and see an angel, standing quite cheerfully at the door of the cockpit, her blonde hair ablaze with light.

"I know you," I narrow my eyes, "I really do know you."

"It takes that little time to forget?" the angel's light shimmers, and fades to a pale glow. She folds her wings neatly, "Jack Hanov Himmerden. How's your wife?"

"She's dead."

The angel stares, "Again? Already?"

"Antoinette," the name comes to me at last, "that's who you are."

"How did you lose her again so quickly? It can't have been ten years since we found her last time."

"About sixty-eight thousand," I correct her, "humans wouldn't have tried to kill your people when I last met you."

"Don't be ridiculous," she laughs, "we can't die." She hesitates, "well, I suppose the earthly angels might be sent to the worlds of the dead." She looks at me suspiciously.

"So how do you not look older, then? Even I look older, and I'm just a spirit."

"I don't know," I shrug, "I just didn't get older."

"Do you actually know this thing?" Libby demands.

"Oh, the atheists of today," Antoinette glares at Libby, "If I hadn't been a sinner once, I'd strike you down for that blasphemy."

"We're not atheists," Karl protests.

"And I'm not a thing. I'm an angel. By a narrow scrape, I have to say, but I am an angel. And apparently quite an established one."

"What were you doing?"

"I was creating," she shrugs, "we all have to. It keeps us going. We make new places, and let them grow." She reaches inside silky robes, and brings out a handful of glowing marbles, "See?"

She hands one to me, and it falls through my hand.

"You fool," she sighs, and catches it before it hits the ground, "you just dropped a universe."

"It went through my hand," I protest.

"Never mind that. You're not supposed to be here, so you'd best head back to wherever you came from."

"Do you know where the black hole is?" asks Libby quietly.

"Not in this universe," Antoinette scoffs, "This is a nice new one. No nasty black holes here."

"Then how did we get here?"

Antoinette's face falls.

"I didn't leave the door open again, did I?" she moans, "I did, didn't I? I'm hopeless. I never should have been an angel in the first place."

Chapter 3 – Stupidity

She takes flight, and vanishes through the ceiling. A few minutes later she returns.

"I have left it open," she sighs, "I always do. I think it's your universe back there, Jack, so if this atheist would follow me, I'll have you all home in a just a sec."

Libby scowls. Karl finishes the blood with a gulp, and Antoinette trips over the fat macaw in a most un-angelic manner as she heads out of the ship.

"Darn bird!" she shrieks, and kicks it. It squawks and rolls over, its legs waving madly in the air as it attempts to turn its great bulk over again. Antoinette snorts regally, and slips out of the plane.

"How did she just trip on a parrot and then fly through steel?" Georgie demands.

"I'd guess," I consider, "I'd guess that if it's alive it's solid to her. Otherwise angels wouldn't really be able to rescue people, would they?"

The ship swings around violently, and Libby stamps on the accelerator. The macaw rolls over onto its feet, and then with a triumphant screech launches into the air, only to fall head first back down to the floor.

The angel, who I met many years ago after a unicorn took me down to purgatory to try and find my wife's soul (it's a very long story), flies ahead effortlessly, occasionally rolling over onto her back and hovering, watching with amusement as we try, in vain, to catch up. Libby starts to go redder and redder, and the ship gets louder and louder, as she tries to make it go faster and faster.

Suddenly, the angel stops. The ship carries on for a few moments, and Antoinette crashes through the windscreen.

"Careful," she snaps, "you'll break the door down!"

Libby sinks into her chair in shame.

"Now you'll have to be very careful," the angel breathes, "go slightly to the left. Just a touch."

There is a rumble as the ship moves about five feet to the left, and stops. Antoinette winces.

"I think it might be better if you let me drive."

She touches the controls, and the ship moves back almost to where it was.

"You might want to sit down," Antoinette adds, "I don't know what it's like for a mortal to go through this."

Everyone joins me on the floor, and Georgie picks up the now unconscious macaw, and strokes its crumpled feathers.

"I miss Sygmom," she sighs.

"I would say you'll see him again, but that doesn't seem to comfort people nowadays," the angel folds her wings up neatly behind her, and the ship moves forwards slowly.

"What's that?" Ollie stands up. I can see what he is looking at – we all can, but I don't think anyone except the angel can answer him.

"Get back down," she says, "it's the door."

She steps back from the controls, and the ship shoots forwards, pulled towards the open door so fast I don't think even light could have caught it.

Then it stops. Everything fades to a bright white except Antoinette – so white she looks like a dark grey smear on the impossible white of this light. The ship grates forwards and when I look at the angel again, she is shivering. There is a grating sound, then a crack, and the ship races forwards again, the white light lost.

"You can get up now," she says, "come and see something no human has ever seen before."

We stand up, and peer past her like a group of curious children. Antoinette steps backwards to let us see, and my heart feels like it's being frozen as she steps through me.

"Sorry," she whispers, and we crowd over the control panel to stare outside.

"We're on a surface," Libby exclaims, "at this speed?"

"The edge of your universe. The division between vacuum and nothing."

"It looks silver," I frown.

"The same as the division between water and air."

The ship pulls away from the wall, as if of its own accord.

"What are we doing?" Libby demands.

"This edge is cracking. Another universe is about to break through."

"What'll happen then?"

Antoinette doesn't answer at first. She walks to the other side of the cockpit, and turns to face us.

"You understand that the vampire is a different version of what Jack is, from a different universe?"

Libby nods.

"There are eight universes with your Earth in them, other than this one. Three Earths have werewolves. Two have vampires. One is dead. One has humans who haven't destroyed anything."

She stops.

"What does the other one have?" Georgie asks the question we're all thinking.

"First, I want you to understand that it isn't necessarily that universe that's breaking through is that one. So I don't want you to panic."

She is going very red for an angel.

"What is there?" I demand.

"They're," she hesitates, "I don't know," her voice goes higher and higher, "they were everywhere at first. They're sort of," her hands move in an effort to explain it without actually saying it, "they're, they're like... sort of...you'd say," she stammers, "a bit like... almost – ish... slightly like...angels, but..."

"Fallen angels?" Libby suggests.

Antoinette sags with relief that she didn't have to say it herself.

"It's probably not that universe," Antoinette says after a short pause, "there's thousands. Most of them are too young to have anything distressing in them. The odds are a billion, a trillion to one that it's that universe that broke through."

"Jacks in this universe," Kathleen puts a hand on Antoinette's shoulder – it stays there, "there is absolutely no way that Jack would be lucky enough to get any other than that one in a trillion."

Antoinette looks distinctly worried. Her face lights up, and Kathleen's hand falls through her shoulder.

"On the bright side, they might not notice. In fact, I'm fairly sure they won't."

She beams.

"So where are we going now?"

"Earth," says Kathleen confidently.

"Earth," confirms Libby.

"Earth." Antoinette looks around at the stars, "there."

The ship turns slightly and accelerates.

"Well, what're we all going to do while we're on our way, then?"

"We?" Libby frowns, "don't you have to go off and do something holy, like turn wine into water, or something?"

Antoinette laughed.

"I can't do that," she snorted, "I'm not a witch. For the next thirteen years, I'm hardly an angel at all."

"Why?" Libby takes a menacing step over the border between free space and Antoinette's personal space, "why aren't you an angel?" She hesitates. "Are you fallen? You are, aren't you?"

Antoinette stares at her.

"Have you ever actually seen an angel after they've fallen?"

Libby blinks silently, and I find Kathleen's mind drawing mine to an image in Antoinette's. I draw back before I can see, and Kathleen gasps and withdraws, reeling.

"You might want to forget that," Antoinette nods in her direction, "and stay out of my head in the future. No, Liberty, I'm not fallen."

"She broke the laws of the macroverse," Kathleen informs us once she has gathered herself, "by ripping a hole between two universes."

"It's like," Antoinette considers, "being suspended from school for a week for writing on the desks."

"Except this is a slightly more serious sentence," I can't help but point out.

"Not if you consider the scale. Obliteration, complete obliteration, is the equivalent of the death sentence. Life imprisonment is your version of falling."

I consider this. Unless someone shot me, life imprisonment would be a very, very tedious business. In fact, it would, so far as I know, it would be forever.

In which case, falling must be extremely unpleasant, if comparing a school suspension to thirteen years.

"What's it like to be obliterated?" Georgie wonders.

"I don't know," Antoinette snorts, "the next obliterated angel I meet, I'll ask."

"I might be able to restore you to being a full angel," Kathleen offers. Antoinette glances at her.

"You probably could, but it would be breaking the rules. It would be a sin for me to let you heal me."

Kathleen takes her hand back, and the ship bellows as it crashes into something solid.

Once the lights have stopped flickering, I stand and look out of the window. A familiarly icy landscape spreads out before me. Home.

"Welcome to Earth," I announce.

The humans stand up slowly, and move to the window.

"I thought it was covered in water."

"This is too far north for that. There's water two hundred metres below us."

"But what about forests?" Libby looks around, "isn't all the land meant to be covered with trees?"

"Not here. In the south."

Georgie throws open the door, and we hear the hatch open.

The rest hurry out behind her. Kathleen and I follow presently, and as our bare feet touch the crisp snow, a deep feeling of belonging courses through my veins.

"It's beautiful," Libby breathes. Georgie nods silently, and Ballsy scoops up just enough snow to make a good sized snowball to hurl at Ollie.

Ollie hurls one back, and misses, hitting Karl instead. Shortly, everyone except me and Kathleen is hurling snowballs – including the angel.

It takes a while for them to feel the cold, and, surprisingly enough, it is the angel that feels it first.

"What temperature is it?" she demands after perhaps ten minutes of snowballs, shaking freshly fallen flakes from the feathers of her wings.

"It's summer," I shrug, "probably minus twelve or so."

"Holy cow," Georgie laughs, "how did we not notice?"

Nobody answers, but the angel wraps her wings around herself tightly as the humans and the vampire troop inside.

"Don't you want to put something warm on?" Kathleen asks.

"I can't. It would fall through me.

"But you tripped on the macaw."

"I change every few seconds. I am not like you, creating energy and matter when you run out. I am energy, and I shift between being solid and hardly being there at all to stop myself from burning out."

"So do angels burn out?"

"If they weren't born angels, they can. When we help universes, we absorb a large part of the energy, and so we survive for another ten thousand years or so."

The five vampire-hunters re-emerge from the craft, wrapped up so thickly that only Georgie, with her dark skin, is recognisable.

"What now?" Ollie's voice emerges from one of the bundles.

"Humans had thinner warmth clothes when I was human," I snort, "how is it you got those?"

"Cost," the bundle shrugs.

I take the glassy ball out of my pocket, and check on the horses. All healthy. I search for the seam, and snap it open with my fingernail. I place it on the ground quickly, and the three tiny figures shake off their slumber, and step out of the hollow sphere. They stay tiny for a fraction of a second, and then, freed of the powers of the box, they explode out to their natural sizes.

Lycanthropy takes off, and the bundle that I presume is Libby screams.

"What is it doing?" she squeaks.

"She's just seeing where we are."

"But she's flying!"

"And?"

"Horses don't fly!"

"She does."

Lycanthropy lands, and mock-starts towards the sun. South, I'd guess, by how far above the horizon it is.

"That way," Kathleen nods, and the humans dutifully follow the horse. Adrastea glances at Kathleen, but Kathleen shakes her head, and the horse moves on.

"I'll fly," Antoinette's wings press down on the air, sending a flurry of snow as she lifts into the sky. She hovers for a moment, then skims ahead to float above the humans.

It takes less than four minutes to reach what Lycanthropy was aiming towards – a village. It seems, at first glance, to be deserted, but then I see lights in a window.

"This looks familiar," I frown.

"It's like a world made of ice," Libby enthuses.

"It's just a covering. Most of them have stone underneath it," I inform her.

"Jack," Kathleen grips my arm, "This is our house."

I consider the weathered structure before me. It is uncannily similar, it is true – it even has stables, in a world with less than a thousand horses. Deserted, as ours would be.

"It can't be," I say at last, "There's too many houses."

"It's entirely possible that it is," Antoinette shrugs, "This Earth could have had a thousand years since you met me."

"How?"

"There is no time in the doorway."

Kathleen takes a few steps forward, and puts her hand on one of the dents in the wall of ice. Her hand sinks through snow and stops.

"It must be ours, Jack," she beams, "It's glass! I'll race you to the door."

As it happens, I win that particular race, but only just. The door is surprisingly clean, compared to the windows, at least, and I push against it.

"It's barred," I exclaim.

"Oh, let me," Kathleen points at the door, and it snaps open.

Someone screams. As my eyes get used to the darkness after the bright white of the snow, I see people. Scores of them, far more than we had dared to hope had survived.

"Who are you?" a bearded man demands.

"I know you," I stare. I do know him. I don't know the beard, or the grey in his hair, but I do know his face.

"Who are you?" he asks again.

"I'm Jack," I reply, "and this used to be my house."

"It is Jack," a woman whispers, "I'd know."

"Imogen," I exclaim, "I thought you were dead!"

"We thought you were," she retorts, suddenly seeming a great deal brighter than the Imogen I knew.

"How long have we been gone?" I ask, peering at her face. At least five years, even if she's aged quickly.

"You've been gone twelve years."

"Not as long as it could have been," Kathleen shrugs.

"You were lucky," Antoinette agrees, landing.

"How many of you are left?" I ask, looking at the surprising number of people around Imogen.

"About five hundred. We found a hundred and thirty bodies."

Fifty, then. Fifty gone in one blast.

Less than I had thought, at least.

The humans waddle up, and Ballsy trips over his feet and knocks us all into the room.

"Who are they?" Imogen asks, "People you rescued?"

"Not the way you hope." I consider how to say this, "They're not even werewolves."

There is a general gasp of surprise.

"We're human," Libby foolishly pipes up.

The surprise turns to anger, and knives come out of various pockets.

"They've led the hunters to us again," A man near the back hisses, "They're working for humans!"

It is a truly hopeless situation. The knives quickly leave hands, and spin towards us. Kathleen seems to act instinctively and the knives turn to falling snow.

"What have you done?" the Priest demands.

"We haven't been entirely truthful with you," I snap, "but that doesn't mean that we're on the side of the humans."

"Only humans use magic," the man at the back calls out.

"Well, did you really think we'd be telling you all we were witches after we got burnt the third time?" I demand. This shuts them up, "These humans are no more dangerous to you than your children."

"Our children are already bitten," Imogen whispers.

"Than your children were," I correct myself, "They were vampire hunters."

"Don't be ridiculous," laughs a familiar voice, "vampires don't exist."

"They shouldn't," I agree, "And they only did in another universe."

"But one of the humans was bitten," Kathleen destroys Karl's protective clothing, leaving him no more covered than the werewolves before me. He shivers, and turns to Kathleen to complain. His mouth opens slightly, and with wolves eyes, all of them can see his teeth. More than one person crosses themself.

"And as much as we enjoyed crashing into other worlds," I continue, "We felt it was our duty to come back and help prepare this world for when the humans come back."

"Why do we need your help?"

"Have you ever wondered how long we've been alive?" I demand. I know none of them have, "Or what we did before the humans left for the first time?"

There are gasps of surprise at this. As far as they were concerned, we'd been there since before any of them were born – but not that long before. They take a while to grasp just how much longer than them we have had on this planet.

"And if you don't mind, it's been too long since I last slept without waking up being dissected, so if you'll all kindly go home, I am going to get a proper rest in a real bed now."

That shuts them up. They all leave, grumbling that they were in the middle of a meeting, but going nonetheless.

"Since when did they hold meetings?" I demand of Kathleen as we clear the furniture to replace it with beds.

"Twelve years is a long time for them, Jack."

"A long time for anybody," snorts Libby.

"Oh, yes," I round on Libby, "I had meant to tell you. There is a time and place to think before you speak. There may be different laws here, but that doesn't mean that sense doesn't apply."

"But it is!" she seems to have forgotten her earlier announcement.

"Not for me," Antoinette laughs from atop an icy ledge, "and I'll be a mere spirit again before Jack and Kathleen get any older."

"Will we get older?" I ask.

"I suppose you might when the whole universe crumbles down to nothing," she shrugs, "who knows?"

I fill the building with heat, and Kathleen quickly separates this heat from the walls.

"Georgie, close the door."

"You could."

"You're right next to it anyway."

Georgie closes the door sulkily.

"And goodnight," I mutter, destroying all the light in the room.

After crashing around for a few minutes, everyone finds their way to a bed.

At around nine the next morning, I let the natural light in again. The humans snore on, but Kathleen's bed is empty, and Karl is staring silently at the ceiling.

"Why doesn't the light kill me?" he asks, as I get up and dress.

"The light didn't kill the vampires in their world," I shrug, "They were killed by dragons who woke up in the light. There aren't any dragons on this planet."

"So basically I'm human here?"

"I know nothing more of this than you do."

I leave, feeling a little guilty at not having done more. I see Kathleen about a hundred yards away, pushing the village away from the house.

"Good morning," I call out.

"Not really," she retorts, "Antoinette's spoken to some of the born angels. They say the humans are preparing to come here again."

I glance at the sky.

"So what are we going to do about that?"

"Whatever we can."

"And why are you moving the village?"

"I'm putting another one in."

With a groan, a large stone church slides into the gap between our house and the village. About thirty houses follow, and then many more.

"How many villages are you bringing?" I demand, jumping out of the way as an igloo – not something I've seen in a long time – joins us.

"Seven so far."

She leaves it at that, and I wonder, as I follow her back inside, how long it will be before all these new neighbours start killing each other.

This may be something you do not understand.

When the human race abandoned us, we lived, at first, in isolation. Most carried silver knives, and when two werewolves of the same sex met, if on a night of the full moon, one would be seriously, if temporarily, harmed. If otherwise, one would be killed.

The only ones that didn't fight would be members of family. It has only been in the last twenty thousand years or so that we have started to live in greater "packs" – mainly because there are few enough human attacks now for this not to be massively devastating. It also gives us better organisation in case of an attack.

However, even with these acceptances of others so close, werewolves do not like to be crowded. And cities are definitely too crowded for them.

But, apparently not these ones.

In fact, as time passes, I begin to notice a number of strange things. The werewolves here all seem to be unconscious in the wolf form – even those who would follow orders last time I saw them change become rabid dogs at the approach of the full moon.

The cold summer winds, which used to drag entire villages out of the ice, no longer blow.

And people from the villages that Kathleen brought know my name.

The humans and the vampire pick up nothing of this. Antoinette spends most of her time in the biting room, tracing her fingers over the bloodstains.

Kathleen is too busy with her plans to notice anything or anyone.

As I do, I get bored. I start to go for walks through the new city, which, considering I'm happiest when I can't see anything made by human or semi-human hands, is just as surprising as some of the previously mentioned oddities. I meet people sometimes – those who aren't listening intently to the humans' stories in between wrecking buildings on the night of the full moon. After about three months, I start to get very close to one of these people.

It isn't what you would call a long relationship. We're walking in the same direction. We start talking – nothing much. Just banter.

It ends up with us both going into her home for a drink. A drink is followed by another indulgence.

It could end at that, but she starts talking. She speaks softly, but clearly. She asks me about space, about people, about women. I realise, after we have talked for a very long while, that, although I know pretty much everything she's killed, loved or eaten in her years as a werewolf, I still don't know her name.

"What is your name?" I interrupt her talk about her (deceased) husband. She looks at me in silence for a while.

"You should know," she chides me; "I was the last one you bit before you went away."

I frown. Trying to remember the rosy-cheeked girl's name – one of those obscure ones you don't hear much, near the end of the alphabet. Vanessa? No, Rosalind, perhaps?

"Xanthe?" I query.

"Polly," she snorts, "Polly, you fool."

That name I do remember.

That name should not be on this earth.

"I didn't bite you," I whisper, "I never bit you."

She laughs, and reaches out an arm to pull me back. I stare at her hand, and suddenly it seems to be all wrong, and not the hand of a young woman at all, not even a hand.

I run. I am a wolf by the time I have reached the door, with no intention of slowing down to answer her screams or demands. Eyes turn on me as I run, but I pay them no heed until I reach the stone church that the humans and Karl have been spending most of the day in, talking.

Only werewolves in here. I turn and continue fleeing until I reach "our" house. I rush inside, and they are all there, Kathleen finally torn away from her plans.

I stand up a naked human.

"Jack, are you alright?" Libby and Georgie stare.

Kathleen rolls her eyes, and stands up. I am dressed by this stage, and she is leaving the room.

"Wait," I pant, "There's something wrong with this place."

"The women not to your taste or something?" the door has almost closed behind her.

"This isn't the Earth we left," I shout.

The door opens again.

"You had to shag someone to figure that out? Twelve years have passed, Jack."

"Not that way. Not the same planet."

The door stops halfway to being closed, and dissolves.

Kathleen stares at me.

"What makes you say that?"

"There aren't any Northern Lights," Antoinette whispers.

"Are you sure we're not just too far south?"

"I've been to both poles. There is no aurora at either."

"And the people here are wrong," I interrupt, "Kathleen, Polly..."

"Polly?"

"I was just... with Polly. A werewolf Polly."

"I don't understand you."

"The girl who left."

Kathleen hesitates. Then it sinks in.

"She could have come back," she swallows.

"She says I bit her."

"We need to leave," Antoinette sticks her head through the roof and peers outside, "as soon as possible."

"I don't understand!" Ballsy screams.

"This place is not Earth," Kathleen snaps, "Jack, get the ship."

I nod, and the walls crumble to allow room for the craft. The horses and the unicorn glance at us through the steamy remnants of the wall.

"On, now," Antoinette snaps.

We obey. I don't even know why, but something in her voice scares me. Even in the deepest, darkest level of purgatory, where the worst sinners known to my universe were trapped, her voice was never so serious.

She slams the door so hard it clips my heel.

"Now get on the floor and close your eyes," she whispers. We obey, and the craft soars away.

As it steadies itself, I open my eyes and stand up. Antoinette is pressed against the window, staring down at the planet. Her face is taut, her fists clenched so hard that if she had any blood, she would have cut herself.

"What are you watching?" I demand. I look out through the window when she doesn't answer, and I see the planet as we left it.

Then it starts to look grey. It seems rather more liquid than ice, and as the oceans become visible, the whole sphere turns to a swirling black mass.

But it isn't just a change of the planet. I feel like my insides are being twisted out of shape as the planet becomes a black cloud of smoke, receding into the darkness of space, as if that transformation has happened both inside and out.

Antoinette lets out a quiet gasp, and turns away from the window.

"You shouldn't have watched that," she whispers.

"Why not?"

"How am I supposed to know? It's not safe if you're not an angel. You lot can stand up now, by the way."

They do, and Kathleen immediately rounds on me.

"Jack what were you doing?"

"I didn't know it wasn't safe!" I protest.

"I'm not talking about that. I'm talking about Polly."

"What do you care?"

"You disgust me."

"What does Polly have to do with you? Without that, we wouldn't have found out that that was…"

"Devil's breath," Antoinette supplies.

"So there is a devil?" I demand.

"That's irrelevant," Kathleen snaps, but Antoinette shakes her head anyway, "Jack, I understand that some good came of it, but why did you do it?"

"What's wrong with me doing that?" I demand.

"What wrong with it? Everything's wrong with it! You had a go at Karl for things like this!"

"I wasn't sleeping with someone of a completely different race!"

"It's the same thing! And anyway, it's disrespectful."

"To who?"

"To Jade, Jack."

I cannot say anything to this.

"And not only, Jade, Jack. It's disrespectful to the women you sleep with. It's disrespectful to yourself, to God, to…"

She trails off helplessly.

"It makes me hate you, Jack."

I say nothing, but look at her in silence. Her mind is screaming at me, making me feel sick at what I have done.

Libby looks at Kathleen, as if deep in thought, and turns to me. She starts to say something, but seems to think better of it, and closes her mouth firmly.

Kathleen leaves the room, the door slamming behind her, cutting off her raging thoughts. I turn to Antoinette, who turns away.

"She'll feel better in the morning," Georgie offers with a sympathetic grin.

"Why did the locator say that was earth?" Libby demands of Antoinette.

"It was told to. Anything that can appear so convincing to the senses – to the point that it kept you breathing without an atmosphere – can easily confuse machines."

"What would have happened if I hadn't found out?" I frown.

"We probably would have all died," Antoinette shrugs, "It basically a toxic cloud of smoke. It's been poisoning us all the while we were there, and if we had been there when it crumbled, we would have all died."

"Even me and Kathleen?"

"Possibly not Kathleen. You certainly – probably a little slower than the rest of us."

"Why does it take that form?"

Antoinette hesitates.

"It's..." She hesitates, "The universe I broke through is a parasitic one. Hell, you might call it. It is full of things that are almost alive, feeding off any negative power."

"What does that mean?"

She hesitates.

"Emotion, really. Feeling, and right and wrong. Anything good, a loving or positive emotion, a good deed, gives out a sort of energy. The energy allows magic. Anything bad or negative, in most universes, just sort of hovers around the edge of nothing. But there are a few very old universes where it does something else. In most of those it gives life to spirit monsters, in the lowest levels of purgatory. In Hell, it forms clouds which are not alive, but have a will of their own, and an intention for evil."

"Is that what a fallen angel looks like?"

"No," Antoinette shakes her head, and her face stretches back in a sort of mirthless laugh, "Fallen angels are agonising to even look upon."

"How do we make sure we don't meet another of those clouds?" Libby demands.

"The chances of landing on another are very remote," Antoinette snorts, "too remote for even the worst luck in the universe to bring you to another."

"But what if we do?"

"Then, if we don't notice it in time, we're fucked, basically."

I think I am the only one that doesn't reel to hear Antoinette swearing. In the brief periods when I could hear her when we met in purgatory, her language was never what you would want to expose small children to.

I don't see Kathleen for another few days. She avoids me – when I am getting my supper, she is making blood for Karl. When we all go to sit down (and, in the human cases, drink) she is feeding the birds.

She doesn't even like birds.

After a week, she stops avoiding me. That doesn't mean she sees me, or speaks to me. She looks right through me in a way no human can, and it is actually quite distressing.

Finally, I corner her in the kitchen.

"Kathleen, I don't see how what I did was wrong," I protest, while she sits at the table cutting garlic. I glance at the dishes, and any dirt on them vanishes. They zoom to their cupboards, and I sit at the table next to Kathleen.

"Kathleen, Jade's dead."

She glances up at me.

"Does that make you think she can't see you?"

"No, not really. But I have needs, you know."

She leaves the garlic to finish chopping itself, and grinds a pestle into a bowl of dried cinnamon.

"Come on, Kathleen," I sigh, "I'm only human."

She glances up at me, and a hatred that I have never seen in her eyes before wells up.

"Stop lying to yourself Jack." We both stand up, and I block the door. She steps to the side, and I move to stop her. She glances up at me as I open my mouth to speak, and keeps walking.

Through me.

I do not go to supper that evening. She cooked it, after all, and so she must be there. Instead I go straight to bed, and sleep.

I don't know how long I sleep for, but when I wake up, I don't feel any less tired. Getting up is a chore, and once I'm up, I can't think of any reason to stay that way.

I make my way to control room, and Georgie, alone in there, glances over her shoulder as I enter.

"Sleep well?" she grins.

I frown. She laughs.

"We went through a pocket of narci-space. You've all been sleeping for forty days. Even that darned angel."

"Forty days?"

"Personally, I think you were all lucky. Your little girlfriend has been very snappy."

"You know she's not my girlfriend. I take it the two of you didn't sleep?"

"Nope. Kathleen and I were in the kitchen when it hit us, so she cast some sort of spell."

"And didn't try to wake me?"

"We tried everyone else. She didn't mention you."

"That was kind of her. Where is she now?"

"On the loo. Oh, she said that it'll go away if you would just apologise."

"What?"

"I have no idea. She wrote one of those sticky notes."

"Postets."

"That's the word! Here, see?" Georgie pulls a note off a chair and hands it to me. The writing is Kathleen's, but it has been scratched deeper into the paper that normal, and the edges are sharper. It reads: Jack. A simple apology and I'll make it go away.

Quite what she'll make go away is unclear, at least, it is until that evening.

Trying not to be tempted back into bed, a little later, I feel a pang of pain in my left arm, and sit down to inspect it. I see nothing, but my skin appears rather paler than normal. I ignore the pain, and pick up the fat macaw, which has just collapsed on the floor of my room. I find Kathleen, and, when she does not pay any attention to me calling her name, I put the macaw down beside her. She glances at in as if in surprise, and looks around the room. Her eyes do not seem to see me, and eventually her attention returns to the hyperventilating macaw. She shrugs, and places a finger on it to heal it.

I leave, and go to the control room. Libby is there, having just woken up. She does not look particularly pleased to learn that she has been sleeping for forty days while Georgie has been in control of the craft.

"Are you alright, Jack?" she frowns, bleary eyed.

"You do look very pale," Georgie nods.

"And badly in need of something to eat'" Libby adds.

I frown. I never need to eat; I only eat for pleasure. I choose not to explain this to them again, and sit down at the back of the room, and watch planets and suns flying by.

"Georgie. Let me fly."

Georgie frowns at Libby.

"Why?"

"I want to see my mother before I die, and we're coming up for an asteroid belt."

"I can do it!"

"Remember when you tried to drive that land shuttle?"

"The lamppost moved!"

The argument is lost. Libby takes over the controls, and we make it through safely.

At twice the speed of light, that's quite an achievement. It's quite thrilling to watch, and it is two hours before I leave the control room – and then only to go to the toilet.

Why do you humans love mirrors so? There is one above the toilet, and one above the basin, and even one on the calling above the bath, and the shower door is made of seven mirrors.

I glance at the one above the basin as I wash my hands, and see something that troubles me. The reflection that moves with me is not the usual one. It is more gaunt, greener, and here and there on the skin are red bulges.

One of these bulges bursts, not far below my eyes, and when I put my hand to it, my fingers come away sticky with my blood. Something moves in the hole, and as the other holes begin to burst, a small, white worm crawls from the hole.

One has burst on my jugular, and it stays open, but my blood does not pour out for more than a split second. It hardly even trickles. I put my red fingers to my wrist, and feel no pulse.

"Kathleen!" I shout, as the reflection continues to deteriorate.

Someone knocks on the door.

"I'm not Kathleen," Libby calls, "but what's wrong?"

"Look for yourself," I fling the door open, and she looks. She frowns.

"I see nothing wrong," she shrugs, walking up to me. I glance in the mirror, and her eyes follow.

She screams.

"Georgie!"

There is a sound of running feet, and Georgie appears, followed closely by every other member of the crew except Kathleen.

"What is it?" Georgie demands.

"Look in the mirror."

Georgie looks. She doesn't scream, but it is a close thing.

"Jack, where is your reflection?" she demands.

"I don't know," I shrug, "it was there a minute ago. Decaying."

"At least you don't look so ill anymore," Libby offers. I nod, and she and Karl take my arms and try to steer me out of the bathroom.

Except that they don't touch me. Their hands travel into my arms, and out the other side.

"I'll get Kathleen," offers Ballsy.

She comes a few minutes later.

"Where is he, then?"

"I'm here," I snap. She doesn't react.

"Jack, maybe you should say –" Georgie starts, and Kathleen stares at her like she's mad. She stops talking, but I understand.

"Kathleen, I'm sorry," I call.

Her neck snaps around.

"Jack? Are you there?"

"I'm sorry I slept with Polly. It was wrong of me."

She smiles, and the mirror cracks. The glass crumbles to dust, and as it does so, my body is returned to me.

"Never do that again," I say, as the mirror recovers, except for a thick crack right down the middle.

"Ditto," she murmurs, and walks away.

Nothing more is said of the incident on the devil's breath planet, or of Kathleen's nasty little bit of magic. In fact, almost nothing happens until Antoinette wakes up,

Almost as soon as she stops snoring – albeit quietly – we go into rapid orbit of an oddly smooth planetoid.

"What are we doing?" Antoinette demands, as the orbit gets smaller and faster.

"I can't say for sure," Ollie, eating pot noodles (which, I must tell you, have been poisoning youths since the days when I was human), shrugs, "But I think we're going home."

"Yes," Libby grins, bursting into the room, "we have autopilot on, and we're about to land."

"Why?" I demand.

"For one thing, I haven't seen my mother for years, and I want to check that Ballsy's father isn't giving her a hard time. For another, we're a little short on supplies."

As soon as the ship touches the ground, everybody rushes to the door. Libby gets between them and it, and stops them.

"Wait," she snaps, "we have to meet again."

"Can't we get home first?" demands Karl.

"Are you going to come with us to Earth?" Libby demands, blocking the keypad as Ollie tries to key in the code.

"Yes," Ollie mutters, giving up.

"Yes," Georgie nods.

"Yes," Karl acknowledges, "I don't really have a choice."

Everyone looks at Ballsy, who nods.

"Well, unless you change your minds, be back at six thirty, to take off at seven. She opens the door, and falls out backwards.

"Stop," Kathleen snaps, and they freeze. She rights Libby with her magic, and places her gently on the ground, and breaks her spell. The other four vampire hunters scramble down the ladder like rats.

"Aren't you three coming?" Libby calls up to us, as the other four compare their watches and, Karl bouncing oddly with every step, head away.

"What is this place?" I demand.

"It's home. It's perfectly safe."

I glance at Kathleen, who shrugs, and Antoinette, who flies into the open air.

"We're coming," Kathleen calls, as Antoinette vanishes gleefully into the violet sky.

The first thing I notice when I touch the ground is how little life there is. Not one blade of grass, not the slightest, most distant buzz of a fly – nothing.

"Where are all the plants?" I ask.

"I would guess that most of them are in gardens," suggests Libby. She closes the craft, and I glance around this vast area of bare – except for occasional patches of lichen – concrete. A few unusually shaped vehicles are dotted over it – most of them, at a glance, intended for short distance space travel.

"Come on," she moves towards the edge of the concrete, "we've only got eight hours."

And that is when me and Kathleen get our first glimpse of the true nature of Libby's home-planet. In the flat surface that stretches across the horizon, interrupted with occasional buildings, or clusters of buildings, we can see that something was different other than the lack of plants. In fact, as we step off the concrete, we can see that there are actually thousands of tiny bromeliads and carnivorous plants, holding on by sticky tendrils to the flat, ungiving, clear surface, for this planet – right through – is made of glass.

The thought makes be dizzy at first, and I lose my balance. The flat surface seems to move away from me, and I tumble to the hard ground.

"You'll get used to it," Libby grins.

"This whole planet it made of glass," I choke, "I won't be getting used to that in a hurry."

"It actually mostly water on the surface." Libby informs us, "come on, get up. It's an experience."

"I'll stay on all fours," I decide, and watch her expression as I become a black wolf. It never ceases to shock humans – even those who have seen it before.

I swiftly discover that it's noticeably easier to walk this way; I don't find myself looking down all the time, although I am, admittedly, at a disadvantage when we reach the water. Libby glances down in a mixture of concern and amusement as I blow water out of my nostrils for the umpteenth time, and as we reach deeper water, I give up on being a wolf and stand up as a human again.

"You know, it's rather unsettling when you do that," Libby points out cheerfully.

There is a loud splash as Antoinette, in one of her solid moments, crashes into the water in front of us.

"I felt that!" the angel exclaims gleefully, shooting from the water like a cork from a bottle of champagne, "I felt that!" She settles on the surface of the water, and walks along beside us, towering above us, some of her footsteps causing fairly strong ripples.

"Is this normal for you?" Kathleen demands, as her feet stop touching the bottom.

"Why wouldn't it be?" Libby laughs, treading water effortlessly.

"Because clothes get wet?" I offer, "And you sink?"

"Oh, don't be so pathetic."

"Does nothing live in this water?" Kathleen frowns. Libby shrugs.

"I don't know. When we left, they were starting to search the oceans for life. Who knows?"

"Just how deep are the oceans, exactly?"

"They think that the Hisgarion goes to the inner core."

I swallow. Earth's oceans go only the tiniest fraction towards the core, and have so far held on to more secrets that we can possibly imagine. A glass earth is probably less fertile, but that is still plenty of depth to provide food and shelter for any huge animal that might live there.

I hurry into shallower water, and become a wolf as I climb onto dry glass. Antoinette steps primly off the water's surface, and smiles sweetly at Libby and Kathleen as they drag themselves dripping from the water.

"I hate getting wet," Kathleen grumbles, "I seem to sink more than anyone else."

On the bright side, I hear her think, at least I can't drown.

I shake my fur dry, and send a silent spell at Kathleen and Libby to dry them – Kathleen always takes a while to get control over water.

"Can Jack understand us when he's a wolf?" Libby wonders, as we approach a wall of multi-storey, glass bricked buildings. I return to human form as a precaution, and nod.

"Cool," Libby considers.

"It would be best if you were quiet about that now," I mutter, as I see people walking towards us.

"Libby!" exclaims a boy, "dumped Karl already?" Libby laughs, and we stop for a while so that she can have a conversation. Antoinette, who flew up into the purple heights as I dried the women, ends the conversation abruptly by landing heavily between the two humans.

"We haven't got much time," she reminds Libby. The boy has fainted, and his friends are staring at the angel in a mixture of awe and fear. Libby shrugs helplessly at them, and moves on.

"We'll go to my mother's house first," she informs us, glancing at her watch, "She'll just be cooking lunch, so she'll be pleased to have someone to share it with.

"What about Ballsy's dad?"

"He's her boss," Libby snorts, "why would she have him around for lunch?"

The house is a homely, almost earthly, with a small garden made up a thick layer of soil over the glass, with a few small trees and lots of shrubs and flowers arranged in no particular order around a vaguely rectangular lawn.

"Mummy?" Libby calls. The door opens, and Antoinette flies back a few feet in surprise.

"You coward," I hiss, as a woman just as homely – if rather large – emerges from the house. Her hair is the same flame-red as Libby's, with streaks of grey like the cooling ashes as the fire cools down.

"Liberty!" the lady exclaims, "you've come home to me!" She hugs her in what looks like a crushing embrace – Libby goes slightly purple, and then the lady notices the angel.

"What company, Libby," the woman exclaims, releasing her and turning to Antoinette. "Are you an angel?"

"Oh, shit, what gave it away?"

This time, only Libby's mother is shocked to hear such words from an angel.

"Well, you must all be starved. Come inside, I've just put a flamingo in the oven."

Libby grins, and we all troop inside behind her – all of us, I think, a little dubious about the thought of eating flamingo.

"Whatever happened to good old chicken?" I wonder aloud.

"Chickens are too difficult to keep on a planet like this," Libby explains, "flamingos are like the plague here."

Still, I feel, looking at the pinkish feathers in a bucket of giblets by the door, a rather too beautiful animal to slaughter and eat.

And, when the oven opens, it certainly doesn't smell as good as chicken, it smells more like slightly like fishy beef.

"So, Libby," The large woman uses a small laser to slice the roast into manageable pieces, "aren't you going to introduce your new friends?"

"Oh, sure," Libby nods vehemently, "This is Jack, and Kathleen, and that feathery thing that just flew out through the ceiling is Antoinette.

"It's funny, you hardly ever hear those two names together," the woman smiles, and chuckles, "It's quite brave of the two of you to be friends, knowing the circumstances."

Libby tries to grin, but stupidly I don't realise what the good lady is on about. Perhaps if I did, I would notice that she is still holding the laser as she hands me a plate, with its restricted beam swinging wildly.

I hear a hiss, and feel a slight pain in my thumb. The woman starts to apologise, but as I put down the plate, it is easy for her to see that there is no wound.

"What are you?" she demands, staring at my unharmed digit.

"Damn," I curse after a few moments consideration.

"Mum, there's no need to panic," Libby jumps to her feet as her mother starts to rummage in the cutlery drawer, "really, mum, please, don't..."

Her mother swings around, with a large, very ancient looking silver carving knife.

"Get out of my house," she hisses.

"Mum, you're overreacting."

"You as well," the woman jabs the knife at Libby, "you have sullied my doorstep with these creatures. You are an accomplice to their evil."

"Mum, they aren't evil –"

"You are no longer my daughter. Go!"

Kathleen and I have, by this time, almost made it to the door, and Libby starts to follow, glancing back at her mother every now and then in the hope that she will change her mind. I hear her cry out suddenly, and feel the thud of the knife in my back. What a lovely mother Libby has.

I reach back to pull it out, and as it comes out, the blood starts to pour. I really hate that woman.

"Kathleen," I gasp, almost tumbling down the last step as my blood all but drains from me. Kathleen glances back, raises her eyebrow in surprise, and touches the wound.

"Jack?" Libby puts a hand on my shoulder, "are you okay?"

"Just never take me anywhere near that woman again," I smile weakly, and then stand up straight again as my blood recovers.

"That's really not like her," Libby frowns, "she used to be really tolerant."

"Clearly, people change."

Antoinette lands neatly beside us.

"Why are you leaving so soon?"

"She didn't appreciate our company," Kathleen informs her, and Antoinette glances back at the puddle of blood on the doorstep.

"You didn't have to kill her."

"We didn't," I snap, "that's my blood."

"Oh," is all Antoinette says to this, before flying away with her toes dragging on the water.

90

"Well," Libby forces back her scowl of annoyance, "We'd better go and get supplies, hadn't we?"

Shopping has changed greatly in the years since your people abandoned Earth. We used to walk around with trolleys, and select what we wanted, and then go to a person with a computer and pay – or at least, those of us who weren't shopping on the internet. When we get to the modern version of a supermarket (more like a factory in appearance, in my opinion anyway), Libby presses her hand onto a smooth panel on the wall, and we wait.

This is probably quite normal to you, as is the mechanical arm depositing a large metal crate on wheels unnervingly close to this panel. For me, it's extremely difficult to trust a machine.

Perhaps there aren't so many accidents nowadays, but I do know that in 2050, when the first fully automatic cars took to the road, road deaths rocketed. When machines were created to do more than one housework task, most of them had destroyed themselves after little over two years, simply by crashing into things or falling off shelves, and sometimes killing their owners in the process.

"Is that your version of shopping?" Kathleen raises an eyebrow, "takes all the fun there ever was out of it."

"Let's go," Libby starts pushing the crate along the ground – one of the wheels has stuck, and makes a horrible squeaking noise as it scrapes over the concrete. It's almost a relief to get back onto the glass.

Fortunately, the crate floats, and apart from it drifting out into deep water when a farmer sends his flamingos splashing past, the journey back to the craft is uneventful.

"You're late," says Karl miserably from under the plane.

"It's thirty-one minutes past six," Libby snorts, "that's hardly late."

Georgie appears at the edge of the concrete, with Ollie slight behind her.

"Why are they running?" Libby wonders, as we help her to heft the crate into a hatch at the bottom of the ship.

"Open the ship," Georgie shouts, "Now!"

Libby frowns at her.

"Why are you in such a hurry?"

"Just open the ship," Georgie pants, stopping in front of us and bending over to catch her breath, "and quickly."

Libby obeys, giggling nervously, and Ollie and Georgie shoot up the steps like the devil's after them. Karl follows at a similar pace, and the three of us stare up at them.

"Get a move on," Georgie shrieks, "I can see them! Quickly!"

Libby walks carefully up the steps, and we follow, glancing behind every now and then to try and see what's wrong. Georgie slams the door as soon as we're through, and the ladder slips into its vault.

"Now will you explain what that was about?" Libby demands. Georgie ignores her, and unrolls a window on the wall.

"Take off!" Karl squeaks, peering over Georgie's shoulder, "quickly!"

We all turn to Karl, and notice the bruise for the first time. A large, cross-shaped bruise near his right eye.

"What did you do, Karl?" Libby demands.

"I told my mother what had happened to me."

"And she just handily had a copper cross?"

"No. She just cried. It was Ballsy's dad."

We peer out of the window, and see the furious crowds below us.

"We still have to wait for Ballsy," Libby points out to Karl, "we can't just leave him there."

"Too late," Karl ducks as a silver cross hits the window, "His father killed him."

"What?" Libby stares.

"Ballsy told him what happened," Georgie informs us, "and once he heard that he'd travelled with a witch and a werewolf and a vampire, he started throwing things. We only just got away."

Libby sighs, and Georgie rolls the window up.

"Get me a rifle," Libby snaps.

The angel materialises in the room.

"What's Georgie doing with a gun?" she wonders.

"Georgie is giving Libby the gun to shoot a murderer," Libby replies, and rolls down the emergency exit slightly.

"You shouldn't do this," Antoinette puts a hand on Libby's shoulder, "He'll haunt you forever."

"He killed his son," Libby snaps, "I'm not letting him get away with it."

"The people will punish him," Antoinette says. A cross flies through the gap, and Antoinette reconsiders.

"Why not let Jack kill him?" she suggests.

Everyone turns to look at me.

"Why me?" I demand.

"You've killed so many people anyway," she shrugs, "You wouldn't have any new memories."

"Why not Kathleen?"

"I'm not killing him!" Kathleen protests, "I've killed too many people already."

"And I haven't? I've never enjoyed killing people, you know."

"It was a phase, and I've grown out of it," Kathleen crosses her arms. Everyone turns to look at me.

"Fine, then," I scowl, "but I'm only doing this so that you don't," I point out to Libby. "What does he look like?"

"He's a bishop," Libby tells me, "with Ballsy's face, and no eyebrows."

I nod. No eyebrows, big hat, and the face of his son.

"Quick death or slow?"

"Just kill the bastard!" Libby screams at me.

I sigh, and drop through the floor.

The crowds don't even notice me at first, but then they realise that there is a person amongst them who isn't throwing everything they own at this shipful of evil. And then they recognise my face.

I watch them coming towards me, looking for the murderer, but all the ones here are well endowed with eyebrows – even the women. I magic myself to being further into the crowd, and try and imagine the face I am looking for.

I have found him. I close my eyes, and I'm there, behind a man with a very tall hat, and a larger cross than anyone else I've seen. He turns to attack me, and his face is a mirror image of the now dead eunuch's. There is blood on his hands – whether actual blood or the stain of murder, I cannot tell, but everything about this man is evil, and I have no trouble believing that he would kill his son. I'm only surprised he waited for an excuse.

"There's one among us," he bellows, and the humans pour in, grabbing at my skin, as if to pull my apart bit by bit. I feel a sting of pain as a silver cross is smashed repeatedly into my back, and a knife – also silver – cuts into my arm.

I reach back with magic, and seize the knife. It lifts over my head, and hangs in the air above the man. He glances up, and I command it to stay above him.

"It'll fall the next time you cause pain," I whisper, and he lashes out with his silver cross. Unfortunately for him, the pain it causes is enough to release the knife. He falls towards me, and his head lands on the ground where I stood, the handle of the knife sticking like a mast out of the top of his skull, the tip sticking out of the opposite side of his neck. The people, enraged, turn all their weapons on me, but I am already back inside the ship.

"I didn't kill him," I tell Antoinette, "He killed himself."

Libby frowns.

"He put a conditional spell on him," Kathleen explains.

"Shall we go now?" I suggest, as Kathleen inspects, and heals, the cuts and bruises the people here have so kindly provided.

"We're done here," Libby nods, "and we shan't be coming back."

She takes off, and once we are clear of that atmosphere, she puts it on autopilot, and focuses instead on unpacking her shopping.

"I'm not comfortable with being flown by a machine," I tell her after yet another sickeningly sharp turn as the ship changes direction at high speed.

"We're in a desert," she snorts, "there's nothing here except light rays and us."

"We're going at eighty times the speed of light," I complain, "surely we won't be in the desert for long?"

"This desert takes up half the known universe," Libby cracks open a small glass ball, and jumps back as several tonnes of rice and pasta fall to the ground, "I think we have time for a quick stock-take.

Judging by the amount of stock, this is going to be a very long stock-take.

After all the packets of food have been taken to their places, Libby tips the remaining contents of the crate – about half – onto the ground.

"What's this?" I peer into one of the balls.

"It's everything other than food," Libby shrugs, "there should be some weird birds in here somewhere, and I think I ordered a dog a while ago, that might be here..."

"You sell pets in plastic balls?" I can't help feeling there is something very wrong with this.

"Says he with three horses in his pocket."

"Only two horses. The one with the horn's a unicorn."

"Same thing. Just a horse with a horn."

I forget that these humans haven't seen much of the unicorn. In fact, they haven't seen it for anything other than transport.

"You probably deserve a warning," Kathleen offers, as Georgie cracks open a ball and takes out several electronic magazines, "Unicorns are very different to horses. They're not herbivores, and they don't die. They eat meat, people or mandrakes by preference."

"Aren't mandrakes plants?" frowns Georgie.

"No," I sigh, "mandrakes are basically human."

And so it goes on, for the next three weeks. Then, finally, we reach the end of the desert, by which time I am quite sick of talking about anything magical.

"There's a wormhole somewhere around here," Libby informs us one evening as we shoot around a small star, "I know there is. It's a tourist lane, for God's sakes..."

Antoinette is being righteous today.

"Thou shalt not use God's name in vain," she points out.

"I might remind you of 'thou shalt not swear'," Libby retorts.

"Oh, fuck that," Antoinette snorts, "There's the wormhole! Turn! Turn now!"

We go straight past.

"You distracted me," moans Libby, "now we have to go around the damn star again."

"It's just after the sunspot," Georgie reminds her as our speed doubles, "co-ordinates –"

"You know perfectly well I can't work out co-ordinates at this speed," Libby snaps, "There!"

We shoot into the wormhole, and after a few moments of dizzying darkness, we emerge the other side.

"Brakes!" Ollie squeals as we hurtle towards an ever-expanding blue dot.

"Locking path," Libby recites, "Earth, here we come."

"Poor little planet," Antoinette sympathises.

There is a hiss as we tear through the ozone layer, and plunge into water. After about a second, we bob up again.

"We should have been shattered," I exclaim, "at that speed, hitting the water surface, we should be scattered across the planet in tiny little pieces of dust!"

"This ship is designed for emergency high speed water landings," Libby informs me, as we all wobble to our feet, "It could survive a head on impact with an ocean at full speed without so much as a dent."

Georgie peers out through the windscreen.

"I don't suppose you recognise this place, do you, Jack?"

I don't. I haven't ever spent much time learning the parts of the oceans. Water tends to look like water wherever you are on them.

"I know I don't," Kathleen looks outside, "How deep is it?"

"The instruments keep changing their minds," Libby frowns, "I don't think they like the salinity."

"Is it actually important that we know?" Ollie demands, "don't we have other things to do?"

"I need the depth to get a rough bearing," Libby explains, "Seeing as there aren't any landmarks."

"Can't you just take off again?"

"I can't take off from water. Even if I could, it takes more fuel to fly than float."

"Don't tell me your lot still use fossil fuels?" I cannot believe my ears.

"No, you twit, we use Beryllium."

I frown.

"How?"

"Querion guns," she replies, as if this answers everything. I choose not to enquire any further, "however, if anyone could give me a rough idea of the depth, it would be very helpful."

Antoinette turns her head towards me, a thoughtful look in her eyes.

"Jack, you know how you can't drown?"

Now everyone's looking at me. Kathleen, for once, is on my side.

"It's completely and utterly irrelevant that he can't drown. There could be something down there that can kill him."

"If we don't move," Libby snaps, "some horrid earth-monster will come shooting out of the water and eat the rest of us."

"You wouldn't have said that if Antoinette hadn't said anything," I complain.

"Oh, come on. What are the chances of you actually getting hurt?"

I scowl. It's all I can do in reply.

It all ends, of course, with me, half a tonne of lead weights, and a very long coil of rope, teetering in the door with nothing on except a pair of a dead man's shorts. I glance into the water. I've always had a peculiar fear of being alone in water. Especially the kind that is crystal clear, but you cannot see so much as a single rocky peak as far as you search with your eyes.

"Please don't make me do this?" I plead one last time. Kathleen has by now given up my cause, and joins the others to cross their arms and look at me sternly.

"Get in there," Libby snorts, "don't be such a scaredy-wolf."

I make an obscene gesture.

"Swivel."

The craft rocks slightly, and I see, as if in slow motion, the chain of weights rolling into the sea.

"Bye," Georgie grins, and I am dragged overboard after them, clutching the end of the rope.

The rope offers no consolation. After it reaches its two hundred metre limit, it simply stretches. Almost indefinitely. And then stays that shape.

And so I plunge rather quickly into the depths. The last time I descended to such a level, I think as the light vanishes, was the last journey my sister ever went on.

I breathe out any air that was in my lungs, and suck in water instead. My pupils stretch out yet wider as my descent speed increases yet further. Something very large and red swims past.

I squeak in shock. I had hoped that there would be nothing of any noticeable size on my descent.

Something tugs at the weights, and they're dragged off. I am moving too fast to be slowed down by that – in fact, their loss seems to speed me up.

My feet come into contact with something soft and slimy. I yelp, and peer down.

A massive eye peers back up at me, and a thick tentacle reaches back to inspect me. I almost collapse in relief as I recognise a giant squid – my sister and I had a brief encounter with one, and it proved to be, in fact, a good deal more amiable than some people we'd met. Not that that's saying much.

It vanishes into the gloom, but not before sending me spinning downwards at a dizzying speed. Something larger and bulkier than it swims past overhead almost as soon as I am tumbling again. For about a minute, the most frightening thing is the complete lack of anything. Then, suddenly, nothingness seems like a very welcome prospect as a gulper eel looms out of the darkness. I find myself changing into a wolf in fright every time anything moves – from a jellyfish the size of my thumbnail with flashing blue lights to a giant swimming crab, perhaps three metres across its back, with a band of red light at each joint.

I bounce off a solid surface, and again after another ten seconds, the second time feeling a sharp pain in my back. I reach behind me and grab onto the surface, and, turning to face it, see that this is a cliff face. Here and there, in the light of a dense swarm of tiny, neon-blue squid, I can see metallic streaks. Silver.

I push away from the wall, and soon sink out of the light of the squid. Something lurches out of the wall, and I find myself folded in half in something's stomach. I stretch myself out, and something tears. Not the rope.

I decide it's time for a little magic. Standing on whatever just swallowed me, I send bright white light from the palms of my hands.

The creature I have just been swallowed by limps out from underneath me, and into the shadows – a frogfish, which has somehow survived being torn open to let me out. I jump off its ledge, and swing my hands to and fro as I sink, sending a myriad of tiny creatures into their dens in the cave wall, and, more importantly, enough light scattering into the void for me to see a good way below me.

I realise, after a third attack by a large, slug-like creature that simply refuses to accept that I am inedible to it, and has a similarly dismissive attitude towards its own demise, that the light is also very good at attracting curious predators – particularly big ones. While it does me no harm to be beset by hundreds of twenty-metre eels no thicker than my little finger, the rope is not so robust. I extinguish the light.

It works, and the rope holds. My feet eventually come into contact with a stony bottom. The cliff face has long since emigrated away from me, so I am fairly certain this time that this really is the bottom. I cannot resist seeing what could be here, but this time, I make the source of light stay thirty metres or so to my left.

In the light, I see something that tells me instantly where we are. The Mariana trench.

What do I see, you might ask. I see my sister's grave. The lowest ever outpost of humanity – where I spent three weeks of my life and my sister spent her death.

I swim closer, and circle the deep-sea station. She was a billionaire, you see, and when fame got too much for her, she retired to down here (shortly after someone murdered her husband). Her retirement was short, for the generators packed in, and the light ran out – so the plants must have died, and so the air lost its oxygen – so she died. I was lucky enough to have left before that.

I enter the code to unlock the airlock, and swim inside. It seals behind me, still working after all these years. The water drains out, and I cough up that in my lungs, and open the gate

Light floods into the airlock, and I almost collapse in surprise - the turbines were destroyed by the current: there should be no power.

I glance around, and see the flourishing plants – kept alive by their miniature biome. The air in here is as humid as ever, and drips of water fall constantly from the ceiling. The floor is covered in soil – when I left, it was bare steel mesh.

I go through to the sleeping quarters. She would have chosen to die in bed, being so fond of lie-ins.

The sheets are rough and crumpled – as if someone recently got up. In here, only here, the floor is as bare as when I left. And there are no remains. Not so much as a fine bed of soil under her sheets.

I go to the observatory.

The computer is on. I reach for the mouse – not a rodent, a small electric peripheral your kind used to have on computers. I don't know what you use now. The screen flickers to life, and a message appears: *Hello, Jack.*

I shut it down, and go to the lab.

And there she lies. In a basin of liquid nitrogen, older, far older, than I remember.

Her arms are crossed over her chest, her eyes peaceful. She would be ashamed that someone saw her this old, if she knew.

I consider the button at the end of the basin. Defrost, it proclaims proudly.

Is she still alive? Dare I find out?

I press it. The nitrogen evaporates rapidly, and she is left lying there, ancient, cold, and, I can smell now, bleeding. Or at least, she was when she died.

She is holding something in her hand. An envelope. I reach for it, and take it carefully from her cold grasp.

"Jack," I read out as if anyone can hear, and open the letter.

"I was a fool, Jack. I'm assuming it's you. I'm not saying about lying to you. I mean about the pit. There is more sea that I thought Jack. Well, I suppose you must know by now, as well. You're a kilometre lower than the bottom of the ocean.

"It's my fault. I found a narrow crack. I opened it up, and it all fell. The whole trench. And they were there. They are asleep again, now I write this, but they've killed me already. Be careful, Jack, if there's anyone with you. Don't make them wake up, please.

"Goodbye, Jack."

I glance at the corpse, and put the letter back down. Pity she hadn't been a little more specific about the "them"s.

I don't have much time to be irritated, because the lights cut out, and a powerful rumbling pushes me off balance. I hurry to the airlock, and peer around in the darkness. My light has also vanished, so I recall it, and something huge and snakelike is briefly illuminated before the light is swallowed.

I dare to conjure another, and this time have the time to glimpse, and be glimpsed by, a giant, horse-like face staring at me from the coils of a truly massive eel, before once again any air hasn't already been crushed out of my lungs is rapidly sworn away and replaced with water, and I am swimming faster than I could possibly have imagined towards the surface.

I can feel it – them – following me, lazily coiling around in the water as I, their apparently helpless prey, lead them to more like me.

When I reach the surface, the world seems surprisingly calm and quiet. I glance around for the ship, and spot it, about two hundred yards away from me. I splash towards it as fast as I can.

"Congratulations, Jack, You're the seventeenth person to the bottom of the ocean," Libby grins when I reach the open hatch, "what luck!"

I shake my head silently as I scramble in, shivering. I try and tell them what I saw, but the only sound I seem to be able to make is the chattering of my teeth.

"We have to go," Kathleen realises, "There's something down there."

"Big," I whisper.

"A sea serpent?" Kathleen stares at me, convinced my thoughts were lying.

I nod helplessly.

"Surely that's just a myth?" Ollie glances from me to Kathleen. I shake my head.

"Well," considers Libby, "I don't really feel like being lunch today. Georgie, take Ollie and Kathleen and be prepared to shoot anything that tries to eat us. The rest of you, come with me."

"How big were these things?" Karl wonders as Libby throws a towel at me and starts the engines.

"Big," I squeak.

"He's petrified," Karl snorts, "the immortal werewolf is petrified."

I glare at him, and he turns back to the controls.

"Karl, push that green button," Libby snaps, "no, not that one. The one below it. Now push that lever down forty-five degrees. And don't splash that stuff on the pressure gage!"

I pass him my towel, and sit down.

A bubble about twice the size of the craft breaks the surface a dozen metres to the right, and Karl flies across the room as the resulting wave hits the side of the craft.

"Seatbelts do have a purpose," comments Antoinette dryly. The craft shoots forwards, and Karl struggles back to his seat to strap himself firmly in.

"There's something coming," he stares at the Environmental Detector screen. Libby glances over his shoulder at the advanced version of radar.

"Big," she considers, "zoom in."

The computer obeys, and suddenly the green blob becomes about thirty thin green lines.

"Not a myth, then," Libby grimaces, "They're going pretty fast."

"Can we go any faster?" Antoinette leans in to look at the lines.

"No, because if we do, we'll break the sound barrier, and it's illegal to do that on inhabited bodies of water, so the whole ship shuts down for five weeks in punishment."

"We hit the water at nearly twice the speed of light," I point out, "why didn't we shut down then?"

"This craft only makes a noise that loud when it breaks the speed of sound or the speed of light."

Something crashes into the back of the craft, and there's a loud hiss from the back of the ship.

Libby punches up a screen to give us a view of behind us. An enormous serpent – perhaps two hundred yards long, is tumbling through the water, lashing out in its death-throes. A plume of red billows out from where its head used to be, and it sinks slowly below the water.

"Jack, go and check everyone's alright back there," Libby orders, as the craft ploughs through a fifty foot wave and into bad weather.

I nod, and pull the door open. I am greeted by not only a wide open door and a foot of water that outlasted the thirty-second emergency shield, but also by a twenty-foot eel.

Twenty-foot eel doesn't really do it justice. It is twenty foot long, with a body about five foot deep and two foot wide, and a mouthful of six-inch teeth.

Antoinette leaps through me.

"Stay behind me Jack."

"And that'll help how?" I demand, as the door behind me snaps shut to stop the craft flooding as we go through another wave.

"It doesn't know it can go through me," she hisses, "It probably thinks it has to eat me first."

"Two lunches instead of one," I frown. Somehow I think that will just make us an even more tempting snack.

It lunges, and its foul breath sends us both stumbling backwards. It is joined by a far more agreeable four-foot eel, and the ship rolls just enough to send all four of us crashing into the door.

The twenty-foot eel slides around for a bit, sending the smaller one to the far side of the room, and starts to slip out of the open door. It lunges out to grab onto anything to stop it falling – which happens to be me. I grab onto the door as I start to fall with it, and the door slams shut.

There is a spray of blood, and Antoinette curses as a tooth flies through her. The teeth through my arm push a little further in, and then let go. I wipe my eyes, and look around.

The four-foot eel flops pathetically on the rapidly drying floor, and most of the head of the twenty-foot eel is rolling around at my feet, twitching. I pick up the smaller eel by the tail, and open the door just enough to chuck it out.

"I hope I never meet you again," I inform it, and toss it into the storm.

"Hah!" shouts Georgie's voice, and a large piece of eel flies past the gap in the door before it slams. We move cautiously towards her voice, and push open the door.

Something large and red hits the screen, and Antoinette swears. Georgie glances back and giggles.

"They've gone," she grins, "those that haven't been blasted."

The windscreen clears, and I can see for a fact that she is wrong. A large mouth is opening almost wide enough to swallow the whole craft. On the bright side, Kathleen, Ollie and Georgie seem far too happy to mind.

"There's something very wrong here," Antoinette considers as Georgie falls over and keeps laughing. I don't answer – I'm looking for a button to get rid of the creature whose tongue is currently wrapped around the laser cannon.

"Look for a big red button?" suggests Antoinette unhelpfully.

There is one, but it is labelled "detach", and I don't really want to be left floating around the ocean with three giggling loons – one of whom has just decided to chew my toe – and a foul-mouthed angel, with an eel the length of a passenger ferry trying to eat me.

There is green switch near the red button, labelled "shield". I move it to the "on" position, and we are presented with a series of small blue sparks and one massive crack as the eel is electrocuted.

Ollie realises that the thing he is trying to get his teeth into is my big toe, and sits up, spitting.

"Yeuch," he spits, as Kathleen and Georgie stop throwing a wineglass to each other. It smashes on the back of my head after flying over Georgie's, and the dead eel relinquishes its grip, and sinks into the sea.

"Switch the shield off," Georgie commands. I obey, and we crash through another wave, removing most of the fried eel-spit from the screens.

"Oh, look, an island," Kathleen comments. The rest of us cram to the window and look. It is small island, but an island none the less, perhaps two hundred and fifty metres across, with a few scattered palm trees in amongst rolling hillocks of grass.

"We could land there," Georgie sighs happily. There is a loud bang, and the island explodes into a ball of lava.

"Or not," Antoinette observes as we bump over a wave and a find the sun glaring down upon us.

"Jack," calls Libby's voice over the speakers, "Are they alive in there?"

"We are," Georgie retorts into a microphone, "Why did you have to send Jack to ask us?"

"The storm cut out internal communications, you bimbo," Libby snaps, "We couldn't leave the aerials out like lightning conductors."

There is a pause.

"There should be a few floating islands about two hours away. If you would all come into the cockpit, we could have lunch on the way."

Georgie shut down the windows, and we traipsed through the blood-smeared hallway, past the almost whole head, and onto the control room.

"Libby's gone to make sandwiches," Karl informs us, engaging autopilot. There is a loud bump from the kitchen to inform us that he is telling the truth, and a stream of muffled words that would make Antoinette blush follow.

"I'll go and help her," Kathleen winces as something smashes.

Karl nods, and takes a swig from his bottle of blood.

"I wonder if you drink animal blood as well?" Antoinette sits down to stare at him.

"Why?" he frowns.

"Because there's about forty litres of eel blood washing around the hall."

Karl does not seem impressed.

"I am not drinking sea-serpent."

"Suit yourself. What if somehow you and Libby end up on the other side of the world to Kathleen, and there's nothing around but sea-serpents?"

Karl glances at the rest of us for help answering this question. Antoinette grins in satisfaction.

"You're a bully, you know that?" Libby comments, as she and Kathleen follow a levitating tray of sandwiches and beer into the room.

"I know," Antoinette looks momentarily remorseful, and cheers up suddenly; "but what would you do?"

Kathleen steers the tray through Antoinette's head.

"Jack, there's your water," Libby chucks the bottle at me, "And Antoinette, if he couldn't drink the sea-serpents blood, the obvious thing that would happen would be that he would try and drink my blood, and I would have to kill him. Simple enough, really."

Kathleen passes Karl another wine-bottle of blood, and puts a hand on his shoulder comfortingly.

"She's just being mean," she assures him.

"Why does Jack never drink alcohol?" Ollie demands.

"Coth he duthn't like it," Georgie teases.

"Jack, do you suppose you would like to demonstrate what happens when you get drunk?" Kathleen holds out a spare can of beer. I back away.

"Better not to," Kathleen nods in agreement, "Karl, do you want a beer?"

Karl downs it quickly, and returns to the blood. Georgie inspects a sandwich dubiously.

"What's in this?"

Libby shrugs.

Georgie bites.

"Bacon," she informs us, "lettuce. Cheese. Butter. More butter. Mayonnaise. Olives. Garlic. Olive oil."

"You don't have to list them all," Karl interjects as Georgie picks an olive pip out from between her teeth, and adds pineapple and pickled onions to the list.

"There's something chewy," Georgie considers, "a bit bitter. Iron-ish."

Libby blushes. Georgie spits out the thing.

"That is quite disgusting," she comments.

"I must have thrown the wrong sandwich out," Libby goes a deeper shade of red.

"It's your fingertip," Georgie seems surprisingly not sickened by the fact. Kathleen destroys the offending fingertip with a glance, and Libby rubs the new fingertip that Kathleen replaced it with.

"Well, one slip with the knife out of twenty sandwiches isn't bad," Georgie shrugs eventually, "not for you, anyway."

"I'm too hungry to care," Ollie admits through a second sandwich.

"You only just finished your elevenses," Antoinette exclaims.

"Do you want a sandwich?" Libby offers her one.

"I'd love one, but I can't eat. It'd fall out of me after five minutes, by which time I'd have knocked a hundred years off my life to hold it in."

She continues to look hungrily at the sandwiches as the rest of us – excluding Karl – eat, and when they are finished, she looks at the plate as if it is the body of a close friend.

"I miss food," the angel sighs. Libby looks sympathetic, and then turns her attention to the ED screen.

"Three thousand feet of water below us," she grins, "think of all those things down there missing food at the moment."

Antoinette glares at her.

"They can eat us when they get us," she points out, "I can't ever eat."

"And I thought you said that the depth wasn't showing," I scowl.

"It wasn't. It is now." She pats the monitor. "Isn't. Damn."

"I'm not going down again. I've been down to the bottom of the sea twice, and that's twice too many."

"Twice?" Libby looked at me.

"And both in the same place," I add.

"That was where you left Jennifer?" Kathleen glances behind as if she'll be able to make out the spot – which is now well beyond the horizon.

"And she lied to me," I add, "She'd shut everything off herself."

"So she killed herself?"

"No, she must have switched it on again not long after I left."

"Was your sister like you?" Libby asks.

"No. She was a normal, everyday human witch."

"Witches aren't normal."

"In my family they are," I snort, "It was one of our great, great, great or something grandmothers who caused all the werewolves alive today. Only she missed the first time and hit her horse. And created horses like Lycanthropy and her mother."

"That's a big spell, in case you were wondering," Kathleen explains.

"So magic is hereditary."

"Yes," I nod.

"So as you had a really powerful great granny, you should be really powerful?"

"It doesn't matter how powerful your ancestors were," Antoinette interrupts, "It's how much magic you were exposed to in the womb or in your early childhood. Even the ways in which you can use magic are affected by that."

"But I grew up in an orphanage," I frown, "there was never any magic."

"Your sister's magic."

"She was three."

"Your sister had a power of hope. It was her hope, and nothing else, that prevented you from dying in your early years. I don't know why she had magic so young. God only knows why –"

"Blasphemy," mutters Libby.

"But she did. And all her hopes were magic. Impossibly powerful magic. And little children have so much hope."

The boat grumbles to a halt, and Antoinette stops her little speech to swear as she gets temporarily stuck in the controls.

"Well, we're there. Anyone want a walk before we take off?" Libby switches off the autopilot.

Everyone agrees that a walk would be good. The island looks a rather pleasant place – a smoothly rounded shape that, according to the ED is a floating island, so not liable to explode. There are gulls flying around, and the occasional cormorant or auk, but not much else.

"A bit plain," comments Karl, shielding his face from the sun as the craft edges begrudgingly onto the island.

We jump down onto the earth, which wobbles ever so slightly, and all of us except Georgie head straight for the shade of five or six large trees near the centre of the island – perhaps fifty or sixty metres from the edge.

I let claws out of the tips of my fingers and climb one to see the neighbouring islands.

"There's twenty-seven islands," Libby calls out to me when I've reached the highest branch I can, "at the moment. About fifty years ago, there were five. One of them sank, and then some more came, almost out of nowhere."

She slaps her palm-top computer as it fails to scroll down.

"Funny," she frowns, "apparently, they were only twenty metres across fifty years ago."

Chapter 4 – Return

I do not answer. From my vantage point, I can see twenty-four other islands, and, without exception, they are all the same shape. A cluster of at least twenty-five identical domes. Almost sounds man-made.

I move a little further out along the branch, and spot the other two islands. The same applies to them.

I jump the seventeen metres to the ground, and the ground wobbles.

"Careful," Libby clucks.

Georgie gives up splashing in the sea, and comes up to us, soaking wet. "Weird roots," she comments.

I glance at them for the first time. A thick mat of roots, spreading out along the surface, barely going below it at all.

"That is weird," I scratch through the soil with a still clawed hand, and after about five centimetres, reach a tough, almost rubbery layer.

"Oh." is all I manage.

"Oh no," Georgie expands.

"Oh no what?" Libby demands.

"Oh dear," Kathleen pushes the rubber with her finger. The island twitches in retaliation.

"Oh my giddy aunt," offers Ollie.

"What is it?" demands Libby, brushing away her own layer of topsoil.

"Oh damn," Karl adds.

"Oh fuck!" Antoinette interrupts gleefully, "Calamari's about to bite back."

"Calamari?" Libby stamps her foot.

"Think of a big," Georgie hesitates.

"Huge," Karl continues,

"Enormous," Kathleen corrects,

"Hungry, probably," Antoinette beams.

"Octopus," Ollie finishes.

"Kraken," I straighten up, "and you three are in grave danger of being digested."

Libby glances at Georgie and Ollie, or at least the spaces where they were a moment ago. They are both currently sprinting as fast as their legs can carry them back to the craft. Libby yelps, and follows. Antoinette swoops after them, cackling almost demonically. Although Kathleen, Karl and I are unlikely to be killed by anything's digestion, I don't think any of us relish the prospect of being eaten, so, with a little assistance from Kathleen, we reach the craft before any of the others.

The Kraken doesn't take too kindly to being sprinted on. In fact, before Antoinette is inside, a huge tentacle snakes up and hurls the craft into the sky.

We all scream for a bit, until Libby manages to steady the craft, and then Antoinette appears, looking rather cross.

"You left without me," she snaps.

"We didn't have much choice in the matter," Ollie points out in between being sick.

"I'll go and close the door," I offer. I only just manage to refrain from puking until I get there. Some poor gull gets in between the half-digested sandwiches and gravity. On the bright side, I should think it will have a good meal once it comes to its senses.

I slam the door shut, and hurry back to the cockpit. Everyone except Kathleen and Antoinette has emptied their stomachs, and Kathleen is looking decidedly green. I send a burst of magic to destroy the mess before we crash, and, would you believe it, Kathleen pukes as soon as the rest is cleared up.

We reach half the speed of light just in time to stop.

"Home sweet home," sighs Kathleen happily, as we land on top of our old house.

"Oops," comments Libby.

"It'll only take a few minutes to rebuild it," Kathleen waves it away, "is everyone fully prepared for the cold this time?" Libby does answer, but I can't hear her through the ridiculously thick coat she is pulling on.

When the doors open, there is a snarl, and a flurry of leathery wings. Karl squeals, and hides behind Libby.

"Oh, don't worry. These dragons aren't the same as the dragons through black holes and mirrors. They're just lizards with wings that occasionally turn into other things." Antoinette flaps her wings noisily at the dragons, which hurriedly vanish into the sky. We scramble out of the craft, shutting the door behind us, and look around.

"Move," Kathleen tells the craft, as I take the clear ball out of my pocket and crack it open. It doesn't open properly this time, and crumbles to tiny pieces of rubbery gravel, leaving the horses and the unicorn expanding rapidly on my hand. I kneel quickly, and they hurry off my hand and onto the snow.

"Jack," Kathleen looks over my head, "Jack, does that horse seem familiar to you?"

I glance up, and see a black horse. Not very unusual.

But then I look again. A black mare, with canines. Normally only male horses have canines, but occasionally, a female does, and these ones are larger than any others I've seen – large enough to stick over her lip.

"That's Hecate," I say, as the unicorn and the two horses turn around, "the little black filly who liked bacon."

The horse whinnies and shakes its head in approval. It turns its head, and screeches with a volume that would have deafened a rock-star. There is a noise of hooves, and a number of unicorns appear, along with two of the horses we left behind – those that have been alive since the time when your people lived on earth.

"There weren't this many when we left," Kathleen frowns.

"These aren't all domestic," I cast an eye over the unicorns, "Most of them are pure-bred."

"Some of them still have the smell of purgatory on them," adds Antoinette, glancing towards the northern lights, "something opened a gate."

"And what of the werewolves?" I demand of her, "Where are they?"

"I'm not psychic," she snorts, "How am I supposed to know?"

I turn to the black horse, Hecate. She walks towards me, until I can feel her hot breath on my face. She is not a large horse: in fact, she's only just fifteen hands. But her presence is larger than Adrastea's, despite the fact that she's almost a metre closer to the ground.

"She's dead," Antoinette breathes, "Jack, that horse is dead."

The horse's eyes study me as I reach out a hand to touch her thick winter coat.

"Warm as life," I whisper.

"She's dead," Antoinette insists.

"I know," I snap, "I buried her."

I try and remember what happened. It doesn't take long. It was still early twenty-first century, when someone related to one of the murderers me and Kathleen had killed had come to kill us. Hecate got in the way, and when we found her, she was as cold as the ground she had died on. A long time ago.

"The wound that killed her is still open," I touch the gash the man had made in her throat, and she jerks backwards.

"Necromancy leaves scars." Antoinette whispers.

Kathleen touches the horse.

"Is she the same horse we left?"

"Apart from the fact that she's fresh out of a grave, yes."

"Fresh?" I stare at the angel.

"A week at most."

The gap closes as Kathleen's magic reaches it.

"Who would bring her back?" Kathleen whispers.

"I don't know that anyone intended it. She might have escaped from purgatory.

"But the gate to purgatory has gone – no-one escapes unless it's been opened by something at least half alive."

"We're talking about a horse's spirit here. The rules of life and death you know are for humans and mandrakes."

"I'm hungry," Ollie grumbles.

Kathleen glances at the shattered house, and flicks her hand at it. The ice swirls up into a rather boring cube, and holes melt for the windows and doors.

"You could at least do the door," I sigh, sealing the shattered glass together again and stretching it to fit the gaps. She glares at me as I start to move past the door, and I twist the door back into shape and push it home.

"And food?" Ollie has a one-track mind.

"There," I snap, conjuring a handful of supply balls from the ship, "Happy?"

Kathleen turns her attention to the stables. She can control wood and stone, so I am not called upon to do anything there. I follow the others inside.

"Is everything broken?" Libby demands, throwing aside half a chair –
the largest piece left, "you live in a tip."

"You're the one that broke it," I point out, snapping my fingers at the
furniture to restore it.

"Jack," Karl says, sounding rather worried, "Jack, help!"

I turn to him. There is steam billowing off the ice at his now bare feet,
and he is swiftly sinking into the ice.

"What now?" I seize his arms, and pull him out.

"It's because he's full of fire. He's giving out much more heat than the
rest of you."

"Is that why I won't live long?" Karl asks, now on the table and thus
unable to do any further damage to the floor.

"Don't be silly," Antoinette laughs, "the only reason vampires don't
live long on their home planet is because it only takes one mistake for them to
get eaten. And as they get to about forty, they start to slow down. On a world
with none of their dragons, you could live to four hundred years."

Antoinette walks carefully along the rim of a chandelier we salvaged
from a crashed luxury space cruiser from Aries.

I stare at her.

"So Dracula wasn't so farfetched, then?"

"Dracula is a crap story about a fictional creature. It is simply because
of similarities between such fictional creatures and Karl's kind that Karl is
called a vampire. It is a coincidence."

"I don't believe in coincidence," Kathleen tells her, as she comes in.

"Well, bloody do."

"I think it's funny," I offer, "that someone so foulmouthed, someone
who actually killed someone, could become an angel."

"You killed someone?" Libby gasps, and they all stare at Antoinette.

"Yes," Antoinette shrugs, "but so did Saint Paul. I stopped sinning and
started doing good things once I was dead."

"How did you die?"

"I think I starved," Antoinette considers, "I can't actually remember. I
may have been murdered. Who knows? Anyway, Jack's not exactly one to
point the finger for killing. He's killed himself once, and goodness knows how
many other people."

"But I'm not an angel," I point out.

"Shhh," Kathleen hisses, "Jack, what can you hear?"

I listen, and even Ollie stops chewing to listen.

I can hear faint noises, but they could be anything, I drop to all fours as
a wolf, and move towards the sounds.

"A ship," whispers a voice, "they must be somewhere nearby."

"Humans?"

"I don't think so. Humans don't come alone."

"But who else would have ships?"

"I don't know. People from Europa?"

"They're human."

"Should we tell them?"

"We'll tell them when we get back. Tonight's special, remember?"

I long to be able to see the faces. A young couple, I can tell that much from their voices, but who – well, how would I know? Who knows how long I've been gone?

"Can you believe it's only ten years," sighs the girl, "since…"

There is a silence. Neither of them wants to speak about the event.

"I wonder what happened to the elders?" she continues.

"They probably got caught and butchered like the rest of them."

"But she wasn't one of us. Why would they butcher her?"

"Come on, no human was ever sane. They probably used her hair for rugs and her skin for shoes."

"Do you ever wonder if any of them survived? You know, managed to escape where the humans live, and stay alive?"

"I don't like to talk about it," says the boy.

"It's funny," the girl giggles, "But I think maybe Polly had the best idea."

"She betrayed us, though."

"No. She just didn't do what everyone else did because everyone else did it."

"Well, I know I couldn't have lived as a human."

"I couldn't either," the girl lies, "It's just… I wonder what Polly's doing right now?"

They stay silent for a while.

"You know," the girl says eventually, "the humans think your father's the son of the devil."

"Maybe he is. Who knows?"

Apparently he has accepted the fact that I am his father in my absence.

"I wonder if your mother knew he was your father."

"I'm sure she did. She was probably trying to protect someone when she lied to me."

"If he's the son of the devil, that means you're the grandson of the devil."

"I hope not," he laughs, "I don't want to inherit hell."

"There is no hell," I whisper, human again.

"What?" Libby demands, and Ollie dives into another bag of crisps.

"Did you hear that?" the girl gasps, and their footsteps move closer to the house.

"What?" the boy hisses, "hey, doesn't the house look a bit different today?"

"It does," the girl frowns, "like someone could have rebuilt it." She giggles, "Hey, you did it, didn't you?"

Apparently I have spawned a witch. That makes three – all my children except Cat.

"I can't do anything with ice," he snorts, "you know that."

"Which means someone else did it."

Kathleen pushes open the door quietly.

"Did you hear that?" the boy demands, and then the two of them are running towards the door. Kathleen jumps out of the way as it is flung open, and Antoinette falls off the chandelier, somehow lighting it.

"Oh, fugg," she swears as she scrambles out of the sofa, "Hello."

The boy and the girl stare speechlessly for a moment, and then they rub their eyes.

"It's an angel," says the girl eventually.

"Catch on fast, don't you?" Antoinette flaps back up to the chandelier, "Can I help you?"

"Since when do angels have spaceships?" The girl demands.

"Angels don't," I point out, "she's not the only one here."

"Well how are we supposed to know that in this light?"

I extinguish the chandelier's candles.

"Charlie," the girl says, "isn't that…"

"Jack," I fill in for her, "and no, I most certainly am not the son of the devil, and no, even if I was, you wouldn't inherit Hell, because there isn't one."

The boy gapes speechlessly. The girl seems to be less shocked.

"How come you know this if you're not the son of the devil?"

"You know, it's not nice to ignore people behind their backs," Antoinette points out, "You haven't even looked at anyone here except me and Jack. And while I am stunningly beautiful, I still feel it's unfair that I get all the attention here. I mean, Libby's not a bad looking girl if you ignore her hair…"

Libby sets fire to the rope holding the chandelier up. Humans are such vandals.

"Look," the girl whispers, "a human!"

"And another one," the boy has noticed Georgie.

"And another one," Ollie raises his head briefly above a mountain of food, only to disappear again.

I hold my breath for what's coming next, and it looks like Kathleen's doing the same.

"Are you from Europa or something, then?" the girl demands.

"Don't worry," Karl offers, "They're vampire hunters. They won't worry about werewolves."

"There's no such thing as vampires," The girl points out.

"What am I, then?"

The girl looks confused now.

"Let's go, Charlie. I don't like your father's friends. I miss that lady with the hair."

"I'm here," Kathleen informs them, "Sorry, but we seem to have forgotten the point of being here. Where is everyone else?"

"There's a tunnel about half a mile north, in a little iron shack. If you get tired of walking, you can slide down it. It's the second turning on the left."

Kathleen nods.

"Thank you. I'll see you again soon."

She leaves, and, like sheep, Ollie, Libby and Georgie follow her.

"Karl?" Kathleen calls, and a full bottle floats into the room.

"Why aren't you three going?" the girl demands.

"I'm too old," I lie. The youths shrug, and walk out.

Antoinette giggles.

"You know what's funny, Jack? Your son is physically about two years older than you."

"Well, he's better off than Sam," I sigh, as Karl starts to snore, "Sam is dust. As is Emily."

"These names are meaningless to me," she shrugs.

"My children. My first child, Cat, is still alive, or was ten years ago."

"Frozen?"

"Frozen."

"I met Emily, you know," Antoinette recalls suddenly, "Did you know she was an angel?"

"A daughter of mine? Too many mixed up genes."

"Your wife must have shone through."

"Can you tell where people are heading?"

"Before I was banned, yes."

"Will you be able to again?"

"Who knows? I might not live long enough."

I stare at her, and she shrugs.

Soon enough, she goes to sleep. She floats while she sleeps, next to the chandelier, her wings folded over her back, twitching every now and then.

Tonight, I cannot sleep. No matter how hard I close my eyes, they always open again. I try to start a dream – but it won't carry itself on. I haven't had a dream since I was seventeen years old, anyway. I even try counting sheep – the problem being that by the time I have remembered what they look like; a real live one has been summoned into the room.

I banish it to wherever it came from, and give up on sleep.

"Jack," whispers a female voice.

"Go away," I mutter, trying to think of something – anything – to keep my mind off the silent loneliness of the night.

"Jack!" the voice is insistent.

"What?" I sit up, and search for the source of the voice. Karl is not a woman, and Antoinette is fast asleep.

"Jack!" the voice repeats, louder this time, "Ja-ack! Are you there? Anywhere?"

I recognise the voice, but I'm not sure where from. It seems to be coming from somewhere nearby, but is slightly muffled.

"Jack!" the voice shrieks, "Jack, if you're still alive!"

Karl sits up suddenly.

"Who's that?" he demands.

"I don't know," I answer, searching the room.

"Who is it?" I call.

"Oh, for Christ's sakes. Who else would be talking on a computer? I could be on Venus, you know, lapping in the sun, but instead here I am, sitting in this pigsty."

"Lena?"

"Yes! How did you know? Now, come down here where I can see you. I don't like talking to the whole of Earth. And quickly, we don't want anyone else to tune in."

I stumble into the tack room, and burn the trapdoor away.

"Jack," Lena heaves a sigh of relief as I come down the stairs, "Now, I have to make this quick, because I'm going to be locked out in…" I glance up above the screen, "forty-five seconds. Who's that behind you?"

I glance back.

"Just Karl. He's a vampire."

"Oh. Okay. Anyway, the humans are coming. There's an army of six million human soldiers coming down."

"Six million? Six *million*?"

"I am fully aware that the current population of earth is eighteen thousand, Jack. You have about six days to get everyone out of the way. Oh, and don't try to call me. They've got a small fleet of warships trained on Europa. We're not allowed to help you, or we'll be blown up as traitors to human – fuck, I have to go. Bye!"

The computer switches off and rolls itself up.

"Six million?" Karl stares at me.

"Sometimes I wish Lena was a liar," I sigh.

"What can eighteen thousand do against that many?"

"I should think it's less than that," I shake my head, "most of the people that survived the last attack were children when we left, or too old to hunt or fight."

"But a journey this far in a quertinak takes at least six years, if not seven. And you met us at least six months ago. Any children over ten then will now be old enough to fight."

I consider this. My son was sixteen when I left. He is now, according to Antoinette, two years older than me. That's what they were talking about, then.

"Ten years," I tell Karl, "we've been gone ten years."

"Ten years ago I was treating girls like monsters who wanted to eat me."

"And now you're controlling the urge to eat them."

"That's one way of putting it," Karl looks offended. I ignore him and swing the chandelier through Antoinette.

She falls to the ground in surprise.

"Antoinette, I need you to go and find Kathleen."

"Iron shack, half a mile north?"

"Precisely. If my son is down there with his girlfriend, come back up and tell me."

Antoinette flaps off.

"What are we doing?" Karl asks as I let the unicorns out.

"We're going to find my son before the scout ships do."

I open the stables, and the unicorns and horses disappear into the night.

"Bloodloss," I call, and the unicorn hurries towards us.

"What about me?" Karl demands, hopping out of the steaming puddles his feet have melted in the ice.

"Hecate," I shout, and a horse's nose rubs against my neck.

"I'm meant to ride that? What if the necromancy wears off suddenly?"

Hecate looks offended, and bites his hand as he reaches out to touch her.

"Ow," he complains.

"Watch she doesn't eat you," I warn, scrambling onto the unicorn's back.

"How will we find them?"

"They were coming south. We'll go further south."

The unicorn has other ideas. After going south for about a hundred metres, he swerves to the right, to the west, and shoots off at full speed, the undead horse hurrying along behind.

After about a mile, he stops.

"Well, that didn't work," I inform him, as Hecate and Karl arrive, and Karl falls off. However, when I try to turn Bloodloss back to the East, he refuses to move. I get off and start swearing at him.

"Why isn't that horse like your other ones?" Karl grumbles as I stop swearing.

I turn to answer him, but I see Hecate walking slowly, deliberately, forwards.

"Is that a fire?" Karl demands, pointing at a small light about a hundred yards off, which Hecate appears to be heading for.

"It is," I reply after a little consideration. The unicorn snorts triumphantly, and I hurry after the horse.

She stops just beyond the reach of the firelight, and Karl stumbles forwards to grab her.

"Stop," I hiss, and he falls over. I pull him back to his feet, and hold a finger to my lips.

He nods, and we walk quietly forwards to where Hecate stands.

Charlie and Rosa are peering into a hole in the snow, created by the fire.

"Wow," Charlie breathes, "what is it?"

"It's a horse's skeleton," she snorts, "Isn't it obvious?"

He reaches in, and pulls out a bone.

I have a bad feeling about this.

"Come back to before your death," Charlie whispers, and lets go of the bone. Curiously, it stays aloft.

"Help," squeals Karl, and a bubbling noise follow. I look towards his voice, and he has disappeared into a quickly freezing over pool of water.

"It's taking a long time," the girl snorts. I grab Karl's wrist as he splashes, gasping, to the surface, and drag him out and onto Hecate's back, before returning my attention to my son.

The bone has been joined by several others, and is starting to look like a horse's back leg. Shoulders and a collarbone follow, and a horse's skeleton quickly forms.

"Hang on," Karl turns his head onto its side, "Isn't there an extra pair of legs there?"

"Oh, shit," I whisper. "Stop," I shout, "Stop, Charlie, if you value your life."

He jumps, and the skull turns to face me.

"Whoa," Rosa whispers, "Charlie, it's alive."

Charlie returns his attention to the skeleton, which has now nearly got wings.

"Its name's Apollo," I inform her, "Undo what you just did, Charlie. Quickly."

Charlie opens his mouth helplessly.

"He can't," Rosa replies.

The skeleton is swiftly growing flesh.

"Do you have any idea how much trouble it was to kill the bastard in the first place?" I demand of Charlie, "Why did you have to bring it back to life?"

They stare silently, guiltily.

"How was it this shallow?" I demand, as if they could know, while searching for a knife to summon before the corpse is fully alive again.

A silver breadknife, two hundred metres down into the ice. It appears in my hand and, as the heart forms, I drive it in.

"Sorry," I breathe, as the flesh crumbles away, and I drop the knife into the hole.

"What was that for?" Karl demands, as the bones are dragged back into the hole by some invisible force.

"That was Lycanthropy's brother," I move forwards a little, and peer into the hole, "Apollo's Moon. Now, Charlie, Rosa, get onto the unicorn."

They stand, staring into the hole.

"Did you not hear me?"

"We don't have to listen to you," Charlie says eventually.

"If you want to be shot and skinned, feel free to ignore me."

"How do we know you don't want to kill us anyway?" Rosa retorts.

"Because if I wanted you dead, I would have let you bring Apollo right back to life."

She glances into the hole.

"You're saying a horse could have killed us?"

"That horse would have trapped you in your own, personal little hell and torn you limb from limb."

It probably seems rather cruel to you to have killed a horse – twice, no less – but if it wasn't for my wife being there the first time this monster attacked me – although we weren't married then – I would have been dead when I was fifteen. As it was, it was this horse that possessed Lycanthropy to bite me in the first place, and this horse has tried to kill me on several occasions, and only luck has saved me.

114

Charlie holds up one of the vertebrae.

"It was just a horse."

"Have you seen Lycanthropy?" Karl snorts. They turn to him for the first time, and then their eyes travel downwards.

"That's the one you did last time," exclaims Rosa, "the one that ran away!"

I glance at Hecate.

"What were you planning on doing once you'd brought her back?"

The two young werewolves look at each other.

"We weren't," she admits.

"I just wanted to see if I could do anything," he adds.

I glance at Hecate.

"Well, bringing Hecate back was quite safe. But you were lucky. Next time, only bring something back if you have to, okay?"

"Can you bring animals back from the dead?" Charlie asks as they, finally, climb onto the unicorn.

"No," I shake my head, "and I have no wish to."

We walk off slowly, Karl not daring to stray from Hecate's back in case he starts melting the ice again.

"Why do we have to sit up here?" Rosa asks after about half a mile, "Why can't we just walk?"

"You know, considering that you're physically my senior, you're a bit immature, aren't you?"

"Well, why can't we walk? It's not exactly comfortable up here."

The unicorn looks offended at this.

"You're not allowed to walk," I reply at last, "in case the humans decide to attack. The unicorn will take you wherever you need to go if anything happens."

"What, we have to run away?" Charlie snorts

"Do you have any idea what they'll attack you with?" Karl asks quietly.

"What?"

"When I left my planet, the latest ALT was about a tonne of nitro-glycerine and two tonnes of silver in a bomb about the length of your little finger. The basic idea was that it would be fired like a bullet, and then when it hit the ground, you'd have three seconds before it blew up and flattened an entire village."

"What's an ALT?" I demand.

"Anti Lycanthrope Technology."

We walk in silence for a few moments, before I – and probably the others – realise how silent it is. There is no sound of any birds, or wolves, or bears, or storms. I glance up at the sky, and it is as black and plain as if it was cloudy, but the air is too thin here for there to be clouds.

I turn to the unicorn.

"Take them home."

And they're gone, with a flurry of snow and an irritated bellow falling over Karl, Hecate and I.

115

"Shouldn't we go, too?" Karl whispers, "I don't want to die."

"Go if you want to," I shrug.

He doesn't.

"Why don't you want to run?"

I consider this. Part of me does long to run, but the other part is even more desperate to stay.

"Curiosity, I suppose," I tell him.

"While you're being curious, we're rather exposed here."

I nod, and a pine forest springs up around us. Karl sighs in relief.

"I wonder how that looked to anyone up there," he chuckles.

"These aren't real. They won't show up on Environment Detection, or whatever you call it."

There is a flash of light, and we both duck, but no weapon lands. About twenty soldiers appear in a tight group on the ice instead.

"Check the forest," one of them barks, and the rest hurry towards us.

Karl stares at me.

"There's a man coming straight for us," he hisses.

He's right. The man's weapon – which looks just as much like a gun as they used to – is loaded and cocked. I am fairly sure there's a silver bullet in there, unless humans are even stupider than I thought.

He is close now. He stops and listens.

And then, very slowly, very deliberately, he edges around the trunk of the tree one away from us.

"He can hear us," Karl mouths desperately.

He's right. The man is now pressed up against my tree, and is edging around it, his breaths coming short.

And then he sees Karl. He squeezes the trigger, and with a quiet pop the bullet sails through the front of Karl's skull. He swings around to face me as Karl falls from Hecate's back, but I am already behind him.

He can hear me still, and his breaths get faster, and more panicked as he swings towards seeming invisible breathing, seeing nothing but one presumably dead werewolf and a horse that isn't at all bothered by the occasional burst from his gun.

Eventually, he decides that Hecate is to blame, and aims his gun carefully at her head.

I can't let her die again, so I seize him around the neck from behind, and sink my teeth through his insulated collar and deep into his jugular vein. He drops the gun, and falls unconscious.

"Karl?" I whisper. Karl sits up, rubbing the patch where the bullet hit.

"That hurt," he grumbles. He looks down at the man on the ground. "Did you kill him?"

"No. He's just never felt pain before." I check the man's pulse, just in case, before trying to justify my actions, "Bastard was going to shoot Hecate."

Karl picks up the bullet that has fallen out onto his lap.

"Lucky he shot me and not you," he sighs. I nod, and glance at where the man came from.

"I don't think much of their scouting party, though," I confiscate the gun, and stow it in my pocket, "shall we go?"

The humans slowly return to their officer, and report that there are no hostiles in the area. Sooner or later, the man I bit will regain consciousness, and after a few days he might remember what happened to him. I'm sure tomorrow night's full moon will help to jog his memory.

Once we have reached the house, I remove the illusion of the forest, and Antoinette swoops down to join us.

"Your son is throwing a tantrum," she grins, "do you need a guide back down?"

"They shot me," Karl tells her, almost delightedly.

"I hope you didn't bite anyone."

"*I* didn't," Karl replies.

"I'm guessing that Jack did."

I look at the ground.

"Better than killing him," Antoinette shrugs, "They'll probably deport him to Earth once they find out. Anyway, wait until you see the new city."

"Werewolves don't live in cities," I stare at her.

"You do now." She waits for me to get onto Bloodloss, who is patiently waiting, and we head north at a gallop.

"Here," she grins, and I reach forwards to open the door of a most ordinary looking iron shack, grumbling from rust.

"Wow," I comment, "that must have taken a long time to dig."

A tunnel about three metres in diameter slopes steeply into the earth, stretching far beyond even my eyesight can penetrate.

"You'd best get off," Antoinette suggests, "You know, they've been digging this thing for eight years. Twelve thousand people digging for eight years to create one tunnel.

"Twelve thousand? But Lena said the whole world only had…"

"Every werewolf on Earth lives down here," Antoinette grins.

Karl puts his feet carefully onto the edge.

"Is it safe?" he turns worriedly to me, "there won't be any copper sticking out, will there?"

"Oh, don't be such a baby," Antoinette sighs, and, in one of her brief solid moments, gives us both a shove.

"Second turning on the left," she calls after us.

At such a steep angle – probably sixty or seventy degrees from the surface – we pick up speed quickly, especially as the ice has been worn smooth by ten thousand people going up and down every full moon for goodness know how long.

After about a minute – but goodness know how far – we pass a turning on the right, and Antoinette appears above us.

"Karl, you're leaving a trail behind you."

Karl pulls the middle finger at her.

"What's in the first turning on the right?" I demand.

"It's a cemetery," she replies, "and they also have the occasional execution there for malicious witchcraft."

"What counts as malicious?"

"I don't know. I've only been down here once."

She rises to the top of the tunnel as Hecate and Bloodloss shoot past, and drops down again.

"First turning on the left is coming up – livestock."

There is a crackle, and the tunnel ahead of us is lit up suddenly.

"Karl, you're on fire," Antoinette cackles gleefully.

"Eff you," he snarls, as we pass the left turning, and Bloodloss scrambles through.

"Next is where witches are allowed to practise magic," Antoinette tells us, as I use a bolt of magic to push Hecate back up so that she can get through her turning. We pass a rather unused entrance on our right, and shoot past the second on the left.

"Damn fools," Antoinette sighs, and I dig my claws into the ice.

"Oh, shut up," Karl snaps, grabbing my ankle and pulling himself to a halt, "You couldn't do it if you didn't have wings."

"You couldn't do it if Jack didn't have claws," she points out, landing in front of us, "and you might want to put that out."

I turn to look at Karl. A roaring fire has taken up residence on his back and shoulders, and he is looking furious.

"I would if I knew how."

Then the water he has melted on the way down catches up with us, and instead of fire, Karl is covered in billowing steam.

"You made it," comments Kathleen, "you really shouldn't have bitten that man, Jack," she hands a clay pot of blood to Karl, and hurries him onto the wooden pavement. "Try not to set it on fire."

Libby and Ollie appear – the latter now carrying a strip of dried reindeer.

"Have you any idea how old that is?" I ask him.

"Don't care," he shrugs, "Why's Karl steaming?"

"He caught fire," Antoinette beams, "where is everybody?"

"Georgie's introducing about twenty werewolves to poker, and another three thousand of them are taking the children and old people to a deeper retreat. About a thousand are further down making crossbows, and the rest are sleeping, mainly." Libby grins, "Although there is a very good restaurant still open on the third turning on the right."

"Not hungry," I inform her, "how're you going to get the ship down here?"

"You are," Kathleen tells me.

"You want me to summon a whole ship?" This is not just impossible, it's ridiculous.

"Jack, you can grow a whole forest in half a second. I hardly think that a single little ship will be a problem.

I sigh, and stare at her.

"You really are nuts."

"Okay, then," she sighs, "sorry, it was just an idea. If you're too pathetic –"

I know she's baiting me – how could I not? – but I rise to it anyway. I close my eyes and concentrate, harder than I ever have before, on bringing the ship here.

"Jack, if you could do it without frying us I would appreciate it more," Kathleen admits. I ignore her, and the crackle of electricity I feel on my skin.

I start to feel the solid materialising, and concentrate harder – I wouldn't want to summon half the craft, and leave the rest sitting on the ice.

"That'll do, Jack," Kathleen calls, sounding very far away.

I open one eye, cautiously. The ship, externally at least, seems to be intact, even if does very nearly reach the ceiling.

"I'll take it from here," Libby offers. I nod, exhausted, and reach out to grab an arm to steady myself.

"You are not coming near me," Ollie wards me off with his dried reindeer, and I find myself falling.

They all peer down at me and I reach out a hand for help getting up – I don't think I could do that by myself just yet. Everyone jumps back except Kathleen, and I latch into her arm.

There is a loud crack, and a flash of blue, and then Kathleen is getting up on the opposite side of the tunnel. Candles flicker on in windows, and faces peer down at us.

"That had better have hurt you," Kathleen warns.

I hate to tell her, but it didn't. Actually, it has made me feel a lot better.

"Sorry," I squeak, getting up and hurrying away from her darkening scowl.

"Oi," shouts a voice from one of the glassless windows, "Magic goes up onto the second on the right!"

Kathleen waves a hand at him and he is struck dumb. In the meantime, she has returned her attention to me.

"Kathleen," Antoinette lands in front of her, "don't do this. You know full well it was an accident."

"He's had this one coming since I met him," Kathleen growls, and conjures a ball of snow around her hand. It turns black in her grip, and starts to hiss quietly, before she pulls her arm back and throws it at me.

It hits me like a rock, right between the eyes, and knocks me against a wall. Once the world has stopped spinning, I stand up, and I am sick, again, and again, and again. When there is nothing left to throw up, I just keep on retching, until I collapse.

It seems that seventy thousand years of anger were not lost by the hex on the plane, and Kathleen's taking it all out now. My head is smashed again and again against the icy floor until I cannot see, and I retch again.

And then, slowly at first, and then more quickly, my entire body starts to freeze. Within a minute, I am rigid, unable to do anything but wait.

It seems that Kathleen relents quite quickly once I can't retaliate, as the ice melts sooner than I expect.. I look up through layers of darkness and cold, and see not Kathleen's face but Karl's

"He's thawed," Karl says quietly, and Kathleen appears.

"Sorry about that," she looks at her feet, "I couldn't melt the ice once I'd made it, for some reason."

I decide it is probably better if I don't say anything for now.

"I think I got a little bit over the top," Kathleen, for the first time since I have met her, looks ashamed.

"I forgive you," I croak, "I probably deserved it."

That was a stupid thing to say, in retrospect. Now she probably thinks she can hex me whenever it catches her fancy.

"Come on," she sighs, hefting me to my feet, "let's get you to bed."

"Bloody magicians," I hear the man she had struck dumb muttering as we stagger towards the ship.

It's difficult to wake up in a sunless city. In fact, I only wake up because at around nine in the morning, I roll over and send a fat macaw flying away with an offended squawk. Antoinette, who is coming through the door, stops to swear at it for a few minutes, before jumping up and down on the bed. Somehow she manages to time it so that every time she lands, she is solid, so I am pretty much rocked out of the bed.

"Good to see you up bright and early," Ollie comments, walking past the door. I growl at him, and try and get back to sleep.

"You do realise that you're going to be fighting in a cross-species war in five days, don't you?" Antoinette dives off the bed and stares down at me, "are you alright?"

"I'm rich!" Georgie exclaims, "I have taught your people poker, Jack. And beaten them at it! Hahaha!"

I ignore her, as well.

"Jack," Kathleen sticks her head around the door, "I've been talking to some of the leaders here, and – Jack, get up, or I'll hex you again."

I sit up sharply.

"What is this," Kathleen demands, "a war or a lie-in?"

"It's not a war until blood is spilt," I point out. Humans are funny like that.

"No," she agrees, "But if we don't all help with the war effort, it'll be our blood. Now, Jack, you have to come up to the surface with me now."

"I'm not dressed!" I protest. She waves a hand dismissively

"You are now. Get a move on!"

To my relief, we don't have to scrabble up the slope – there are poorly defined steps along the edge of the tunnel, which Karl does his best not to melt as we hurry upwards.

"Oh, get a move on," I grumble as Kathleen stops to think for the umpteenth time.

"On the slope," Kathleen grins, jumping onto it herself, and sliding upwards.

"That is disturbing," Libby puts one foot on the ice, and slips. After her yelp of pain and cold, she shoots upwards.

"Bye," Ollie and Georgie jump on at the same time.

"I think I'll walk," I say eventually. I'm still feeling seasick from the last time.

"If I could have your body for one day," Antoinette sighs, "I'd be up that slide like a shot."

"You can have mine anytime," Karl snorts.

Antoinette shakes her head at us in pity, and flaps away swearing to herself.

"You took your time," Kathleen scolds when we reach the top.

"We're here now."

"I can see that," Kathleen sighs, "Now, as I was saying to Libby, "what we really need to do is find out exactly what we have to our advantage. I propose contacting Lena and asking her if Europa could send its army."

"No point," I remember, "Europa's under siege. If it helps us, it'll be destroyed."

"Okay," Kathleen sighs, "so we have five horses, nearly a thousand unicorns, and about twelve thousand werewolves, one me, one vampire, and three humans."

"And one angel, for what it's worth," Antoinette points out.

"And one angel," Kathleen nods, "Antoinette, would you like to tell Jack?"

"Well basically, we're fucked," Antoinette tells us gleefully.

"Not entirely," I interrupt, "where are the rest of the horses?"

Kathleen stares at me.

"Lapping in the tropical sun and having the romp of their life near Kenya, I suspect."

"I don't think so," I shake my head.

"The thing is," Karl considers, "even if we could muster six million intelligent creatures to fight, we'd never win. Humans have better training, better weapons and the advantage that they can all speak to each other."

"I think it's a pity we're not nearer the equator," Kathleen sighs, "There's plenty there to help us."

"You mean the reptiles?"

I never can refer to them as dinosaurs. In my mind, dinosaurs were wiped out sixty-five million years before your lot left earth – in reality, of course, I was responsible for unleashing them on the world again. On the bright side, they didn't have much interest in eating people.

"They wouldn't fight," Antoinette sighs, "they'd just eat anyone on either side who had killed someone."

"The only thing we can do," Libby offers, "is scare the heck out of them, kill a few of them, and run like crazy before they can kill any of us."

Kathleen doesn't react at first, but then she looks at Libby as if she has just sprouted wings and a halo and become a less foulmouthed version of Antoinette.

"You're right," she whispers, "It could work!"

"Except, of course, that they'll find the hole and wipe us out," I point out.

"Oh, that's easy," Kathleen laughs, "all we have to do is get rid of the village above the ground, and hide the way to the city underground."

She points a finger lazily at our house, which crumbles into a billion snowflakes, and turns to each of the ice houses in turn, destroying them without leaving a trace, and then to the iron shack.

"I can't do it," her shoulders sag. I glare ate it for a moment, and the iron vanishes, leaving the hole gaping up towards the sky.

"Now just hide it with a nice sprinkling of snow, and they wouldn't know for a moment that it was there," she waves her hand, and a gust of wind blows a thick covering of snow over the hole.

"Now can I go back to bed?" I yawn.

That afternoon, after I have slept a little more, the thirty-seven leaders of the werewolves from across the world translate Kathleen's plan into the thirty-six other languages – if you include American as a language. Thankfully, there are only seven or eight Americans strutting around as if it was their plan in the first place, and they have before won thousands of wars against the humans.

They take it upon themselves to organise the war effort – and introduce conscription. As I wander down yet another confusing street, one taps me on the shoulder.

"Hey, kid," he drones, "you gonna sign up for the war or nut?"

"Nut?" I frown at him for a while before I realise what he was talking about.

"Come on, kiddo, I ain't got all day. Us adults have stuff to do, ya know?"

I have never had such a strong urge to hit someone in my life.

"Sorry, sir," I smile as politely as I can, although I have a feeling my teeth may be showing, "My name is Jack Hanov Himmerden."

"Thank you, kid. And date of birth?"

"January the twenty-third, nineteen ninety-three."

"You sure that's right, kid?" he sniggers.

I glare at him, and it's all I can do to stop myself from loading the glare with hexes and curses enough to kill him on the spot.

"Look it up," I hiss.

Trust the Americans to still have electronic technology – although I can't really talk. He pulls a computer from his pocket, types in my name, glances at my face, and faints dead away.

What a relief.

You have to understand, I don't hate Americans. I don't even dislike them. I have, in the past, got on very well with some Americans. Unfortunately, most American werewolves decided not to have children shortly after I ate the human ambassador, and the only ones who carried on breeding were exactly the sort that should be forced off the planet for the sake of the gene pool. The unconscious one was a result of the combination of two such people, so he had no hope.

Down at the seventh turning on the left, there is no talking. The only American witch – a plump lady with a deep, jolly voice – has one hand on a thick red log, and the other about the same height off the ground next to her. Every three seconds, an identical log appears under this hand, and another werewolf comes and rolls it way for processing. A Scandinavian is sitting opposite her, carefully handling newly made crossbows, and muttering something to her every time he finds a fault. A little deeper into the shadows, along with several hundred carvers, the Scandinavian's wife and his teenage daughter are stringing the crossbows by drawing lines with their fingers, where string appears.

A long way back, a Chinese man is sweeping up the sawdust left by the carvers, and, whenever he has enough, he stoops down and presses it together to become bolts for the bows.

"This is a tight operation," Libby giggles behind me, "isn't it a bit pointless, though?"

"In what way?" I ask.

"If you attack them outright, the crossbows will kill about a thousand, tops, before they find out where you are and wipe you out."

"Eit's defensive," says the American witch, "mah husband might be getting' all axited about some war or other, but this is in case they discovers us. We ain't gonna go looking for a faght."

Libby appears surprised.

"What about the hit and run idea?"

"With these? Don't you be a loon, gal."

Libby turns to me for an explanation. I shrug.

"How am I supposed to know?"

Eventually, we find Kathleen, jumping up and down on the American who took it upon himself to sign us all up for the army.

"And you say I have no self control?"

"You would not believe this guy," she snaps, relenting, "anyway; it can't do him any harm. He's a werewolf, after all."

Somehow I think she has missed the point.

"The stress could kill him," Libby checks the man's pulse quickly.

"Fine," Kathleen touches the man's throat, and the magic seems to target his brain, "as far as he knows, that never happened."

"What happened to the plan of nipping out and picking them off?"

"It's been scrapped. We're playing defensive – see if they go away, and if they don't leave before we run out of supplies, then we'll have to attack them."

She picks up the man's now smashed computer, shrugs, and tosses it into the tunnel.

Over the next few days, the most exciting thing that happens is poker. In between conjuring haystacks and rats, we all do our best to learn Georgie's beloved game. I don't think I am alone in still not understanding the first thing about it after she has had us playing it for eleven days.

At every available opportunity, we go up to the surface, and check for any sign of the invading army, but they seem not to be coming. After a fortnight, we stop waiting.

"I'm going up to de surface dis night," grumbles a young Brazilian girl, putting her crossbow away, "Dey're not coming."

Her ideas are echoed by a large number of young werewolves. A few geriatrics mumble something irrelevant, but there is really nothing we can do to stop them. They have every right to be bored – in fact, we don't even complain as we follow them up into the evening.

They reach the surface as the moon rises, and plunge into the night as wolves.

"I wonder why they've given up," Ollie sighs, "I was almost looking forward to the war."

A loud howl breaks the air, followed closely by several more.

"They found nothing," I shrug, "what else were they supposed to do?"

"Those teenagers are being a bit loud," Libby winces as a wolf howls close by. Karl swigs at his bottle of blood before replying.

"It's all the hormones all over the place," he offers, "They need to get out and shout every now and then."

I scan the horizons, and notice an unlikely obstruction.

"How sure are we that the humans haven't landed?" I demand.

"No-one's heard anything," Kathleen tells me, "or seen anything."

I stare harder at the obstruction and after a while I can make out the shapes. Buildings, big, heavy buildings, surrounded by a high wall, right where the twenty humans Karl and I saw landed.

"How have they not noticed that?" I point, and Kathleen stares towards it.

"I see nothing," she shrugs.

"Let's go closer, then," I sigh, and lead them all about two hundred metres towards the thing.

"I can see it," Antoinette calls, "It's huge! They must have landed their entire army here!"

"Can any of you see it?" I demand, turning to the others.

"No," is the unanimous answer, so I move them all closer.

"A bit of an outline," Kathleen offers, "against the sky, there's this patch that looks out of place." She hesitates, and walks back into the tunnel.

"It's simple," Libby snickers, as we get within twenty feet of the thing, "There's clusters of cameras on each side, and corresponding projectors on the opposite sides. People have been trying things like this since the twenty-first century."

"Why could I see it before you?" I wonder.

"Because your eyes were not human when you looked," Libby kneels in front of the wall, "Wolves' eyes see slightly differently, and these were designed for human eyes, because werewolves are human most of the time."

"So they can all see it now?" I enquire.

"Oh, yes, I should think so."

I walk up to the wall, and peer at the tiny lenses and screens, quite easy to see now that we're this close up.

"It's just a coating," Libby informs me, "A roll-on sheet. You can get it for ships, as well, if you're planning excursions into hostile environments."

I reach behind the web of cameras and projectors, and wrench a considerable number of them off.

"Back!" Libby shrieks, "get back!"

And an eight foot silver spear shoots out of the wall to lodge itself in my stomach.

"I told you to get back," Libby squeals, as I stare helplessly at the blood trickling out of the wound, and slowly, unstoppably, everything goes black.

I open my eyes to see an icy wall.

"You fool," Libby snaps, "you could have died, just for a little scrap of sophisticated wallpaper."

"It hit your aorta and the edge of your stomach," Kathleen informs me, "And if it wasn't snowing, there would be a trail of blood all the way here."

I sit up.

"They can't trace that, can they?"

"They won't be expecting you to be hiding behind witchcraft," Georgie snorts, "they know that werewolves hate witches."

"I am, however slightly concerned," Kathleen glances up at Antoinette, "There were three bodies found in the snow, but there are five people missing."

"Bodies? The humans attacked us?"

"At about four in the morning," a middle aged woman informs me, "they opened fire on a group of twelve that were trying to bring down a straggling reindeer. The reindeer and three of them got away, and we found four more dying, and three dead, at the site."

"Could the other two have run off?"

"The only tracks around were the humans' and those that got away. They're being questioned at the moment, and will be locked up once they have finished recounting their tale."

"Locked up for what?" Libby frowns.

"Reindeer aren't supposed to be hunted at the moment," the woman sniffs, "for ten years the law has stated that they may only be culled in summer, and only once healthy populations have been ascertained. The punishment for breaking the law is three years imprisonment."

"And what of the other two?"

"We're going to try and retrieve them," The woman turns on her heel, and walks away.

Shortly after she has left, the American that Kathleen jumped up and down on appears.

"What do yous think ya're doan' in the Haspittle sec-shun?" He barks.

"Oh, go spit-roast yourself," Georgie snaps.

"A yuman daires say thet to mah faice?"

"What are you doing here, then?" Kathleen challenges.

"Lookin' fur yous. I 'ave to teal ya thet wun Kathleen Anchor, a Karl – damn, wart is thet surname?"

"Smith," Karl offers.

"Thet's the wun. A Karl Smith, a Liberty James, and a Jack with a lang surnaime, they's supposed ta be reportin' to law enforcement section thiys afternoone."

And he leaves.

"I hate that man," Kathleen says eventually. There are murmurs of agreement, and we get up to leave.

"What time is it?" I demand.

"Late morning," Libby glances at her watch, "the sun should be rising soon."

"Don't count on it."

"Why do they want me?" Libby wonders, "And not Georgie or Ollie?"

"I'm hungry," Ollie comments.

Once Libby's watch tells us it is twelve o'clock, we leave Georgie and Ollie to poker and food, and head down to the sixth turning on the right, Antoinette flapping along to watch.

"Ya're laite," snarls the American.

"Are you the only other one here?" Kathleen scowls.

"Nwun Eilse is heire yit."

After about five minutes of his mind-melting accent telling us how terrible we are, other werewolves start to arrive. I see Charlie and Rosa in the distance, but I don't recognise any of the others.

"Werewolves," a voice called, and I turn to its source to see the middle aged woman who was in the hospital section, "and others. The three hundred of you here are those who we believe are probably the most useful members of our defence team."

Everyone looks puzzled at this. The woman smiles apologetically, and continues.

"Due to your many different… gifts, the board and I feel that you are the best wolves for the task in hand," she hesitates uncertainly. "The humans appear to have captured two of our kind, and if they torture them, they may discover how to find us, despite Kathleen Anchor's illusion. With your skills, we hope you will be able to penetrate the human base, and rescue the two captives."

And she leaves.

"This is ridiculous," Libby hisses.

"Why isn't she telling us what to do?" demands someone.

"What's ridiculous?" Karl wonders, fiddling with the laces on his shoes.

"Werewolves don't like witches, right?" Libby turns to me.

"They didn't used to," Kathleen nods slowly.

"They're trying to get rid of you. Just so you wouldn't realise it, they put some who aren't witches with you, so that those "gifts" could mean anything, and send you out to kill two birds with one stone. They get the captives back, hopefully, and in the meantime, manage to drastically reduce the number of witches."

"But why would they do that?" I laugh, "Magic is the greatest weapon any of us have!"

"Humans have similar ideas," Libby shrugs, "when I was in the military, for about a year, they said that if the only way to win a battle was to ally ourselves with an evil creature – such as werewolves – we should lose. It's a similar situation."

"But not all the witches are here," I laugh.

"When there's only a few, they can force them to do their bidding, without being their allies."

I stare around at the confusion, and see that it is starting to come to order.

"This conspiracy theory is all very fun," Antoinette sighs, "But there are only a few hundred witches on this planet. If they wanted to get rid of them, they would have done so long ago. The only reason they didn't tell you what to do is that they don't understand what magic can do, so they can't tell you what to do with it."

"So why are there normal werewolves here, too?" Libby demands.

"Because magic wasn't the only gift she was referring to," Antoinette shrugs.

"There are only five here who aren't witches," I look around, "that American, Rosa, Libby, Karl, and that dark girl over there."

"How do you know the dark girl isn't a witch?" Libby demands, "And that everyone else is?"

"There's something about witches," I shrug, "you can sort of tell after a while." I can't explain how I know, I just do.

"What da you tink yous lookin' at?" the girl demands in a thick Caribbean accent. She raises a crossbow suspiciously, "Do you tink I's nat so good as yous because I's bluck?"

"Oh, oh no," Libby wrings her hands worriedly, "No, Jack just said that you're like me, one of the ones who isn't a witch."

"I's nat yuman. You's nat like me. But no, I's nat a witch, neider."

Then the American jumps up and down and tells us all to get a move on, or we'll find his crossbow bolt up one of our "lezzy asses". With Kathleen pulling a middle finger at him under her hair, we all collect crossbows, and walk out.

Kathleen bewitches the slope, and it doesn't take long for people to realise that it no longer takes them downwards, so most of them take that way.

"Do nut you twos tink it wood be fasdar?" the Caribbean girl asks, when only she, Karl and myself are left.

"I don't want to catch fire again," Karl shrugs.

"And what about Jeck?"

"Jack," I correct her, "I just don't like it."

"I gets a littel dezzy, and cunnut shoot stret."

When we reach the surface, everyone else has arranged into ranks. We slip in behind Kathleen and Libby, who are arguing ferociously.

"Hello, Dad," says a voice beside me.

"Charlie," I glance at him, "when did you decide that I was your father after all?"

"A Polish fortune teller – she's over there."

The woman – about fifty, I'd guess – is looking distinctly nervous, and doesn't seem sure about how to hold the crossbow.

"Naw the beist whey ah can see is to atteck theim atraight," says the American, "We're gonna murch up, and fire in a good oarderly fashion."

"Can I shood heem?" the Caribbean girl demands.

"Feel free," I shrug.

"Pity dere's no silva cups on de bowlts," she sighs, "Is dere a wetch heir who can maik silva?"

"There's no point killing our own kind," Rosa snorts, "Apparently, he organised the Americans into an army against the humans last time they came."

"So dat's why dere's only liddle childrun and heis family from de stets, den?"

Rosa has no answer to this.

"Sir," Antoinette calls, "With all due respect, sir, this is suicide."

"Are yew part of theis upperation?" he demands, staring up at her.

"No," she glares at him.

"Then yew gut no raght to teill me what tu do."

Someone sets him on fire. Sadly, someone else puts it out.

"Most of these people are little more than children," Antoinette tries again, "and what's three hundred against six million?"

"Shut UP, ya pesky little crow!" he bellows.

"Oops," comments the Caribbean girl dryly, "do you tink he forgot about de yumans?"

Libby swallows. We are scarcely a hundred yards from the human fortress now, and they are sure to have heard him.

"Get closer to me," Kathleen shouts. An alarm sounds within the fortress, and everyone clutches their ears.

"Don't yous be breakin' the rainks," the American warns, but it's too late. The witches – most of them in their teens or early twenties – are hurrying towards Kathleen, forming one thick mass of petrified, half deafened bodies. Kathleen murmurs something, and an impenetrable shield is thrown up around us.

"Can any of you transport yourselves?" Kathleen demands, "If so, go home."

About fifty of the witches vanish, and Kathleen nods in satisfaction.

"Deserders!" screeches the American, and catches fire again. Someone sniggers.

"Do you surrender?" calls a voice. We all stare up to the top of the wall, and see the humans.

There must be well over two thousand of them, all taking careful aim with rifle-like weapons.

"Werewolves niver surrender!" barks the American.

The humans open fire.

"I can't keep this up for long," Kathleen calls, "Jack, can you give us a forest?" I nod, and we are surrounded by trees.

"Make it bigger," Kathleen gasps, sending another pulse of magic to keep the shield up. I obey, and the forest stretches for three miles behind us.

Kathleen whispers something to the girl beside her, who turns to whisper it in her neighbour's ear.

"Can someone create an illusion?" her voice asks us all, "an illusion that we are all still here?" there is a pause, and then; "now everyone that is afraid, leave," whispers the voice, and I hear a multitude of feet leaving. Beyond the shield, I see occasional figure rushing through the trees, but they disappear into the trees within moments.

"Why aren't they fighting back?" demands a fat human, popping up briefly.

The Caribbean girl smiles, aims, and fires.

"I's neva bin too fund uf dose who leads frum de buck."

I turn to see the fat man falling from the wall with a bolt through his eye.

"Cover!" screams Kathleen, "I can't hold it anymore!"

The shield vanishes, and a rain of bullets falls down on us. The witch next to Kathleen ducks down beneath the crowds, and over two hundred of the others just vanish.

"They's gun!" exclaims the American, too stupid to realise that he should copy those that remain and take cover.

"Dat was luck," sniggers the Caribbean as the American collapses bleeding to the snow.

"I'm scared," whispers someone behind the tree next to us.

I glance around – Charlie and Rosa are huddled close behind a large oak.

"You should have gone when you had the chance," I hiss.

"But that would have been cowardly," Charlie retorts.

"Fire at will," whispers a girl's voice in everyone's ears.

"Jeck, and da vampire, if eider of us dies now, et was good ta meet yous."

"Karl," the vampire in question hisses, "my name's Karl."

"Melody," the Jamaican smiles.

She loads a bolt into the bow, steps out from behind the tree, and fires.

"Well, I's nut ded yeet." Melody grins, and loads another bolt.

"Did you get one?"

"Four. Went nicely up de barral as he shut at me. Big bung."

I glance out from behind the tree.

"How do you shoot one of these things?" I demand of Melody.

"You aims and you lets go," she jumps out from behind the tree and sends one bolt through two humans.

"Jack," whispers a voice, "where's Libby?"

I glance around.

"Libby?" I call.

Karl stares up into the tree as if she might be there.

"Libby?" he shrieks, stepping into the line of fire.

"You fool," hisses Libby from another tree, "where did you think I was?"

"Oh," he sighs in relief.

"You's doin' preddy good," Melody grins at him, "I tort dat vampires had de same weakness as us does."

Karl glances down at the bullets that have fallen to the ground around him.

"Oh yes," he realises, and turns to the humans, "I don't think I can aim one of these things."

"You really are hopeless," Libby hisses.

"Can you aim a gun?" I demand.

"I could if I had one," he frowns, "but we don't."

I hand him an automatic.

"Careful with it, it was my sister's, I think."

"Where'd you pull dat wun frum?" Melody demands, firing another bolt into the human masses, "dis is ridiculous. Where's de man who was settin' de American alight?"

"I think he went home," Libby whispers.

"Grett. Nuw what's we supposed ta do?"

Kathleen has stood up, a little way along, looking slightly unwell.

"Jack," she calls, "How are we supposed to get past them?"

"Dat's why dere were so many uf us."

"Three hundred against six million?" Kathleen laughs, "come on, are you mad?"

"I'm out of bullets," Karl gasps, sitting down.

"Geev it to me," hisses a Russian witch two trees away.

He does, and she throws it back to him instantly.

"Done."

The Russian fires a bolt into the humans, misses, curses, and ducks back behind the trees.

"How long are the trees going to keep you safe?" Kathleen demands.

"If I die, they'll vanish," I shrug, "If I don't, they won't change until I want them to."

"Don't die, den," Melody laughs.

"Easier said than done," Kathleen snorts, and turns to shout abuse at someone who just hit her in the eye.

"That hurt, you little fuck!" she screams.

Antoinette, for her part, is distracting the humans by fluttering around in frown of them, and, every now and then, knocking one over.

"Yumans, dey die like de flies," Melody chuckles, "dere's enuff of dem dead on de ground to warc raght up to de top uf dere wall."

Kathleen looks, sheltering her eyes from the raining bullets.

"Not yet."

"Stop shooting," screeches some heavily decorated man, "Now!"

He cocks a small gun.

"Why are all ze generaghls male?" demands the Russian, shooting a bolt into one of the soldiers near the man.

"How do you know he's a general?" demands Charlie, crouching ever closer to the Earth.

"I know sings. It's my majic, like yours is breengink back se dead."

"These are your captives," the general snaps, pointing to two teenagers "If you do not stop firing, I will shoot them."

Melody considers it, and shoots the gun out of his hand.

"We'll only stop shooting when you stop," Rosa bellows.

The general's shoulders sag, and he barks out a command. The rain of bullets peters out and stops.

"He's lyingk und cheatink," the Russian whispers, "breeng more trees!"

I obey, and then we can hardly move for trees.

"I'll find the whisperer," Kathleen hisses, scurrying through the maze of trees.

"Is nut dis pissful," Melody stretches out on the snow, "Yous would nut know dere was yumans on de planet."

"Gather," whispers the whisperer's voice, "follow the footprints."

The seven of us look around for footprints "We're the centre," Libby whispers, realising that all the prints lead to us.

Soon, others appear – forty-four others, including Kathleen.

"Se humans are not goingk to shoot de captives," the Russian whispers, "dey vere tryingk to deestruct us so sat dey could come into se forest and vipe us out."

Melody giggles and releases a bolt. There is a yelp of pain, and she returns her attention to the Russian.

"What will they do?" asks one werewolf who can't be older than seventeen.

"They will find those of us here," the Polish fortune teller smiles, "but what will happen then has not yet been decided."

"Crossbows are useless at short range," a Brazilian points out; "We need something that doesn't take so long to load.

"I have a dagger," offers an Egyptian girl.

"Pass it to me," a middle aged Canadian Red Indian holds out the palms of his hands. Unwillingly, the Egyptian hands it over, and he runs his finger along the blade, as if searching for a seam.

"There," he pulls it apart, leaving him with two identical daggers in his hands. He hands one back to the Egyptian, and splits the other in half again.

"That's not enough," whispers Kathleen, "we need something longer."

I think back, deep into my memory, and remember a pair of twin swords we had when I really was only twenty-four, and the man that murdered my wife.

"Here," I whisper, "they're rusty." The Russian strokes them with her fingertips, and they are repaired. I hand them to the Red Indian, and soon there are thirty pairs.

"They cannot divide any further," he whispers.

"Jack," Libby considers, "do you remember the gun I had on board?"

I think back.

"Describe it."

"A hefty little sub machine gun. Sixty second century – titanium?"

I picture it in my head, and it falls into my hands.

"Thanks," Libby scrambles onto the lower branches of a tree, and takes it.

"Sey are close," the Russian whispers.

"I can send some of them to sleep," offers another Egyptian.

"You need to go west north west," Kathleen whispers, "knock out as many as you can in that direction."

"Who needs to go that way?" demands the younger Red Indian.

"As many as possible," Kathleen snaps.

"Since when are you in charge?"

"Since I am the oldest person here."

"You're not the oldest. My dad's older than you."

Her father leans to her ear and whispers something to her.

"Oh," she murmurs, and stops protesting.

"Thank you," Kathleen nods to the father, "Now, you, Isis," she points to the Egyptian with the dagger, "you stay with me. Jack, Karl, Libby, you stay with me. And you," she points at Melody and the Russian, "I don't know your names, but you stay with me. Who is it made the illusion?" another Brazilian raises his arm. "You stay with me as well."

"What about the rest of us?" Rosa asks.

Chapter 5 – Hate

Kathleen turns to the Egyptian boy.

"Are they asleep?"

"They should be."

"Alright. The rest of you get into the trees, and head West-north-west. Do not come out of the trees, and those of you without anything other than your crossbows, stick near someone with a weapon." They quickly scurry into the trees.

"Wait," Kathleen calls, "Rosa, do you know why they sent you along?"

"They didn't," she blushes, "I came because I didn't want Charlie to be here without me."

Kathleen sighs, and turns to the seven of us that are staying with her.

"I need someone to have a plan," she says after a long silence.

"Sey're too close," the Russian girl informs us, "No time to hide."

A bullet shoots out of the trees, and hits Karl in the chest.

"Karl!" squeaks Libby. Kathleen pushes her to the ground as a bullet shoots past where her head was but a moment earlier.

"Where's the vampire?" Isis demands in all our ears.

"He hus jumped." Melody glances upwards with a smile and fires a bolt towards where Libby's bullet came from. A human thuds into the clearing, panting.

"Don't speak," whispers the Brazilian, "He can't see you."

Karl drops back down to the Earth, behind the human.

"I know you're there," the man hisses, "show yourselves."

"Who, me?" Karl whispers, putting a hand on his neck.

The man spins around, but it is too late. Karl sinks his teeth into his neck, and after a brief spurt of blood, the man collapses, and Karl is wiping his mouth.

"That's dealt with," he spits, "he tasted disgusting."

"He vas on steroids," the Russian woman whispers, "Sey all are."

"Disgusting," Karl repeats.

"Ve nit to head tovards seir building," the Russian decides, "kvickly."

And so we hurry off towards their building, the Brazilian letting go of his illusion as we go. Naturally, being me, I am hit by a branch that Melody pushed aside so that she could get through.

"Don't you move," a very deep, female voice commands, "Or I'll blast your cursed brains out."

I look up. A woman with the build of a carthorse is pointing the long, black barrel of her gun at me.

"Now, very slowly, I want you to stand up."

I do so, wondering what to do now.

"Don't you try any magic tricks, neither."

"Either," I correct her. I have every intention of trying a "magic trick" – she can shoot one of me a lot more easily than, say, forty of me.

She pulls the trigger, but by this time, I am no longer that easy to kill. Part of me drops dead, and the rest of me, now snakes, slithers away over the freezing ice as fast as my coils can carry me.

I reassemble behind Kathleen.

"Kathleen," I call, looking at the stump that was my arm before I became the snakes. "I need a bit of help here."

"How did you do that?" she demands, gripping it as she continues running.

"Ve cun't go any furser, or sey vill shoot us," the Russian whispers.

"I'll distract them," offers Isis. She leans to my ear and whispers.

"They're inside."

There is a cacophony up above and the Russian waits a moment, smiles, and nods at Kathleen.

"Hide us," Kathleen tells the Brazilian.

He nods, and we rush out into the open. There are no guards on the wall.

"Here," Kathleen touches a large door, "it only opens from the inside."

Melody considers for a bit, and then turns to the Russian.

"Weire's de bowlt?"

The Russian points, and, after another moment's consideration, Melody fires her crossbow at the point

The door swings open, and Melody smiles in satisfaction

"There's too many people," Kathleen glances at Isis, "could you tell the prisoners we're coming to find them?"

Isis nods, and leans to Libby's ear.

"We're going to rescue you."

"Where are they?" Kathleen demands of the Russian girl.

"Se seventeence cell on se right, in se sird row on the left, undernease se prison buildingk."

"Very good. Now, you, Isis and Paolo are going to go home."

They protest, but Kathleen glares at them and they leave, vanishing after a few steps, their disembodied footsteps heading into the trees.

"And who do you think you are?" drawls a voice from above us. Melody points her crossbow in the direction of the voice and fires. A skinny dwarf tumbles to our feet.

"Why are you so happy to kill them?" I demand, closing the gate.

"Dey killed me mudda, me farda, me sisda, me sonne and me dorta. I's just gettin' evan."

I suppose that makes sense.

"Nobody kills anyone unless they have to, okay?" Kathleen rounds on us, "That includes you, Jack. We don't want to attract any attention."

"What did I do?" I spread my palms, "I haven't killed anyone today."

A soldier spots us, and starts to come towards us, his gun at the ready.

"Stop," Kathleen whispers at him, and he freezes.

"Into those barracks," she snaps, "quickly."

134

We edge past the shouting crowds, and slip through the barracks. Kathleen closes the windows with a glance, and Melody locks the door carefully behind us.

"I've been expecting you," Antoinette comments, "In fact, I've even managed to lock the soldier that was hiding under this bed in the bathroom."

I turn to look at her, and something catches my eye. At first, I think there's someone standing at her shoulder, and then I see the acrylic casing. I look at the other beds, and beside all of them are similar situations.

"They're frozen," Libby informs me, "This way, they don't have to feed six million. They probably have about one million awake and active, and if one of them dies, they are replaced by one of these."

"Dat's sick," Melody levels her crossbow to one of the frozen human faces, and then lowers it again, "Cun't shoot a soldya in hees slip."

"Where do they keep their spare uniforms?" Kathleen asks Libby.

"There should be a small button on the ceiling," Libby reaches up and presses one. Something along the lines of a bookshelf comes down – clothes on the top shelf, a gun and ammunition on the second, boots, cap, brushes and polish on the bottom, along with a well thumbed book.

"Look at the frozen people for size," Libby glances at the frozen man beside the bed, and then at me and Karl.

"Jack," she says eventually. Kathleen is delighted to find that there is a frozen soldier slightly shorter than her, but not short enough to mean that the woman's uniform is too small.

Libby quickly finds a suitable uniform for herself, and Melody finds one on the second turn, apart from the boots.

"Karl?" Libby turns to check on him. He is staring into one of the frozen soldier's faces.

"My brother," he whispers, "in there."

"Yous ded nut knuw dat hey hud joined de army?" Melody frowns.

"I knew. I just didn't expect him to be... here."

Libby takes him by the arm.

"We'll come back and get him," she promises, "but now you need to get dressed, and help us to find the captives."

Karl nods quietly and stands up. Libby pulls down the clothes from the same bed, and turns to Melody.

"You don't want to take that with you. It'll stick out like a sore thumb. Pass it here."

Melody scowls, and clutches the crossbow.

"Give it to me," I sigh, "where do you live?"

"Tree hundrad und sevanty-two, secund flur."

I banish the crossbow.

"It's waiting just inside the front door. Now take a gun, and let's go."

Melody passes me her clothes as well, and I banish them too.

"Jack," Kathleen considers, "Jack, I have a problem."

Kathleen is looking very distressed indeed.

"My hair, Jack. No human has hair like this."

135

"You could wait here," I offer.

"You know I couldn't. You'll have to cut it."

She puts her hand to her hip.

"Not above there."

I nod, and summon a pair of scissors.

"Could I just have a minute, first?" she pleads. Kathleen and her hair are very close.

After a few minutes of holding it tight to her, she stands up straight, and holds her head high.

"Please do it quickly," she pleads. I nod, and lift her hair up on my arm.

"Below or above the waist?"

"Above," she breathes in deeply and closes her eyes. I look at the scissors, decide against it, and summon a short sword instead.

"Ow!" she yelps, and half her hair drops to the ground.

Then she opens her eyes.

"You said make it quick," I shrug.

"Let's go," she sighs, giving one last baleful look at the glistening pool of black hair on the floor, "It's just hair, after all. We slip outside, Kathleen checking the ends of her hair, looking almost tearful, and this time nobody looks twice at us.

"Attention!" shouts a fat, important looking man, "Soldiers! There are five intruders within the ground. Private Jenkins saw them not half an hour ago, and it is believed that they are still present. If you see them, you are to call for reinforcements immediately, for they will not hesitate to kill you.

There are murmurs of surprise, and Libby shouts out.

"Werewolf scum!"

The nearby soldiers mutter in agreement, and Libby grins at us.

"Now they won't notice that they've never seen us before."

"Oi, you!" shouts a less fat, but still quite portly fellow, "You, the midget with the hair!"

"Yes, sir!" Kathleen turns to face him.

"Have you registered?"

A young woman has appeared behind him, and holds a finger to her mouth.

"Well? Don't just stare into space, young lady! Have you registered as active?"

The woman shakes her head slowly and deliberately.

"No," Kathleen nods, "Sorry, no, sir."

The young woman makes walking signs with her fingers.

"We… we just walking – going?" Kathleen guesses. The woman shakes her head, and hold up two fingers.

"We were just going to!" Kathleen exclaims triumphantly. The man glances over his shoulder, and the woman ducks swiftly. He turns back to Kathleen.

"Good. Could you please take these to Madame Benita." It isn't a question.

"Captain, sir," the woman behind the portly gentlemen salutes, "I'll take those, sir."

"Thank you, corporal, but these privates are heading that way anyway."

"Yes, sir. But, sir, they are only just awoken, and they might get lost. I am loath to allow your documents to come to harm."

"Of course, corporal. Thank you, corporal."

"Thank you, sir."

The captain walks away, and the corporal grins at us briefly.

"See you, Jack."

I stare after her.

"Stop gawping, you'll swallow a fly," Kathleen snorts.

"Maybe you had an affair with her," Libby suggests.

"I don't think so," I frown, "she would have been hardly sixteen last time I had an affair."

"Excluding the one on the fake earth."

"Excluding that one."

A platoon of soldiers thumps past, and we press against a wall to avoid being trampled.

"How can anyone wage war from such chaos?" I demand.

"Are you going to register?" A boy – about eighteen, at most – grins nervously.

"Er," I turn to Kathleen.

"Yes," she says tentatively.

"Good. I can go with you, because I'm completely lost."

"We're lost, too," Libby assures him.

"Totally, completely, utterly lost," Karl adds.

"We can be lost together," he grins, and falls in behind Melody, "So," he says to Melody, "How long have you been in the army?"

Melody looks at Kathleen, and back at the man.

"Tirteen munts," she lies.

"Wow. That's a long time. I only joined up when they said they needed more people for some war."

"Damn, I really need the loo," Kathleen decides suddenly.

There are murmurs of agreement.

"I don't need the loo," the boy frowns, "Here, I'll look after your stuff while you all go."

This is hopeless. After discovering that the bathroom windows are too small to escape through, we go back out to where he is patiently waiting, and set off again.

"Look," Melody points, "de preson buildun'."

"Cool?" the kid suggests.

Nobody makes any reply to that.

"It's coded," Kathleen scowls, "I hate codes."

I glare for a bit at the lock, and turn to Kathleen.

"Eight zeroes."

"Why are we going in here?" demands the boy as the door swings open.

"No reason," Libby lies, "did she say underneath the prison building?" she asks Kathleen, looking down at a trapdoor.

"She did," Kathleen nods, "Down we go."

"Where are you going?" the boy demands.

"Oh, it's a secret assignment we're supposed to do before we're registered," Libby shrugs apologetically.

"I'll help!" offers the boy.

"No, you really don't want to," Libby assures him, "It's gory."

"Come on, I'll have to learn to face gore, won't I? We're at war here."

And so he follows us down the ladder below the trapdoor, and into the basement of the prison building.

"Third row on the left," Kathleen considers, "Does this count as a row?"

"I think probably row of cells," Libby frowns, "Hey, the ones on the right have got numbers!"

"It probably applies to both of them." Kathleen nods, "Okay, three… Here!"

"What are you doing here?" demands a voice. Kathleen glances up at the white-robed man, striding towards us as fast as his fat legs will carry him, "This building is off limits to soldiers!"

He stops in front of us.

"Now leave. If you are out of this building in ten seconds, I will not sound the alarm."

"We have a duty to carry out down here," starts Libby.

"There are no duties authorised down here!" he bellows, spraying spittle over us.

"That is disgusting," Kathleen wipes her face and turns to me, "Jack, can you shut him up?"

I nod, and he collapses to the ground with a surprised squeak.

"Dude," the soldier comments, "That's not right. Seriously, man."

"He's not supposed to know what we're doing," Libby seems to have elected herself minister of lies, "It's better for him this way."

"We should probably knock you out, to," Kathleen shrugs, "We're not supposed to let anyone else see this."

"I don't know anyone here. Who am I going to tell?"

Everyone, I think, but say nothing. I would knock him out, too, but then he would definitely find himself implicated in it.

"Seventeent cell," Melody reminds us. We hurry onwards, glancing up at the numbers above the cells.

"There's not many people here," the boy shudders, "I'd be pretty scared coming in here alone."

"Jack," Karl stops at a cell with a man in nothing but his underwear, "Isn't that the man you –"

"Yes," I interrupt before he can finish, and then Kathleen stops.

"Poor, poor children," she sighs, "what have they done to you?"

"Why have they got kids in here?" demands the boy, "that's just not right."

"Do you even know who this war is against?" Kathleen demands.

"Not really," he shrugs, "I know it's on some planet that people were on pretty early."

"It's against us," I inform him, "Our entire species."

"We's werewurves," Melody informs him, "as is dese childrun."

The boy looks at us for a minute.

"But," he stammers, "but you just look like normal people... you can't be – them."

"Here's the thing," Libby puts hand on his shoulder, "werewolves are normal people. It's just that at some point in their lives, they got bitten by someone who had turned temporarily into a wolf."

He shakes her hand off.

"That's a lie," he points at her, "werewolves are the grandchildren of the devil."

"Oh. Okay then," I consider, "so how would you prove that to us?"

He looks confused.

"Well," he stammers, "I... – you couldn't touch a symbol of God without burning!"

And then he notices that Melody is wearing not one crucifix, but five.

"She can't be a werewolf," he points at her. Then he notices that everyone except me is wearing a crucifix, "None of you can be except," he points an accusing finger at me, "you."

Melody hands me one of her crucifixes, which I hold in the palm of my hand and begin the change. The boy screams, and stumbles backwards.

"We won't bite you," I promise, holding back a laugh as I straighten up again.

"If you're not demons," he says eventually, as Kathleen kneels to try and reach the prisoners, "why is there a war?"

"You do know that your species once tried to wipe out angels?" I remind him.

"You're not saying –"

"No, he's nut sayin' dat werewurves is engels," Melody sighs.

"It was an example of how happy your species is to wipe out any other. They automatically think that everything is going to attack them. So they attacked us first."

"At first it was just for the fur," Kathleen gives up on trying to reach the unconscious forms, and smashes the door down, "And then they took some of us for scientific experiments. Jack and I escaped, and Jack foolishly bit someone who blackmailed him."

"Jack, as in –"

"Jack Hanov Himmerden," I confirm. He crosses himself instinctively.

"And presumably because of that, there was an outbreak. So they thought we were attacking them. And they decided to come and wipe us out." Kathleen touches the forehead of one of the werewolves, and shudders.

"They've put something in his blood," she whispers, "It's destroying his mind."

"How do you know that?" the boy demands.

"We need to drain his blood," Kathleen turns to me, "I need a knife."

I fish around in my memory until I find one, and hand it to her.

The unconscious form shudders as she puts it to his neck, and the blood pours out onto the floor.

"You've killed him!" exclaims the boy when the blood stops trickling.

"No," Kathleen puts her hand back on his forehead, and passes the knife back to me, "I've saved him. Karl, you do not want to drink that."

Karl was halfway to dipping a finger in the blood.

"But it's suppertime," he complains.

"Just hold on one minute," Kathleen waves her free hand as the werewolf below her hand opens his eyes.

"There, now," she pats his head, "are you better?"

He nods nervously, and stands up.

"If you want to leave, kid, do," she addresses the human soldier, "Jack, could I have a bottle?"

"I want to leave this army."

"I'm sorry, but I have no power over that." Kathleen waves her had, so I hand her a bottle, and she hands it to Karl, half full, "That'll have to do."

"I could live here!" he looks desperate.

"Why did you suddenly change your mind?"

"I don't want to be in this war!"

"Who are you?" asks the healed prisoner.

"She's clean," Kathleen announces, and starts healing the girl.

"No, she isn't," Libby reaches down, and plucks what looks like a mole from the girl's neck, "She was bugged."

"They said they were going to let us go," the first prisoner tells Kathleen.

"So they made you too weak to fight, and bugged her," Libby nods, crushing the bug between her fingernails "And then they would have come and wiped us all out."

"Wake up," Kathleen whispers to the girl, whose eyes open slowly, "You're better now."

"We have to go," Libby glances around, "they'll know we're here by now."

"Please can I come with you?" begs the soldier.

"Oh, fine, just shut up. And act like you know what you're doing."

"How are we going to get these two out?"

"Jack?" Kathleen turns to me, and I present her with two uniforms.

"They'll have to do," she tells them, "put these on, and quickly."

"Couldn't you change their faces?" suggests Libby.

"While we go," Kathleen nods, and the boy's red birthmark across his cheek vanishes. The girl's dark skin and green eyes turn to pale skin and blue eyes, and her hair loses its curl. The boy's nose gains a roman bridge, and the girl's double canine vanishes.

"De moon will be risan in only farve minetes." Melody informs us, "We do nut wunt to be heire when dat harpens."

"Then we'd better hurry," Kathleen holds the door open, and we all slip out, letting it swing shut behind us as we head back to the gate.

"There's a back gate behind barracks block F," whispers a voice in all our ears, "Titania says the combination is seventy-two, eighty-three, forty-six, eighty-seven."

"Block F?" Kathleen glances around.

"That's my barracks," the soldier points, "over there."

We hurry towards it, but a soldier blocks our path.

"Where are you going?"

"To our quarters, sergeant," Libby answers.

"There's no time for that! There's fugitives! Start looking for them!"

"Yes, sergeant." Libby nods.

"Well, turn around and start looking for them."

"Dere's no time fur dis," Melody mutters, and shoots the man dead, "can yous nut feel da moon?"

"I said no killing!" snaps Kathleen, and we step over the body.

"Hurry," Antoinette lands behind us, "move, you fools! From thirty metres up I can see the moon!"

"What was the combination?" Kathleen demands.

"Sevan," Melody recalls, "tow, et, tree, fore, seex, et, sevan."

Kathleen pushes the door open, and a siren screams out.

"Slip well," Melody grins, and she and the two newly released captives bound off into the night, leaving their uniforms behind them

"I thought you were all werewolves, not just her," the boy frowns.

"Only Jack's a werewolf," Antoinette hovers beside him, "Kathleen's immortal, Karl's a vampire, and Libby's a human. I, of course, am an angel."

"Does that mean that God's taken the werewolf side?"

"No, it means I have. The thing is, it's only because of Jack that I'm an angel at all, so I think I owe him something."

"The uniforms can be traced," whispers a voice in our ear, "take them off."

There is a mad scramble as we strip of the uniforms, and the boy looks at us.

"What are you doing?" he demands.

"We feel like dancing naked under the full moon," says Libby sarcastically, "anything that the army provided you with, take it off. Quickly."

He obeys, and is soon standing there in nothing but his socks and underpants.

"Boy am I glad I kept my stuff on underneath," Libby sighs, "Now, they will have deactivated our guns. Jack, give me mine."

I summon it and hand it to her.

"Goodnight," whispers Isis in our ears.

"I have mine," Karl, like Libby, kept his own clothes on underneath the uniform, with the gun I gave him earlier in one of the larger pockets.

"Do you know how to use one of these?" I ask the soldier, holding out my sister's revolver.

"Where did you get that from?"

"My sister had it with her in the Mariana trench," I reply, "Can you use it?"

"Is it loaded?"

"Yes."

"So I just cock it, point it and pull the trigger?"

"Pretty much, yes."

He takes it carefully.

"This looks ancient," he breathes, as I summon the twin swords, which I had stuffed under a bed in the barracks.

"Do you need anything, Kathleen?" I ask.

"No, no, I'm fine. Which way's home?"

"That way," Libby points carefully.

"Go," Kathleen summons a weak shield around us.

"There's a warship coming," the soldier squeals, as we hurry off in the direction of Libby's pointing.

"I'll go and distract them," Antoinette takes off, and we hear her giggle as she lands again.

"I don't want to know what you did," Kathleen snaps.

"You're not how I expected an angel to be," the soldier confides in her as she flaps along behind him.

"I'm not how I expect an angel to be," she shrugs, "Look out!"

The shield shatters, and a ball the size of my head hits Karl.

"Throw it away," Libby shrieks. Karl throws it, and it hits a tree and explodes.

"Next time try and get rid of it in the process," Kathleen snaps, turning her attention to the soldier, who has about forty small, silver blades in his back, "You're not dead, you ass. Get up."

She takes her hand away as he gets up, the last of the silver having fallen out, "from now on, Karl's at the back, and I'm at the front."

We run on, and then, quite suddenly, there are human soldiers all around.

"Deserter," one waggles a finger at the half-naked boy as she takes aim. "You'll get frostbite like that.

"You first," Kathleen waves a hand at the woman, and she freezes solid.

"Now, unless the rest of you want to die, leave now," Kathleen snaps.

"You can't kill us all," one sniggers, and they charge at us.

"Try me," Kathleen sighs, before pausing to consider how best to go about it.

Kathleen snaps her fingers, and two of them turn to ice. Libby opens fire on them, and another ten fall bleeding to the snow, but it's not enough. She gets shot in the shoulder and the neck as she starts to shoot again, and crumples like paper.

"Goodbye, werewolf," sniggers the man who shot her, taking aim at her head. Karl snaps his teeth into the man's neck, as he prepares to pull the trigger, and the gun swings up, shooting instead one of the human soldiers.

"It doesn't work!" the boy yelps, dropping my sister's gun as he ducks under a spray of bullets.

And then the only sound is the double thud of one of the humans hitting the ground after one of my swords swings through his midriff.

There is a low rumble, and everyone looks up.

"Holy mother of God," whispers one human, just in time for giant reptile to plunge its head down and swallows him.

Then the screaming begins. The five of us press up against a sturdy tree as the head plunges down again and again, and Antoinette flies up, screaming, to have a look at it.

And then, apart from Antoinette, everyone has stopped screaming. There is a series of tremors as it leaps away, and we peer around.

"Everyone's gone," I whisper. Antoinette lands beside me and nods, still screaming.

"What was that?" Libby is clutching the tree.

"Was it a dinosaur?" the soldier swallows, "because they said – they told us – they only live near the equator."

"That was not a dinosaur," I swallow, "they normally stay near the equator, too, but that animal is much, much newer."

"A chimaera," says Kathleen when she gets her breath back, "from Peru." Antoinette, still screaming, flies up for another look.

"It's a long way from home," I swallow, "they must have known about the war somehow."

"Why didn't they try and eat us?" the boy demands, as Antoinette lands in front of us, panting.

"I don't know," I stare up at the sky, and see a chimaera folding its wings and diving towards the human fortress.

"They did last time they saw us," Kathleen points out to me.

"It's because," Antoinette stops screaming to gasp, "because you weren't moving. They're nearly blind. They rely on movement to catch their prey, unless the main head is hibernating."

"The main head?" the boy turns to Kathleen for help.

"A chimaera has three heads," Kathleen tells him, as we stand up, "the main one, which you saw, and two smaller ones. The main one eats meat, but when there isn't enough meat to sustain it, the two smaller ones wake up, and they are herbivorous. They are said to look like goats heads, but I don't think anyone's ever got close enough to see."

A small bomber drones overhead, powering towards us, and a Chimaera flies out of nowhere to snatch it up.

"I don't like them," Libby decides.

"Here," Kathleen says, stopping, "Now, you, soldier, whatever your name is –"

"Nicklaus."

143

"Nick, then. Before you go one step further with us, you have to promise me that you will not try and rejoin the human army or tell anyone anything that could be harmful to us."

"I promise," he frowns.

"Are you sure? Bearing in mind that if you break this promise, you will turn to stone?"

He swallows.

"I promise," he confirms.

"Very good," Kathleen nods, and he sinks two feet into the snow.

"It's not cold!" he exclaims.

"It's not real," she replies, "except to anyone who I do not wish to get through. Walk forwards."

He does, and he disappears.

"This is cool," he exclaims. Karl lifts his feet out of his deepening puddle, and we all walk through the snow, and into the tunnel.

To Karl's dismay, we have not managed to walk onto the steps. He curses and swears enough to make Antoinette swell with pride, and catches fire.

"I hate this!" he bellows, as the soldier whoops somewhere ahead of us.

"You've gone too far," Kathleen calls to the soldier as Libby and Karl grab onto my legs. There is a screech and a pop as one of my claws is wrenched out of my fingertip, and we scramble through the second turning on the right.

"Will someone put me out?" Karl begs, and Antoinette adds to the problem by fanning the flames gently with her wings, "and will someone else shoot that damned angel?"

Libby leans against a wall, clutching her shoulder, sliced open on one of my claws as she sped past in the tunnel.

"Where's Kathleen?" she demands, trying to stem the flow with her blackening fingers.

"Here," Kathleen and the soldier come through the entrance, and she puts out the fire with a blast of icy water, "he's hypothermic."

"I'm bleeding," Libby chokes. Kathleen glances at her, and touches the sore.

"I'll deal with the frostbite later," she promises, and returns her attention to the deserter.

"Karl, could you bring some clothes for this man?"

Karl hurries off, and Georgie and Ollie appear around a corner.

"You have no idea how boring it is when everyone has gone furry," Georgie informs us, "Who's the guy?"

"He was a soldier," Libby gasps, "could I have something warm?"

"Ollie, go and get a blanket. I'll make hot chocolate. Can you believe they have plants growing on the livestock level? Someone has some sort of power with light, so they've got an entire cocoa plantation down there, with pretty much every nice plant you can imagine…"

Libby snores quietly, and Kathleen turns to her.

"Shit," she swears, "Jack, take Nick into the hall."

I obey, and she starts healing Libby.

"In there," she points at the village hall as Karl arrives with clothes.

"I wish I could do magic," Karl sighs, shaking the deserter awake, "here, get these on,"

"Why?" I ask, as we go back outside.

"Because with magic you don't have to worry about things like this," Libby snaps, awake but grumpy.

"I can't heal," I shrug.

"Well, there's always at least one thing in life less to worry about, then," she stands up, and wraps herself in the blanket that Ollie has brought.

"Am I not amazingly quick?" Georgie has returned with seven mugs of hot chocolate, "the fact that there's a hot spring down here has nothing to do with it."

She puts the tray down, and sips one.

"And I didn't even forget the sugar," she adds after a moments consideration.

"Did everyone get back?"

Georgie pauses.

"Before they all went mad and hairy, they did a head-count," she considers, "I think they said they lost one man – some American guy that they needed for his military skills. I can't remember his name, sorry."

"Charlie and Rosa got back?"

"Ages ago."

I haven't been this relieved in three thousand years.

With my fears quelled, I retire for a night of comfortably dreamless sleep.

The next day, I am awoken by a slightly euphoric Kathleen.

"You were right," she beams once she has shaken me awake.

"Wonderful," I turn over and go back to sleep.

"Jack, wake up," she hits me with a pan.

I sit up.

"Why?"

"Because you were right," she snaps, "The horses were coming."

"You could have said earlier what I was right about," I notice her hair; "that grew fast," I comment.

"Titania – the Russian girl – she restores things."

"Like with Karl's gun?"

"Exactly like with Karl's gun."

"Can she heal people, then?"

"She can't. Only dead matter."

"Do you know why the horses took so long?" Kathleen teases, turning her back as I get dressed.

"No. Why don't you tell me?"

"They were leading the chimaeras here."

"That was them?" I hate to think how many of them got eaten.

"You see, the chimaeras can't harm werewolves. You'd just pass out the other end."

"Unpleasant image there, Kathleen."

"And you know what the best thing is?" she turns around and grins, "Not one of them got eaten. Not one, Jack!"

I consider the odds of this.

"That isn't possible," I decide after a few minutes, "they probably lost foals or something."

"Not a single one was eaten. A couple of them did die from old age, but otherwise, every single horse that was part of that herd in our absence is alive and well and in the livestock section."

Of course, we have to visit them. There are a rather shocking number of foals – even without chimaeras on their tails, this would be a lot of foals. A lot of the horses are very thin, though, and some of the older ones look almost dead from starvation. Animals that unwell could not have survived being hunted by chimaeras all the way from Peru.

"They're starting to look better already," Kathleen considers, patting one of the thinnest, "It's quite weird seeing them grazing underground."

"When did they arrive?"

"Midnight, I believe. Everyone was quite surprised. A lot of them have never seen normal horses." On that note, I realise that I haven't seen anyone other than Kathleen since I woke up.

"Where is everyone?" I demand.

"That's the other thing I was supposed to tell you," Kathleen closes her eyes and breathes in deeply, "They're – well, there's no point telling you. You would have to see it to believe it."

She leads the way up to the surface level, looking over her shoulder every now and then to make sure I am still following. She really doesn't have to worry. She has my curiosity aroused, and curiosity is quite possibly the biggest driving force in my life.

"Everyone's been up near the surface since about ten. It took a while for them to feel safe enough.

"What time is it, exactly?"

"Well, it was about ten to eleven when I came to get you, so probably – half elevenish?"

"Half eleven?" I exclaim, "You couldn't have woken me earlier?"

"You only got to bed at four in the morning," she points out.

"But half eleven?"

"We were a bit," Kathleen reaches the surface, and breathes in deeply, "distracted."

I come out into the light, and once my eyes have recovered from the initial shock of the sunlight, I start to see the shapes against the sky.

"Mary mother of Christ," I cross myself, and stare up at them. A hundred, probably more, thickset, dark green-brown bodies, facing away from the sun, their immensely long necks curled to their backs, their wings –

unthinkably huge wings – spread like sails, angled to catch the suns heat, sitting as still as stone around the entrance to the cave.

"Are they alive?" I whisper.

"See for yourself," she waves a hand at the nearest chimaera. I walk carefully up to it, through the thick, gasping crowds, and underneath the massive chest. I reach up as high as I can, slightly left of the centre of its chest, and touch the scaly skin.

When I feel the thump, I almost scream. The beast shifts slightly – I pull my hand away from its chest and move out from underneath the animal as quickly as possible.

"Their other heads do not look like goats," Libby is standing the other side of the beast, hand on hips, "They look like tortoises with horns."

"Kathleen said they were *said* to look like goats. What happened to the trees?"

"Some witch or other cleared them in this bit."

I peer past the sea of wings, and see the edges of my imaginary forest.

"For an illusion, your forest's pretty solid." Libby congratulates me.

"It's an illusion to all the senses except taste."

"Why not taste?"

"Have you ever tasted pine?"

Libby considers for a moment.

"Point taken," she decides at last, "Have you seen Kathleen's hair?"

"I have," I glance at the chimaeras; "they're moving. I don't like this."

There is a drone in the sky, and a chimaera leaps into the air. The drone intensifies, and there is a loud crunch as the animal lands again.

Perhaps I should explain about chimaeras. They aren't the goat-sized creature of Greek legend, although they were believed to be a legend for a long time outside Peru and Brazil. Peru and Brazil were first really plagued by them in the early twenty-first century, which was also when I first – and last – encountered them. They have two ways of catching food, other than their herbivorous heads. They can either, after warming their wings up in the sunlight, which takes a long time in dense rainforests, fly after their prey, which is normally successful but uses incredible amounts of energy, or they can leap.

And for a five tonne reptile, they can leap pretty well, as the pilot in the plane that has just been swallowed could testify is he was still alive.

"That is pretty cool," Libby turns around to look behind her, "now where has Georgie gone?"

"Here," Georgie calls, "Libby, I don't like being here. I know they can't hurt anyone else, but they might – I don't know – mistake us for the other humans."

"Libby's right," Kathleen calls, "Even if they didn't mean to, they could destroy you. Five tonnes leaves plenty of room for accidents."

Libby scowls, and stomps over to the tunnel entrance.

"Ollie!" she shouts, "Ollie, you little peedletwip, where are you?" Ollie peers out from behind one of the chimaeras.

"Have you seen how much meat there is on these?" he grins, "If we could just kill one without the others noticing, we could eat for weeks…"

A chimaera glances down at him, and cuffs him with a wing-tip.

"I do nut tink dat yous wood leve fer lung if yous keeled one uf dem," Melody picks him up off the snow, "Evan if yous onlei traid to keel wun uf dem."

Suddenly, all the chimeaera's heads turn to stare into the north.

"What's got into them?" demands a thin Indian boy.

Nobody answers him. Everyone is searching the horizons for the cause of the beasts' concern, but the horizon, even to my eyes, is clear of any disruption.

"They are coming!" screams Titania, "The humans!"

There is a moment's hesitation as this is considered, and then panic. Total, blind panic as everyone runs for the tunnel, and the chimaeras take to the air.

"Ah see nowun," Melody raises her crossbow warily, "De yumans cunnut hide demselves, cun dey?"

"Technology," Libby squeezes herself out of the swarming masses, "can do almost anything."

There is a deafening bellow, and a chimaera collapses to the ground.

"Jack, stop staring, and get underground," Kathleen calls. I point at the twitching monster dumbly.

"I'll deal with it," she snaps, "Now get underground!"

I hurry to obey – it's easy enough now that there's only Karl, the four humans, Melody and me trying to get down.

"I think I've broken a rib," Georgie grunts as soon as we are under the ice.

"Kathleen'll fix it," I promise her.

"I hope she hurries up," Georgie prods her chest and winces, "It feels like one of my lungs has been punctured."

"I'll tell her to hurry up," I turn to go, but Karl's hand grabs my ankle as I scramble towards the false snow.

"Let me."

I nod grudgingly, and he scrambles up.

"Karl, get out of the way!" screams Kathleen's voice, almost hysterically, from quite a way off, "get out of the way!" Karl ducks back into the tunnel, his eyes wide, "Get back!" he commands, pressing himself against the tunnel wall and walking backwards into it as it melts.

"Get in!" he calls as he disappears.

"What?" Georgie frowns, "Is Kathleen coming?"

"Get in! Quickly!" Libby obeys, and Nick and Melody take one look at Karl's face and follow suit.

"It's cramped," complains Ollie, squeezing in, and then –

And then there is a deafening sound not unlike thunder, and something huge and mud green bursts through the hole. There is a scream, and Georgie disappears after it, and then, before anyone can react, another, and another, and another, and then, after goodness knows how long, Kathleen.

"Sorry," she stands up on the slope, "they were dropping like flies. I couldn't keep on healing them all – what's wrong with you lot, have you seen a ghost?"

"Georgie," Ollie points dumbly into the tunnel, "She –"

Kathleen takes a few moments, but realises without having to read more than our faces.

"I'll find her," she promises, and plunges down into the tunnel.

We follow, and within ten minutes we reach the end of the tunnel where, lying like a broken doll in the widened hollow, is Georgie's body.

"She's dead," whispers Kathleen, looking up. Libby chokes behind me.

"She can't be dead," Ollie snaps, "Isn't there something you can do? Isn't there something someone can do?"

"Your son!" Karl says after a few seconds where the only sound is shocked silence, "He could bring her back!"

"Our rules of the afterlife are different from those of horses," I interrupt, "you wouldn't get Georgie back, even if the body came back to life."

"Well you can try," snaps Libby, "It's all your fault she's dead, after all!"

"You can't blame me for this!"

"It was you whose species we came to save – you who we were bringing home! You and your stupid dwarf!"

For once Kathleen says nothing.

"And it's your fault Ballsy's dead!" Libby screams, "And that Karl's a vampire! And it'll be your fault when Ollie and I die as well, along with your whole stupid planet!"

"Shut up!" I bellow, "You cannot blame me for this! It wasn't my fault you ended up on the wrong Earth! The only reason you're still here is because we stopped you from going into that forest! And it was our horses that carried you back to your ship when the vampires found out you were human – and our magic that stopped them from tearing the ship apart to kill you! It was you – not me – who decided to go back to your planet with a werewolf and a vampire in tow! If it wasn't for me you would have stayed on the devil's breath and been destroyed then! All of you!"

"At least we'd be together!"

"Libby, be quiet!" Karl shouts.

"We cun doe nutting gud bah sharting," Melody adds, "She es deyd, and dere's nutting we can doe abowt dat."

"The only thing we can do is give her a good funeral," Karl says softly. Libby opens her mouth as if to scream at him, but thinks better of it, "Do you want Jack to carry her up to somewhere better?"

Libby nods, and Karl glances at me. I pick up the body carefully, but there is no way I could stop her shattered limps from dragging. I start to summon some sort of board to lay her on, but:

"No magic," Libby snaps.

There seems to be an unspoken agreement that we should take her back up to the craft, and the walk is a long one. Just outside the habitation level, Libby starts to cry more noisily.

"Georgie can't be dead," she whimpers, "Georgie's always been there."

"She's gone," Karl puts his arm around her, and she pushes him away.

"Jack," calls a voice, "I hope you didn't leave the body down there."

We all look for the voice, and I think we probably all see it at the same time.

"I have a spirit here," Antoinette grunts, "I don't know who it is, and unless it's someone who we want dead, I don't particularly care."

"What should I do?" I demand, "Should I lay out the body in some special way? Do I need to get some sort of herbs?"

"The only thing you need to do," Antoinette flaps her wings and adjusts her grip, "Is find your son before it escapes."

"I'll go," Kathleen rushes off, and disappears round a street.

"Whoever this is," Antoinette struggles to stop herself from being pushed into the ceiling by the fleeing spirit, "They are one of the luckiest dead people I've met."

Libby sniffs.

"It's Georgie."

Antoinette ignores her, and concentrates instead on pushing back out of the icy wall.

"He's here!" Kathleen calls, and Charlie runs up to the body.

"But I can't bring back anything but animals!"

"When a human spirit hasn't yet reached purgatory," Antoinette grunts, "They behave the same way as an animal spirit that is in heaven. The only reason you can't bring back humans normally is that the doorways are closed to their dead unless God or one of the archangels dictates otherwise."

"She means try," Kathleen translates, and I put Georgie's body down on the ground, wincing as the broken femur pushes through her skin. Charlie studies my face carefully before putting a hand on Georgie's arm.

"Come back," he whispers, avoiding the dead gaze of the wide open eyes, "Come back to before you were dead."

After a few minutes, he takes his hand away.

"It's not working."

"How can you be so sure?" Antoinette has landed now, "have you ever done this before?"

"I gave her my magic, but she should have reacted by now."

"Humans are ridiculously stupid animals," Antoinette snaps, letting go completely of the spirit, "her body might take a while to realise it's alive."

"How long?"

"I don't know, but it would probably be quicker if she wasn't mangled."

Kathleen reaches out a hand, and glances up at Antoinette, who shrugs.

"It can't hurt her."

Kathleen puts her hand on the smashed chest and closes her eyes.

"She's gone," Libby buries her face in the vampire's chest, "cold and gone."

Kathleen frowns, and then opens her eyes.

"My magic is going somewhere, but there's no pulse or anything."

We watch in silence as the bones slowly reorder themselves, the wounds closing, until finally a perfect, undamaged body lies there, as cold as the ice, with no pulse or breath, and glassy, staring eyes looking through everything in their path.

"She's dead," Kathleen says eventually, "in perfect health, but dead." Libby reaches forwards to hold the cold hand, and the eyes move slightly.

"Did you see –" Ollie whispers, and then, suddenly, the body is no longer a cold, emotionless corpse but, living, gasping Georgie.

"Jesus Christ," she curls into a ball, and then looks up, "what happened?"

"You're alive!" Libby squeals, and knocks her flat again, "You're alive! You're alive!"

"What else would I be?" Georgie groans and shoves her off, "how did I get up here? And why have you been crying? Is everyone else dead, or something?"

"What's the last thing you remember?" Antoinette considers, "before being here, I mean?"

"About three seconds ago, I think, I was going down the tunnel –"

"Towards a bright light?" Libby prompts.

"Not that tunnel," Georgie snorts, "the ice tunnel. I was in front of a chimaera, and it was trying to stop, and then the end was coming up, and it was pulling out its wings and then –"

"And then you were here," Antoinette nods, "That makes sense, in a way."

"In what way?" I frown.

"In the way that your son brought her back to before death. As far as she is concerned, she didn't die at all."

"Die?"

"We found you shattered on the end of the tunnel," Karl tells her apologetically.

Georgie looks quite pleased about this.

"I am undead! Does that make me, I dunno, a vampire? A zombie?"

"You're not exactly undead," Antoinette hesitates, "I'm sorry to have to tell you this, but you're still dead."

Georgie frowns, and puts a finger to the side of her neck.

"I have a pulse. I can't be dead."

"Karl has no pulse, and Karl isn't dead. A pulse means nothing when you're talking about magic."

"So I'm dead, but it's exactly the same as being alive? How does that classify as dead?"

"Not exactly the same," Antoinette glances at Charlie, "I'm not entirely sure how to say this."

"Your spirit is glued inside your body," Charlie offers, "It's like if you had a toy with two parts which can come apart. You lose one of them, so when you find it again, you stick it back on."

"And they don't come apart anymore," Georgie nods, "so I can't be properly dead again?"

"Not unless you're liquidised or burnt," Charlie apologises.

"So if you want to see Sygmom again, you do have options," Antoinette tells her brightly.

Georgie winces, and changes the subject.

"What happened with the humans?"

Kathleen glances into the tunnel, and we all fall silent. Over the muffled sound of our breathing, the sound of planes can vaguely be heard.

"I suggest that I go up and look," Antoinette offers, and disappears up the tunnel with a leisurely flap.

Presently, she reappears.

"They're doing their best to bomb the magic away," she informs us, "it's holding, but in about half an hour they'll have melted through deep enough to get around it."

"What are they bombing it with?" Libby wants to know.

"Some sort of flaming ball thing," Antoinette shrugs.

"Very helpful."

"What will happen when they get down here?" Georgie turns to me as if I know.

"Dey well keel evaryting," Melody answers for me. There is a short silence as everyone considers the likelihood of this.

"They won't kill us," Nick protests.

"They don't know that you're still human," Kathleen shrugs, "And just because you're not a werewolf, it won't stop silver from killing you."

"We have the grand total of half an hour to get ready to stop them," Libby considers, looking at the wall, "Is everyone who can't fight still in the eighteenth turning on the left?"

"And a thousand healthy adults as well," Kathleen nods.

"Can you seal the tunnel off – completely, I mean – with ice?"

"I'd have to be there, but I shouldn't see why not."

"Antoinette, find Isis, make her tell every werewolf who is fit and free to fight to go into the seventh turning on the left. Jack, go to the first turning on the left, and take every animal there down to the sixth on the right, and send them right to the back." Antoinette flies off, and after a moment's hesitation, I drop to all fours and scramble as a wolf up the tunnel.

The horses, upon seeing me, rush into the tunnel, and vanish into the darkness. The unicorns follow at their own speed, and the fifty or so reindeer huddle in the back of the cavern when they see me, millennia of being savagely attacked not forgotten through a mere six years of domestication. I follow behind them, and they run, panicked, into the passage, and disappear from view.

I hurry after them, and soon I hear Libby shout;

"Stop them! The sixth, you fool!"

There is a flash of blue, and the reindeer are sent tumbling up towards me, and into the sixth.

"Jack?" Libby peers at me as I stop at her feet, and nods, "Good dog –" I growl, "– I want you to go up and shout down when they break through."

"Perhaps it would be better if I did that," offers Karl, "he could get killed."

Libby sighs.

"True. Now, where's Kathleen?"

Kathleen and a golden-skinned girl scramble out of the darkness below us as Karl vanishes into the darkness above us.

"Everyone who can't or won't fight is in the ninth on the right."

"Have you sealed it off just after the eight on the left?" Libby barks.

"I have, sir."

"I don't think you understand the seriousness of the situation for the rest of us. Isis," Libby turns to the Egyptian girl who came up with Kathleen, "can you ask whoever set fire to the American to stand in the opening of the seventh turning on the right?"

We hurry down the tunnel, and Isis whispers in Melody's ear as we go. When we reach the seventh, we hear a distant bellow from Karl, and a short Indian boy of about twenty is sitting in the opening.

"You're the fire witch?" Libby demands.

"I set fire to General Furtoe, yes."

"Good. Can you control the fire properly?"

In answer, he sends a ball of fire into the air, which swirls around me until I am surrounded by a blanket of fire without burning me.

"Very impressive. Now, could you melt a cave big enough to contain everyone here in between this level and the one below?"

He sends a ball of fire into the floor, and after about twenty seconds, it reappears at his wrist.

"You've got about ten minutes," Karl gasps, patting out the fire on his clothes as he scrambles through the opening, "before they get here."

"Isis, tell everyone to get down this hole, now."

Isis whispers in the Indian boy's ear, and there is a sudden rush of people towards the hole. In less than five minutes, they have all dropped through, and we follow, Libby glancing out of the hole behind us before dropping into the knee deep water with us.

"Kathleen, close this hole. You – what's your name?" she demands of the Indian.

"Adnan."

"Adnan, please open a hole between here and the eighth level, coming out just above the entrance."

He starts to obey, and she stops him.

"It doesn't have to be above, so long as it's a clear shot."

He obeys, and once the water has drained through, we see the edge of the tunnel.

"Jack, could you please become human again? You're making me uncomfortable."

I change back, except my eyes. Vision is currently more important to me that her comfort.

For about twenty minutes, we hear nothing, and Libby chides Karl for panicking her. Then, suddenly, we hear voices, and footsteps, above our heads. Someone screams, and Libby silences them with a glare.

"What was that?" a voice demands above us.

"Where are they, captain?"

"They could be anywhere. Probably waiting for stragglers to eat."

Kathleen stifles a giggle.

"Do you think they ate the hostage?"

"They're aliens, son. I have no idea what they'll have done."

"My mum says they're basically like humans."

"Your mum is filling your brain with fairytale nonsense."

"Yeah, private, your mum's a sympathiser."

"She says my great, great, great, great grandma was bitten by a werewolf."

"Private Sterning's a werewolf! Werewolf, werewolf! Don't bite me, private!"

The voices move, and a multitude of footsteps move away, and down.

"They must be in here!" calls the captain's voice, and we hear feet running on the ice. I can see a crowd of men and women, bristling with weapons, charging into the tunnel.

"Up," whispers one woman with her eyes closed, "Up. They're up."

They all stare upwards, but this deep below the ice, they cannot pick out the hole in the uneven ceiling, even with their night-vision lenses in. Libby taps Melody on the shoulder, and makes a gun with her fingers, and points it down the hole.

Melody is only too happy to comply, and with my sister's revolver, takes very careful aim, and fires a single shot.

"Up!" screeches the human witch again, "they're up!"

I think we all feel pity for them in this moment, as they realise that we are not as completely stupid and unprepared as they had been led to believe. Melody alone seems without conscience, and is soon handing the gun to Titania, the eight spent bullets marking one life each.

"There!" someone points to the hole, and Libby squeals

"Away from the hole!" she shouts, and everyone presses themselves against the walls.

Nothing happens, and an Egyptian man leans forwards.

"Are you sure they've seen us?" he asks, Libby peers forwards, and pulls her head back swiftly as a volley of silver bullets thunder up the tunnel.

We turn back to the Egyptian, who, his head shredded, collapses with a hiss of air escaping from his open neck. The other eleven Egyptians I can see follow his corpse with mournful eyes as it slides slowly towards the hole, and down.

154

Another shower of bullets comes up, and everyone turns away as the corpse is pushed back up the hole.

"Come down and fight like humans," shouts an officer. Isis leans forwards, her eyes closed, and gives the body a gentle push towards the hole.

"Tell them," Libby turns to her as exclamations of horror and the occasional sound of someone vomiting come up the shaft, "Tell them that we will not kill anyone who drops their weapons and holds up their hands."

I hear a million identical whispers from below us, and an officer makes an indignant squawk;

"Not if you want to live, soldiers!"

Nonetheless, there is a loud clatter of guns on the ice, and out of the twenty of so people I can see, three raise their hands.

"I'll kill you!" the officer comes into sight, and aims a gun at one such soldier.

"I wouldn't do that, Commander Bryce," Libby calls, keeping her face shielded from the tunnel, "I really wouldn't."

"And why not?"

"Because your soldiers are just children. They've seen computerised deaths plenty, but they haven't seen war."

"Our soldiers will flatten you beasts like flies!" the officer roars.

"May ah?" Melody begs. Libby nods, and with a quiet pop, the officer collapses to the floor. There is a bang, and one of the soldiers howls and clutches her foot.

"We can send someone down to sort that out if you promise not to shoot her," Libby calls. The answer we get it a volley of bullets through the hole. Once they have stopped, Melody stands up, and shoots every visible human holding a weapon.

"Those of you who do not want to be here," Libby calls, "leave." Isis whispers the same thing in Kathleen's ear, to ensure that everyone hears. There is a rather apologetic shuffle as several hundred humans weave their way through the crowds, one of them hopping.

"This is your last chance," Libby warns, "Do you really want to die for someone else's cause?"

"You cannot win," laughs an officer, safely out of Melody's range.

"Victory isn't much to celebrate when you're dead," Libby retorts, and several thousand – hardly a dent in the impossible numbers below us – shuffle out, their heads low, avoiding spittle and blows from other members of their army. Once the movement has stopped, Libby checks her gun is loaded, and turns to Karl and Kathleen.

"Which one of you will go first?" Silence. "If anyone else goes first, they'll be shot to pieces," she hands Melody her gun absently, and ignores the steady thrumming as the Caribbean cuts a considerable chunk out of the human forces.

"Damn this," Antoinette swoops through, and Karl and Kathleen scramble through after her. Before the humans have a chance to recover from the discovery that their bullets don't work, the rest of us plunge through behind them.

I get hit in the leg as I drop through; the only soldier that didn't notice that Kathleen and Karl are unharmed fired as I fell through the air. Less than a second later, the roof of the cave crumbles, and everyone who hadn't already dropped through the shaft is here, and fighting for their lives.

Kathleen bellows as if she's been stabbed, and vanishes into the crowd amongst tumbling ice manikins and spraying blood. I find myself slashing wildly at the crowds, hardly noticing their own rather feeble attempts to stop me. Melody has dropped Libby's gun – Libby has charge of it now – and has instead got a sickle in each hand, some of the many unusual weapons that have been summoned and replicated. I try not to look at what I'm slipping on, or to feel the sticky warmth of the stumps my ankles keep colliding with.

Melody groans as a human shoots her, and then grins wildly.

"Dat's yous beast?"

The unfortunate human loses both hands for the insult before his head tumbles. Somewhere behind me, I feel a wave of heat, and a massive ball of fire rolls through the human crowds.

Everything stops to stare at this, and then fifty or so humans simply collapse and fall to sleep. Titania screams in pain as someone sticks something into her side, and lashes out wildly with a machete,

Another fireball decimates the human army, and then there is a scrabbling sound behind us. Nobody stops, but suddenly, with us, there are unicorns, their horns and claws decimating the humans, even after they have fallen once, and should be obedient to their killers, they are getting up and continuing to slaughter humans. A Chimaera, cramped though the cavern is for it, scoops up half a dozen men in its cavernous mouth and bites down on the unlucky creatures.

I duck as another fireball and a round of Libby's bullets fly overhead, and glance up to see, for the first time, how reduced the human numbers are. In the cramped cave, with mainly firearms, they have been easily destroyed. The floor is awash with blood, and the humans outnumber us only three to one now. The cave is starting to feel a lot roomier, as many of the bodies are now nothing but ashes.

Someone runs at me, and one of my swords swing so out, lopping their head off. Through the frenzy of fighting, I can hardly even make out whether my attacker was male or female – but it's too late to care now, and I am back in the fray.

"I've lost my shield," Kathleen gasps, collapsing at my feet. I leap over her, and run two humans through before turning back to her.

"Shield?"

"I've been shielding us all. Not very effectively, it must be said, but I think it helped."

A wave of werewolves appears out of nowhere, and as one steps through Kathleen, I realise it is an illusion. A thunderbolt – not an illusion, strikes at me, but does little harm. The human witches are far less effective than ours, clearly.

I slash through another human, and Ollie appears beside me.

"I'm scared," he whimpers, as a human who has somehow acquired a sword slashes at him.

"Join the club," I lop the woman's head off, and hand Ollie her sword. I blink to avoid the spurt of blood as he stabs a soldier in the chest, and turn to slash off a row of human heads.

I feel a sharp pain in my left side, and a sword is poking out the other side of me. I look up, and see a human savagely twisting the handle. I slash the little bully's hands off, and leave it at that. Melody glances at me, pulls out the sword, and whoops wildly as she plunges into a shrinking circle of humans.

"Well, I'm not alone then," Kathleen comments as I find myself staring up at the ceiling, "was it a human or an accident?"

She lays her hands on my side, and the wound closes. I sit up slowly, groggily, and there is a clash above me. Georgie leaps over, and with repeated slashes manages to drive a human man against the wall.

"Surrender?" she offers hopefully.

"Swivel," he stabs at her with his sword, and she cuts him in half.

"He could have cut your head off," she warns me, and someone blasts a hole through her chest with their gun.

She turns to look at them, and they look at her. She looks down at the hole for a moment, as if thinking, and charges at them with her sword with a disturbingly cheerful yell.

"We'd better get up," Kathleen heaves herself to her feet, and a crowd of humans tumble like dominoes in icy prisons. I glance around, not knowing what to do, and stab out as someone comes near me.

"Fool," sniggers Melody, "Dat's jest steyle. Yah'll neid selvar to meck mih blidd,"

Karl has frozen nearby, and is staring into the face of the man who is pumping him full of silver. Eventually the human looks up.

"Why won't you fucking die?" he curses, and then stops. I duck an incoming bayonet, and snip the owner's Achilles tendon with my sword before returning my attention to Karl and his assailant..

"You don't have to fight," Karl pleads.

"Why are you helping the beasts?" the man – presumably Karl's brother – demands.

"Because they're not beasts," Karl replies, "they're humans that don't always look like it."

A passing officer swings the back end of a gun at Karl's head – it shatters, and I run the man through.

"Sleep," whispers an Egyptian behind Karl, and his brother tumbles unconscious to the ground.

"Everybody stop," calls a quiet, distant voice. Isis leans to the ear of the human that has stopped dead in front of her, and bellows in everyone's ears, "STOP!"

70689AD

An angel – not Antoinette – is suddenly above us, higher than even the new opening in the ceiling should permit, and she is crying. Someone stabs a sword through me.

"Do not spill another drop of blood," she shrieks, "Stop!"

There is something about the urgency in her voice that makes everyone, absolutely everyone, stop. I put a hand to the wound where the sword went in, and feel the blood trickling out.

"Not one more drop," the angel seems to recite, "may touch the ground."

I glance up at my attacker, who catches the drips of my blood from his sword in the palm of his hand. I clutch the wound desperately, but through my hands, I see the blood trickling gently, and a drop is forming. It falls, and I have never seen anything fall so slowly in my life. Everyone's heads turn to me as it crashes to the ground, and the angel lets out an agonised scream.

"Too late," she moans, fading into the ceiling, "too late."

"Bred bitch," Antoinette snorts, "everyone – I mean everyone – stop fighting. That classy little cow wouldn't have come anywhere near us if there wasn't something seriously wrong. Humans, I speak for the werewolves here, you will not be harmed further unless you cause further harm."

"Everyone drop their weapons," Libby calls. The twenty-five thousand or so humanoids obey silently, and there is a loud clatter as guns and blades fall to the ground. Kathleen scurries around, reviving the dying – a similarly short human seems to be doing the same, as well as a very tall Kenyan werewolf. The chimaeras and unicorns filter out, and the humans and werewolves slowly gather together, differences temporarily forgotten, under the spot where the angel appeared.

"What's wrong?" whispers a human girl beside me. I glance at her – a pretty thing. Kathleen catches my eye, and I look guiltily at the floor.

"Too much blood," I shrug. Silence, aside from the healers' footsteps, and everyone stares at the blank ceiling.

"What will happen?" she whispers at last. I shrug, and pull my eyes away from both the ceiling and her face.

"I personally don't want to find out," comments Georgie on her other side, "What will we all do now?"

"Well, most of these soldiers will start screaming in about thirty-seven seconds," Libby glances at her watch, "the moon is rising."

"No blood," calls Antoinette as the thirty-seven seconds ends, and silhouettes start to change, "no biting, no harm."

The werewolves slip away, and we are surrounded by humans.

"I'm not comfortable," says Karl eventually, and Libby nods.

"We won't harm you," calls the most important looking of the humans.

"That's generous," laughs Libby nervously, "after you lost so many compared to so few."

I would hardly call two thousand bodies few, but in the circumstances, it's a miracle.

"You killed Bryce," a voice returns from a way across the cavern, "you're lucky we haven't canonised you."

"How come you haven't changed?" all the humans are suddenly looking at the six of us suspiciously.

"Human," Libby shrugs.

"All of you?"

"Not me," Karl glances down at the floor. His brother, awake again, cocks his head to stare at him.

"But you're not a werewolf."

"Vampire," Karl smiles uneasily.

Several humans cross themselves, and Kathleen returns to us, dusting her hands of dried blood.

"Everyone else is dead," she says quietly. A good deal more humans are standing now, and a good deal less werewolf bodies than I thought are scattered amongst the human corpses.

"Six humans and a vampire working for the werewolves? Why?" the officer frowns.

"Four humans," Kathleen replies, "me and Jack tried working for the humans a long time ago."

"Funnily enough," I add, "we were left behind when they turned this planet into one frigid block of ice."

"I hardly think you're in a position to call Earth frigid," Kathleen murmurs, "Judging by the number of children that could be yours."

"Jack?" a human soldier queries.

"As in Jack Hanov Himmerden," Kathleen nods, "and Kathleen Anchor."

"Are you really – you know?" a nearby human boy struggles to say the words.

"I know what I really am," I shrug, "tired. Does anyone else want to sit down?"

And so it happens that at around ten in the evening, nineteen thousand human soldiers, four rogue humans, a werewolf, a vampire and an immortal all trudge up to a less bloody scene, to the eight thousand human deserters, and a row of icy chairs.

"So, aren't you a werewolf?" queries one of the nearest soldiers once we have all sat down.

"I am," I nod.

"So how come you don't change?"

"Because that's how I turned out."

"How do we know he's not just changing slowly?" asks another human, "we can't see anything but his shadow."

A bright light fills the room, and I yelp in pain and cover my eyes.

"How come the vampire isn't afraid of daylight?" demands the witch who brought the light.

"It isn't the light that kills," Antoinette swoops delightedly past the witch, "It's what the light awakens."

Karl grins as if this is somehow his fault.

"What do we do now, then?" the human officer demands.

"Go back home?" suggests Kathleen hopefully.

"We can't just do that. We're supposed to stay on earth until we are told that we can leave. Which is apparently only when every last werewolf is dead."

"Can I just ask what we did to deserve this?" I can't help thinking that one little bite isn't important enough to merit an entire war.

"Your people made an entire solar system inaccessible. First there was your little invasion on one of the landing satellites, and then there was the outbreak on the holiday destination of Alyeon."

"Alyeon?"

"Someone bit an innocent girl, apparently."

"She was not innocent!" I exclaim, "She was blackmailing me!"

A very familiar human soldier – a witch, I think – stares at me.

"That was you? How did you manage to get halfway across in so little time?"

"Who are you?" I demand, "And why did you protect us in the base?"

She glances at the rest of the humans, and then turns back to me.

"I was born to werewolf parents," she shrugs, "I suppose it's difficult to kill the race that produced me."

"Polly?" Kathleen spots it before me; "You came back." She doesn't look like the last Polly I saw, but then she is, presumably, the real one.

"I don't want to be bitten," she backs away from me quickly, "I didn't even mean to sign up – I just did, and then realised that I couldn't kill a werewolf."

"If you'll stop your banter," the officer calls, "I'm afraid, soldiers, we must camp down here for the night."

There are angry protests at this.

"We won't harm you," Kathleen smiles slightly, "We are not the savages you want us to be."

"Are you really in league with the devil?" demands one. All of us, including Nick, sigh.

"No," we all say together, before Kathleen continues, "Most werewolves are Christian."

"What will happen in the night?" I wonder, "If we let you stay, will you come to us in our sleep and wipe us out?"

"They won't," Kathleen shakes her head, "They're not going to risk more blood."

"Not after the angel," adds the officer.

"Would they really kill you if you returned to your base?"

"The generals have a strange habit of not believing in anything that isn't easily proved by science. They'd probably execute us for cowardly desertion."

"Well," Kathleen considers, "The second turning on the right might have a few nasty little spells hovering around, but I'm sure nobody would object to you staying there until you can leave."

"We can never leave, unless we want to die."

"Tomorrow morning," I inform him, "I will take a unicorn and tell your leaders that there will be no more fighting. I will make out that you have all been taken prisoner, and will be returned if they promise to leave us alone. I will take some of you with me to show that we haven't killed you all."

And so it happens that twenty-seven thousand humans are allowed to remain in peace in the very heart of the werewolf sanctuary.

I don't sleep at first – I only feel safe enough to start to sleep well after midnight, and even then I keep waking. Then I hear Kathleen snoring quietly, and if she feels it is safe, it must be. I let my eyes close properly this time, and darkness even my eyes can't penetrate surrounds me.

It is a relief to wake up still alive, and I hurry out of the craft to look around. Our guests, it seems, are paying a visit. Werewolves and humans are milling around, in tightly separated groups, but there seems to be no violence between the two.

"Quite spectacular, isn't it?" Kathleen is standing at the foot of the craft, "If they attacked us now, we'd drop like flies."

"How many people did we lose, in the end?" I ask eventually.

"About five, six hundred."

I whistle. The usefulness of witchcraft is incredible.

"I've said we'll go to Titania's funeral this afternoon."

"I didn't see her fall."

"She was stabbed with a bayonet somewhere near the beginning, but her blood was all over the cavern."

"She didn't die at first?"

"She was still warm when I found her, and the wound was almost clotted. If she had just a little more blood, she would have lived."

"Even without healing?"

"Even without healing. She would have been weak for about a month, but she would have got better."

Kathleen seems to feel that this is somehow her fault.

"Anyone else I know?"

"Melody was dying when I found her. Isis had been shot through the head."

"Is she dead?"

"She would be if the human girl hadn't healed her. She was paralysed, but fully conscious."

"Surely she would have just stayed that way?"

"Her heart was paralysed as well. Paolo had a hole the size of your head in his back, but he's fine now, and Georgie hadn't realised that she'd lost her left arm."

Considering that Georgie is left handed, this is quite something to miss.

"Shouldn't she have bled out?"

"Whatever cut it off was hot. The wound had sealed. Not to mention the... thing."

We are walking through the crowds now, and I notice that there a lot of humans missing. Kathleen seems to be reading my mind again:

"They're mostly down on the eighth level. Apparently they're not allowed to leave bodies behind."

"So what exactly are they doing?"

"They have those little power-balls like Libby has, except they're coffin shaped."

Space economy in coffins? Humans really are strange.

Antoinette appears in front of us, looking indignant.

"Why is nobody talking to me?"

"What?"

"Georgie's helping to pack away the dead bodies, and Ollie's gathering up the weapons, and Libby and Karl are talking to some random guy."

"That random guy is Karl's brother."

"Whatever. Anyway, as soon as I tried to join in the conversation, they give me a look like I'm intruding, and tell me to call you."

"Why do they want us?"

"I don't know, do I? I'm just like some stupid errand girl."

"I'm sure they didn't mean to offend you," Kathleen assures her, "It's probably just an emotional time for them."

"An emotional time? How come you're supposed to join in the conversation, then, and I'm not?"

Kathleen sighs. Antoinette is getting rather over-sensitive to things like this.

"Come on, Jack. Antoinette, I'm sure you can come too."

· "Oh, no," she scowls, "I'm not going to be told to go and fetch Georgie as well."

As I follow Kathleen towards the third level on the right – every part of the city except the homes – we are stopped by a broadly grinning young lady.

"Ah do nut tink I's tanked you."

"You're welcome," Kathleen beams, patting Melody's back and gasping for breath through the suffocating bear-hug, "It was... no bother... at all."

"Tankyous!" Melody calls as we hurry into the darkness, "A tousand tarms tankyous!"

"How on earth is she that strong?" Kathleen demands, "She doesn't look particularly big."

"She probably spent her youth beating up sharks," I shrug, "who knows?"

"Her youth? She's hardly twenty!"

"Her mental youth. She's seen too much to be twenty."

"This is where I left them," Kathleen pushes open an ice door into a deserted café, and three heads turn.

"Jack, Kathleen," Karl stands up, "I'd like you to meet my brother Robert."

"Bobby," the human holds out his hand, "pleased to meet you, Jack, Kath."

"Kathleen," Kathleen corrects him, "I don't like to be mistaken for a Catherine."

We all sit down, and there is a short silence before Bobby asks.

"So, are you two like –"

"Married? No," I scoff. Kathleen closes her mouth and looks away.

"Funny," Bobby looks up at the ceiling, "all the books always said that you were the son of the devil and she was your evil human wife that you made immortal."

"Bobby, there is no devil," Libby murmurs.

"Kathleen's lived for so long because her mother wished for her not to be dead after she died of kidney failure," I tell him.

"Black magic, then?"

"It was God's power that brought me back to life," Kathleen snaps, "Don't believe everything your teacher told you."

"Right. Right. So is it like witches are better than humans? Somewhere in between humans and angels?"

"Not at all," I interrupt, "my great, great grandmother or something caused werewolves to exist in the numbers they do. Witches are just people, good or bad, with different amounts of power."

"Your great great grandmother? So it's hereditary?"

"She wasn't a werewolf, she created the curse that exists nowadays after her daughter was bitten by an old version of the werewolf. When you can only see one thirteenth of the moon, at the stroke of midnight, there will be a silver snow."

"Which carries your curse?"

"Exactly."

Bobby turns his attention to his brother.

"Is that what happened to you?"

Karl doesn't answer at first; he is searching for his wine-bottle. He finds it, hands it to Kathleen with a sheepish grin, and turns back to his brother.

"I've already told you, Bobby, I'm not a werewolf."

"What are you, then?"

"A vampire." Karl takes a sip of blood from the bottle, and wipes his mouth, "I got bitten by a vampire in a different universe."

"So what exactly is a vampire, then? Do you turn into a bat from time to time, and die only if silver or wood goes through your heart? Can you not touch crucifixes?"

I notice that Bobby is rolling my sister's revolver around in his hand like a toy, and turning the chamber round and round with his fingers. I catch a glint of silver, and there is a dull thud as something is dropped into the empty chamber.

"Not silver," Karl, oblivious, laughs, "you shouldn't believe everything the legends say. Copper's the real one to kill vampires with."

I see a flash of red, and stand up.

"I really wouldn't do that, Bobby," Kathleen leans back and stretches.

"Do what?" he stares up at her.

"Shoot us. You really do not want to get me angry, and seeing as you'd have killed three of my friends, I think I'd have reason to be angry."

"If I was planning on shooting my brother," he retorts coldly, "I'm sure I'd manage to kill you in the bargain."

"You wouldn't, believe me. And then you would most certainly die, probably slowly and painfully."

"Kathleen's just joking," Libby assures Bobby uncertainly, but Bobby lifts his arm and shoots Kathleen.

"That was irresponsible," Kathleen picks up the silver bullet, "Jack?"

As Bobby points the gun at me and squeezes the trigger, I hold out my hand and catch the gun.

"There is no need for this at all," Kathleen smiles politely, and empties the bullets into the floor; "You do carry an assortment of bullets, don't you? Copper, silver, and iron?" Do you have gold in there as well?"

He stands up, and I hold the tip of a sword to his throat.

"If you get your silver dagger out, Jack will be forced to take your head off. And we really wouldn't want Karl to see his brother die, would we? Even a brother that was going to kill him."

She calls the bullets up out of the icy floor and holds the three of them up for everyone to see.

"Now, we don't have to expect any more of these attempts, do we, Bobby?"

He sits down, very red, and Libby and Karl stare at him speechlessly.

"Now, Bobby, we'll forgive you this time, but if you do that again, Jack will bite you."

"Will I?" I turn to her.

"You will. So, Bobby, we'd rather you handed us the dagger than we had to take it from you."

He slides it across the floor to her feet, and she picks it up, sniffs, and hands it to me.

"Get rid of it, Jack."

I nod, and it vanishes. I can only imagine Georgie's reaction when she discovers that there is a dagger in her trousers.

"What are you two looking so shocked by?" Kathleen smiles at Karl and Libby as she sits back down, "Wouldn't you be a bit distressed to discover your brother was now undead?"

For the rest of the day, Bobby behaves himself admirably – although Libby and Karl don't seem to want to be alone in the same room as him after that incident. They take every possible opportunity to get away from him, and when he asks to come to Titania's funeral as we get dressed for the event, both of them shout "no" with such vehemence that everyone within a hundred metres turns to stare at us.

"No," Libby repeats, more quietly, "you didn't know her, and so I feel that it wouldn't be right for you to go."

They have managed to isolate the human that killed her, and as a sign of respect, the poor boy has to help carry her white-robed body, his place the closest to her beautiful face, her fine features made ugly by a frozen expression of pain and anger.

"I'm sorry," he practically sobs to her mother, who doesn't seem to feel any resentment, and clasps him to her and soaks his shoulder in her tears.

"We are gathered here today," says the Russian priest sadly, "to say our last farewell to Titania, daughter of Anya, sister of Maria, mother of Olga. She was not known by many, but those who did know her will not forget her. Goodbye, Titania."

"Goodbye," whispers the assembly, and the body is laid gently into the grave. I feel an intruder, a cruel intruder, to be here but unable to cry, unlike the werewolves who knew her and the human who killed her.

"Let's go," whispers Kathleen, and kissing the dead girl's forehead as custom dictates, we leave.

Chapter 6 - End

There is a peculiar quietness about the underground city this afternoon – a united but lonely silence. Humans and werewolves line the benches along the walls, grieving for those they knew, all sins, it seems, forgiven in the names of those who were sinned against. It is not unusual for me to see a human and a werewolf clutching each other in a desperate embrace for the one that one of them took the life of.

Unfortunately, there will always be a few who carry resentment – I cannot deny that both Kathleen and I were those once (hence my eating the human ambassador), and both of us will have the chance to resent for far longer than anyone else here. We cannot, therefore, stop them – all we can do is help those who are harmed by this resentment as best we can and prevent any real harm. By the time the evening has fallen, even the most rebellious souls seem to have given up on hate.

Of course, this cannot be. In the morning, I am awakened by a sickeningly bright light, and a stinging sensation all around me. When my eyes have grown used to the light, I realise I am being dragged along the snow in a sack fashioned out of silver wire mesh. It doesn't take long to work out who is doing the dragging.

"What exactly are you doing, Bobby?"

He glances around at me and forces a smile.

"Liam, our little pet's awake."

The other man looks around and grins far more convincingly.

"Well?" I demand, starting to melt away the silver wires.

"I wouldn't be melting that if I were you," the other man warms, and I see the gun in his hand.

"You think you could kill me with one little bullet?"

"Why ever not?"

My answer is a cacophony of hissing.

"Very clever," Bobby kicks me, and I return to a human form, "The thing is, that wouldn't be one little ball of silver coming out of there. It would be hundreds. And you would be splattered like so many little snakes on the snow. You don't want that, do you?"

"So what are you planning to do with me, then?"

"Hand you over to the generals. I'm sure they'll see you as a useful hostage, and pardon our returning without wiping your people out. And then they can, using you for experiments, manufacture a weapon that will wipe you and your kind out, whatever your magic can do."

I doubt it somehow, but I let him keep thinking this. When we reach the human fort, it seems that most of his allies believe the same thing, and as I am cut out of the half-melted mesh and marched away to the prison building, I can hear my kidnappers being praised as brave and heroic.

I, on the other hand, am spat upon. There are hundreds of shouts of "scum!" as I am marched past, and occasionally, I am hit by their breakfasts.

Humans are some of the best creatures alive at being prejudiced. It is almost a relief to be pushed into the prison building and down into the basement, considering whether or not to hex the twelve accompanying soldiers.

"Sit!" orders one of them, pushing me into a cell. I look at him in what I hope is an unfaltering, unafraid manner. Knowing me, I probably look like I am about to wet myself.

"Sit, or I'll shoot you in the kneecaps," he bellows.

I shrug, and wipe his spittle from my face.

Eventually, he gives up, and sits down opposite me, allowing the others to go away, and I amuse myself by leaning on the front door of the cell and changing features of his face. After a little while, I grow bored of the conventional colours and turn his eyes bright red. I then give him an overbite almost large enough for a small squirrel to fit through without him noticing, and pull out the roots of his now bright blue hair.

The scream of anger as he goes off duty almost makes me glad to be in this cell.

My new guard is an incredibly fat woman who, nonetheless, moves with the elegance of someone a third of her weight. Not that a third of her weight is exactly thin, but it's considerably thinner.

"So what are you planning on doing with me?" I ask casually as she polishes her gun.

"Oh, I don't know. Probably a public execution in the centre of the free universe."

"Which is where?"

"Ursula 4."

"Why do you people have to make everything sound like a military operation? Next thing, you'll be calling this planet Earth Three."

"Where'd you come up with a name like that?"

"What do you call this planet?"

"Same as everyone. Fera 3."

"Fera?"

"What else?"

"Well, I always felt that Earth was a name that would stick. It was the accepted norm long before I was born, and that's what we still call it. I'd much rather remember the planets as My Very Earnest Mother Just Sent Us Nine Potatoes than Fun Female Friends Fill Funny Files For Fat Fools."

"Why do you need to make a sentence out of it? All you have to do is count from the sun."

"Doesn't that rather take all the interest out of travelling around a space system? I mean, it doesn't sound half so interesting when you realise that mould got to Fera 3 from Fera 2."

"You find *mould* interesting?" she looks understandably surprised.

"No, it was just – oh, forget it," I sigh, and search my brain for something else to entertain myself with. Finally, I hit on something that is probably sensitive. "Your weight," I consider eventually.

"This gun is loaded, you know."

"You wouldn't shoot me. It would mean at the very least demotion for you."

"What about my weight?"

"Is it a genetic thing, or do you just eat too much because you like food?"

"Genetic. Why do you care?"

"I could make all that weight go away, you know. I am a witch."

"I saw the last guard; I know you're a witch."

"Well?"

"Well what?"

"Well should I get rid of it for you?"

"Why do you want to?"

"Because I'm bored."

"Listen, whatever your name is, I've lived thirty-seven years with this fat, and even if I did want to get rid of it once, I certainly don't feel the same now that I'm living on your ice-cube."

"Thirty-seven. Jesus."

"What are you blaspheming about?"

"I would have said you looked more like twenty-seven, personally. For a fat person, you're in good shape."

"Very good shape," she waves her gun warningly, "round is my favourite shape."

She glances at a clock on the wall.

"Shouldn't you be getting furry by now?"

"Do you want me to?"

"It's the full moon tonight. Traditionally, your lot get mad and hairy when there's a full moon."

"Only if I want to."

"That's a bit pointless, isn't it? Why didn't you just get your buddies on Europa to let you into our society as a fake human, then?"

"First of all, someone might have recognised me."

"Big deal. Say it's an uncanny likeness."

"Secondly, I'd be betraying my people, and third – just take a guess at how old I am."

"Lookin at you? Twenty-four, twenty-five, at a stretch."

"Nearly seventy thousand. Did you actually study history in primary school?"

"I spent most of my time passing notes. I roughly got the gist that werewolves are some ancient race created by the devil."

"Well, you really missed out, then. I used to work for the humans, in the early twenty-first century."

"You know, for someone as old as you, you don't look too bad."

"Oh, you're just saying that. Anyway, when your lot left, they didn't like me anymore. They started believing in werewolves just soon enough to leave me behind."

"When you say you worked for the humans, who do you mean?"

"This policewoman – she became a president of one of your settling ships, I think – called Alice Kerrow."

"Alice Kerrow? You knew her?"

"I spent most of my youth in and out of her police station whenever some friend or relative or other had been murdered, and most of my adult life – before I was fired, of course – killing people she didn't want to risk delicate little humans on capturing."

"She was just president of one ship?"

"Isn't that a lot to you?"

"When you consider that she's now Empress of the entire Milky Way? No, not really."

"Just how many galaxies have humans taken over, then?"

"You expect me to remember numbers? You don't think I chose to be a soldier, do you?" She realises how close she is getting to the bars of my cell and pushes her chair back against the empty cell behind her.

We remain silent for a while, and then I grow bored of silence.

"What's your name, then?"

"You're going to try and control me, aren't you?"

"I've only ever tried that once, and that was on a dead body. There'd be no point, anyway, seeing as I could get out without you."

"Oh really?"

"Really."

"I dare you to."

"That's pathetic," I snigger, standing next to her. She screams, and I return to my cell.

"So why don't you escape?"

"I don't know. Possibly because the outer wall and windows are magically sealed, and if I did get out of this cell for too long, the doors would lock, and I couldn't penetrate them with anything short of a comet."

"That's a good enough reason, I suppose. I take it you noticed the cameras?"

"They weren't here on my last visit."

"That was you that broke in?"

"Well, a girl called Melody did the breaking in – I just tagged along."

"I'm surprised no-one noticed you. You're hardly the least distinctive looking person."

"A uniform does wonders. Anyway, one of the people that helped us get in used to be in the human army."

"I didn't know anyone had been left here last time they came."

"They didn't. She brought me back here after I saved her boyfriend's skin in a dragon world."

"Dragon world? What dragons went for you?"

"Not the dragons we have here. These ones fed on humans. Well, these particular ones fed on vampires, but that's beside the point."

She waits with me until eight o'clock in the morning, and then, after she has had fried eggs, bacon, toast and lots of sausages, and I have not had something that looks rather like diluted vomit, she leaves to shrink the bags under her eyes.

"You'd best eat something, you know," she calls as she leaves, "otherwise you'll starve."

"Believe me, I won't. Good morning."

The other guard is not the same one I attacked yesterday – this one is a much skinnier, nervous looking man.

"I thought they were going to do experiments on me," I yawn as he sits down.

"I dunno," he whimpers. I grin. Another timid little soul to discourage from ever coming within a hundred yards of me again.

"So, how long have you been in the army?"

"Eleven years."

"How old are you?" I wonder, "twenty-nine, thirty?"

"Twenty-eight."

"I pity you. Someone as young as you shouldn't have to be in such a dangerous situation."

"If you try and get out, I'll shoot you."

I widen my grin enough to show pointed canines. Part of me feels a bit guilty as he cringes against the back wall – most of me is too bored to care.

"Oh, I don't have to get out. If you are exposed to me for too long, you'll start to become a werewolf."

"You're lying."

I am, as a matter of fact, but he doesn't see too convinced of it.

"Well, I could be. If you're O positive, though –" it's just a guess, "– then I'm not."

He presses against the back of the cell behind him.

"You've read my file!"

"How would I have done that? I've been in here, and your file's…" I consider, "What's your name?"

"Steven Jafred junior."

"Okay, so now I have your file," I hold it up, and sit down on the metal bed to read it, "Oh, how terrible. You're O positive. And your mother was a hooker? I'm sorry. I really am. So, what's this she died of?"

"Ursteads Syndrome."

"Which she caught from one of her clients? Well, it was bound to happen, wasn't it?" I look up at him, and find to my satisfaction that he is already halfway to shooting one of us in the head.

"I have to go," he scowls.

"So soon? We were just getting a conversation going."

He runs away as fast as his skinny legs can carry him, and I burn his file. For about ten minutes, I am left without a guard, so I get out of the cell and wave at the camera for a bit. As soon as someone comes to check what I'm doing, I hurry back into my cell and smile stupidly at him. He points a gun at me warningly, and sits down.

"I can see you're not much of a talker, are you?" I twirl his keys around my finger. He starts to move forwards to snatch them, and thinks better of it, shooting my foot instead.

"Now that wasn't very friendly," I scold, digging the bullet out of my heel and throwing it to him, "That'll scar!"

He grunts, and I sit back and sigh. After a while, an idea strikes me, and I send one of my fingers slithering towards him as a snake. He doesn't notice at first – it's not a very big snake – but soon enough it has scrambled up on top of his cap, and I peer down at his startled face from up there.

"Holy crap!" he swears, and throws it at me. I snigger, and it rejoins the rest of my hand to become a perfectly normal finger.

"Are you scared of snakes, sergeant?"

He mutters incoherently, and sits down again. I smile, and hold out an empty hand.

"What about spiders?" A tarantula appears, its legs draping over the sides of my hand, and I let it crawl up my arm and onto my shoulder.

"Get rid of that thing," he points a trembling gun at my forehead, and I comply.

"Sissy," I snort.

He squeaks, and falls silent.

For the next few hours, I emulate him, and say nothing, aside from a comment on the poor service when a young soldier brings us both food. He shrugs, and drops mine on the floor.

Finally, at about six in the evening, the sissy leaves – not without me growling goodbye first, and the fat lady returns.

"Missed me?" she grins, sitting down to her supper, "Have they done any experiments on you yet?"

"Not unless they were counting to see how many people I drove mad. When a certain Steven Jafred junior commits suicide, could you tell me?"

"I'll make a memo."

There is a short silence as she consumes what looks like spaghetti.

"So, tell me about Alice Kerrow."

"Alice Kerrow? Why do you want to know about her?"

"Well, I've only seen her once, and it was a pretty big thing to see her on my home planet, so I'd like to know more about her."

"It was over sixty millennia ago."

"I won't sue anyone if you get it wrong."

"Very well," I sit down and think, "the first time I met her – when did I first meet her? I know, it was just after my late wife's parents were murdered."

"Why did you meet her then?"

"She had to arrest my next-door neighbour – he was the murderer. A werewolf, too. That was how my late wife – of course, she was just my girlfriend back then – that was how she first learnt about werewolves. I don't think I was a werewolf yet by then. I can't really remember."

I think about it.

"Actually, I was. And that wasn't the first time I met her. The first time I met her was before I was a werewolf – by about six hours. We were riding along some cliff-top path, and the horse I was on fell off."

"Ouch," my guard grimaces, "did you have to shoot her?"

"Nope. She was shattered. Completely. We still have her – or at least, we did before I was kidnapped. Anyway, Kerrow was the one who got to throw a wobbly when a man with a pickup truck took the horse to the zoo instead of bringing her home, and then she had to tell us that our horse had been fed to the lions."

"So how did you become a werewolf, then?"

"That evening, I was in the horse's stable – she was my favourite, you see, and she came flying home –"

"She flew? I thought she was dead?"

"Dead? I just said she was shattered. She wasn't a normal horse – you did hear me say we still had her?"

"I assumed you meant the body."

"Yeuch. Why would we keep a body for that long? Anyway, she came flying home, and her brother, I think – we owned the whole family – possessed her to bite me. She was a carrier of the main werewolf curse you see nowadays, you see."

"So when did you next meet Kerrow?"

"Probably when a group of Celtic-Catholic nutters kidnapped me and crucified me. She, with a bunch of my friends and her secretary, came down and found me. Well, actually, I lie – Kathleen found me, but Kerrow was generally doing a lot of running around these stone walled tunnels and nearly getting eaten by their security."

"Werewolves?"

"No, mainly sharks and crocodiles. I saw her in court before that, though, while they were trying my neighbour to see if he was guilty of being a four hundred-year-old murderer. There were loads of occasional meetings and all that rot, you know, Christmas dinners, children's christenings, my wife's funeral – casual meetings. Then she picked me up from the scene when I killed my late wife's false brother who had murdered my wife."

"Hence the lateness."

"Yes." We both fall silent for a moment, and then she apologises:

"I'm sorry, I didn't mean to make a joke out of it. I've never really lost anyone, so I shouldn't really…"

"Oh, it's alright. I can scarcely remember her."

It makes me sick to realise that this is true. She and I were inseparable – I killed myself to bring her back from the dead – and now I've nearly forgotten her.

"It still wasn't my place."

"I hardly think you need to worry about etiquette," I hesitate, "thank you, though."

She falls silent, and seems to be thinking.

"What do you think will happen when you get executed?"

"You're talking as if you know it's going to happen."

"What are you going to do, escape?" she activates her radio – a little wart-sized dot on her cheek.

"I might," I shrug. She repeats this into the radio and switches it off.

"It's a pity. I'm rather getting to like you, Jack."

"Well, there'll be plenty of time for something to happen before you get back to wherever you're going to execute me. I might even die without anyone else's help."

"Of what?"

"Old age? Space sickness?"

The conversation then steers towards space-travel, and then breakfast arrives, so execution isn't mentioned again until that evening, after I have learnt almost her entire military history – from an intelligence agent for a private planet to a double agent for the space federation, to private for the federal army – and still do not know so much as her initials.

On the thirteenth day of my imprisonment, she informs me that there is an epidemic going around.

"Are there any biting insects around?" She asks while spraying insect repellent all over the cells. I can't help laughing.

"Insects? Can't you feel what the temperature is? If it wasn't for technology *you* would have been dead long ago from the cold here."

"Bats, then?"

"Last time I saw a bat was a frozen one three hundred years ago, three hundred miles further south. Nothing that small can survive here outside a heatwave. And this isn't a heatwave."

"Well, something has been biting people, and by the time we find them in the morning, they're stone dead."

I think about this for a while, and then something dawns on me.

"Did you bury the dead from when we attacked?"

"All the bodies were stored, if that's what you mean."

"Is there a list anywhere of the missing?"

She takes out a palmtop computer, and fiddles about for a moment.

"There's a list of everyone dead."

"Can you get rid of anyone who's been... stored?"

"Which leaves us with everyone who went down to attack you."

"Can't you get rid of them as well?"

She presses a few keys, and then stares at the screen.

"Bloody thing," she whacks it against the wall, and presses a few more keys.

"That's impossible! Every single body has been stored, you dumb machine!"

She slams it against her thigh, and glares at it.

"How many names are there?" I inquire.

"Two – a woman called Lisa Tetron, and a man called Serje – I can't pronounce his surname, so you'll have to go on first names."

"Names are unimportant," I sigh, and sit down heavily. She senses that there is something very amiss with these missing dead people.

"What is it?" She demands, leaning against the bars of my cell and peering down at me.

"Do you have copper bullets?"

"Why bother with copper when there's titanium?"

"That's a no, then?"

"Obviously. Why do you care?"

"The epidemic that's going around isn't really killing them."

"I've seen the bodies, Jack. It really is killing them." She chuckles, and her belly wobbles dangerously.

"Give them a few weeks, and they'll start to feel warm again. Then they'll get a fever. And then they'll start sweating and steaming, even floating, perhaps, and then they'll wake up."

"So it's basically harmless, is that what you're saying?"

"If any of the victims get off this planet, the human race will be wiped out."

"But wake up a few weeks later. Big deal. We go temporarily extinct."

"No, you'd all die properly not long afterwards. They're not human when they wake up."

"What are they, then?"

"Vampires."

She bites her top lip, and her nostrils pinch. Her eyes narrow from the bottom up, and her cheeks swell, before she finally bursts out laughing. She keeps laughing for a few minutes, "Good one, Jack," she giggles at last, "You really had me going for a minute there." She wheezes as she struggles to get her breath back, and her body rocks dangerously in merriment.

I elect to stay silent until the laughter – and the resultant tremors – has subsided before I try to speak again.

"You might recall that my pilot's boyfriend had to be saved from vampire-eating dragons."

"In another universe," she chortles, "probably your imagination. No real dragon would ever harm anything bigger than a mosquito."

Considering that this woman will not do anything to stop my death, which she considers imminent, I decide that the human race – your race – can look after itself. Everything has to go extinct at some point.

So for a few weeks – with her occasionally rattling up a small earthquake by remembering that conversation, we stick to the most trivial subjects I could possibly imagine. My other guards cease to arrive for duty, and are replaced with a wrinkled old hag with charms and superstitions up to her ears. She takes up residence in one of the empty cells – from where she has a clear shot of me – and doesn't leave it even to sleep. I'm not entirely sure she can talk – at least, she never responds when I wish her a good morning after screaming to wake her up. However, she cannot be completely senseless, because she has filled her pockets with copper and silver bullets.

174

I'm afraid to say that the usual guard takes no such precautions, and every day I become more surprised to see her – especially when, as she notes on the eighteenth day of my imprisonment, the ice starts to melt and a shallow puddle of water starts to creep into the cell.

"Is it global warming?" she wonders.

I say nothing.

"It's really weird – it's only the compound and outside it for about twenty metres that's melting. After that it's as solid as it ever was."

She turns to look at the other guard, who snores loudly. I say nothing.

"Don't be such a pig, Jack, tell me what's happening."

I let her fidget for a minute or two while I consider whether to speak or not

"I have actually," I stop, and wipe away the warm trickle that has crept out of the corner of my mouth. I must be really desperate if I'm drooling for someone this… horizontally unchallenged.

Surprisingly, her expression is of concern, not of disgust, and she is not looking at my crotch either, but at my hand. I follow her gaze, and frown.

"Blood," I say eventually. Well, gargle is more along the lines of what I do, as a mouthful of iron-sweet liquid accompanies the word on its outwards journey. I retch. More blood gushes to the floor, and the guard's head snaps around to listen to a sound that has joined the groans, snores and drips that were already established. Footsteps, coming down to our level.

"Get in the cell," I gargle, "quickly."

She pays no heed, but stares instead at the people who have appeared. They are not running, as their footsteps were a moment ago, but walking forwards with their bodies hunched ever so slightly and eyes focused on her neck. Stalking her.

"Get in the cell," I spit out another mouthful of blood.

She doesn't seem to hear. Her pudgy face has turned pinkish-white with fear, and she doesn't seem to be breathing.

I hear a tinkle, and turn back to the intruders. One of them is flipping through a ring of chip-keys outside my other guard's cell. She turns over, but doesn't stir. I hear the fat guard's breath at last, short and fast, over the gargling of my own. The door to the other guard's cells swings open, and she sits bold upright, screaming, and firing wildly into the vampires, for that, of course, is what they are. One of them screeches and collapses, and then her gun stops firing. She stares up at the intruders, her eyes wider than a doe's, and with a final scream loud enough to make the walls shake, she disappears under a mass of vampires.

I can't see what is happening to her – although I can hear squelches and there is blood trickling out of her cell – but I would guess that she is being torn apart. A section of intestine lands in my cell, and confirms that theory.

I hear a click behind me, and realise that my surviving guard has finally come to her senses and locked herself in a cell.

"Get their keys," she hisses. I close my eyes obediently, and with a little more effort than usual, the chips fall into my hand.

"There's one marked eight," she whispers, "There should be six more identical to it. Could you get them, too?"

I close my eyes, and after a few moments of concentration, two small chips tumble into my palm, followed by another three.

"That's all I can get," I hand them to her. She nods with a weak smile.

"So what do I do now?" She wraps her fingers around the bars between us and stares over my head as the vampires abandon the dissembled, bloodless, corpse. I gargle helplessly, and find myself flat on my back on the bench at the edge of the cell. The vampires glance in at me, and move on to the guard's cell. She trembles as their eyes work over her, as if she can already feel their hands tearing her apart.

"What's wrong, Soph?" asks a male in a quiet, kind voice. She steps forwards, and I hold up a hand to stop her.

"You're dead, Alex," she swallows, "I've seen your body."

The vampire laughs, the kindness in his voice gone, and she presses back against the bars between us.

"You're not Alex any more, are you? You're not even human."

At this point, I realise that I cannot hold my hand up anymore, and it falls to the ground with a solid crash. The guard's head snaps towards me, and she swears under her breath.

"Jack, what's happening to you?"

I have to say that for not the first time in my life I haven't a clue. On the bright side, I don't have any blood left to lose, and my lungs fill with bitter, polluted air. It's always such a pleasure to breathe, even if I don't have to.

I sit up, feeling more than a little bit nauseous, and lift my hands up for a look.

"Oh," I comment. I feel even sicker now. Even the vampires have stopped clamouring to get through the bars to the guard to stare at me.

"Holy Kerrow," one of them swears, "What the fuck are you?"

I don't answer. I don't know that anyone could: my little fingers have been replaced with reverse thumbs, and my most of the flesh on my hands has withered away. What is left is a dark purplish grey, stretched tight over the bones. At the ends of my fingers, the bone, blacker than pitch, has emerged from the necrotic skin, but instead of any vaguely human bone shape, the bones are curved over into thick, stony claws.

"I need Kathleen," I whimper, trying hard not to watch as the skin dries and peels away from the darkening flesh on my arms. I don't think any hears me, other than myself. The vampires' hunger has got the better of their curiosity, and they are scrambling up the bars to try and break through the ceiling of the guard's cell.

"Switch on your radio," I order, as the flesh on my claws recedes further, and the bones in my arm start to change shape. She reaches up to do so, but with a whimper drops her arm and crumples to her knees to pray.

"Switch on your radio," I repeat, and slam a hand against her bars. She stops praying, and stares in silence at the remains of titanium bars. The vampires don't stare for long this time, but they do stare.

"Switch it on," I snap. The thought has occurred to me that below ground, the humans probably still have some of their radios on. The guard obeys.

"Now call Kathleen Anchor," I continue.

"Kathleen Anchor?" the guard whispers into the myriad of noise, "Kathleen Anchor? Are you there?"

There is a fuzzy reply.

"No, but I can take her a message. Who's speaking, and why? Over."

Libby, I believe, on the other end.

"Sophia Brooks. Jack Hanov Himmerden wanted to speak to her."

"Tell her to seal Karl in the ship," I snap. Sophie passes it on, and I feel a wave of pain coming over me. The flesh on my arms, that which is left, anyway, is as solid as stone, but rotten. There is a grating sound, and it parts to allow backward hooks to press through, and I am driven to my knees as my entire body is enveloped in pain.

"Done," Sophia switches off her radio, "What was that for?"

I hold up my hands and concentrate.

"Get down," I grunt, and a tiny, yellow grain of sand appears in my hand as she obeys. I close my eyes and blow on it gently.

"What's he doing?" wonders the vampire called Alex, and then I feel the burst of heat, and the creature swoops out of my hands.

The screams don't even manage to start before the dragon dwindles back to a tiny yellow ball. Sophia whimpers, and I can see her patting out fires on her clothes as she stands up. I try and follow suit, but I cannot.

"What's wrong?" she demands. I try to shrug, but through the pain, I seem unable to tell my body what to do. The ash settles, and she steps back in surprise.

"Jack?" she asks uncertainly.

"Who else would it be?" my voice sounds like a stone being scraped on a blackboard – if you don't know what that is, it's a wooden board covered in black paint that teachers used to use chalk on up until the twenty-first century, to write notes for the children to copy. Chalk could make a bad enough sound on it, but nails and stones made an unbearable sound.

She nervously reaches out a hand, and I take it carefully. She squeals in pain as she pulls me up, and when my hand comes away, I can see the deep gauges my claws have left in her hands and wrist. She sucks the blood out of the wounds, and shrugs.

"I'll live."

I slash through the bars with my claws, and watch as they fall to the ground.

"I can't let you escape."

"Stop me, then."

Clearly, something else doesn't want me to leave, because another wave of pain hits me, and I almost crumple to the ground again. When it subsides, there is a sword buried up to its hilt in the left side of my chest, and my clothes have been replaced by a black, scratchy robe.

"If you go, they'll kill me," Sophia tries.

"If I stay, you'll kill me," I snap, "You can come with me if you must."

She hesitates, and I give up trying to unbolt the trapdoor and smash it. Sophia grabs the yellow ball and blows on it as the vampires swarm in, ignoring me, and this time the dragon escapes.

We wait for a while, and then, eventually, a slightly larger yellow ball rolls down the steps. Sophia, who had hurled herself to the floor, stands up again.

"What were those bangs?" she demands. I cannot answer, but when we get outside, the answer presents itself. The human ships have been destroyed, by fire, it seems, and the compound is deserted.

"I don't think I'm going to be attending my execution, somehow," I comment, and Sophia nods miserably.

"And I'm stuck on this damned planet."

I am pushed forwards by some invisible force, and fall face-first into the snow. There is another burst of pain, and when it ceases, a great weight is holding me down. I push with as much effort as I can, and come back to my feet. I start to fall backwards, but I instinctively move the weight, and regain my balance.

"Jack," Sophia's voice is below me now, "Is that normal?"

I look towards her voice, and see that I am in fact slowly floating back down to the snow, and I can see what the weight is – two huge, black-feathered wings jutting out of the dead flesh of my back, just below my shoulders.

"No," a worrying idea is starting to form in my mind, "No, it shouldn't be."

Sophia sighs, and puts a foot in a bubbling pool of water.

"It's warm," she comments and I grab her arm to pull her away from it.

"This is Earth," I explain, "Don't touch anything unusual."

"You're right, so I think I'll get into the hot spring and out of the forest on the ice."

"The forest is just an illusion," I snap, "I'm going home now." I flap the wings experimentally, and lift off the ground again. Once I have cleared the tops of the trees, I stare around to get my bearing, and see the bare patch of ice indicating the tunnel in the near distance.

It seemed a moment ago like it would have been so easy to fly straight there. Unfortunately, I have no such luck: my wings fold involuntarily; and I plunge down to the earth.

"What now?" I demand as Sophia comes to look down at me.

"I'm not sure how to say this, Jack," she frowns, and tugs something. My lower back screams in pain, and I see what she is holding up.

"Is that part of me?" I demand, snatching the blackened string of vertebrae from her; the burst of pain confirms that it is indeed attached to me. It's not that I'm not used to having a tail – I'm just not used to having a tail three metres long with less flesh on it than a fast-food restaurant's chicken nugget.

After about a hundred yards of it dragging in the snow, I decide flying is the better option. Now, however, I only fly high enough for my tail not to touch the ground – low enough for it not to hurt too much if I fall again.

It doesn't work. I land with my tail underneath me, the vertebrae complaining as several of them pop temporarily out of their joints.

"What's happening?" I demand. Sophia puts a hand to my head and brings it down with a thick wad of hair to explain.

"I can live without my hair," I shrug, and take off again, my tail creaking back into place as I do so.

And, just when I think perhaps the burst of pain have stopped, my wings start to move in maddened frenzy way as a series of bursts of pain rattle through my body.

"Jack?" Sophia ducks as I almost hit the ground, and then regain control, "Jack, are you okay?"

"I'm fine," I retort, landing carefully to inspect what damage.

"That looks painful," Sophia winces, and reaches out to touch my face. I look down to where her hand stops, and see curved black tusks sticking out just above my top lip, curling back slightly towards my ears. She puts a pudgy hand next to my eyes, and I realise something must have happened there as well.

"What is it?"

"They're not your eyes," she frowns, "there are no whites left – they're too bloodshot. Your pupils have gone like a cat's."

"Anything else?"

"Your face is changing shape. It's weird – only a bit – but it looks like it's being stretched a bit."

I swear, for no particular reason, under my breath, and look around.

"We're here," I announce in relief, "finally."

"Where exactly is here?" Sophia snorts. I choose not to reply with words, but walk into the mouth of the hidden tunnel instead. Sophia's eyes widen.

"It's just magic," I snort, "Can it really be that shocking."

And then I notice the direction of her gaze. It's not towards me, but towards the sky far above me. I follow her eyes, and see a tiny black dot growing rapidly larger above me.

"What is that?" I demand. She doesn't answer.

"It's falling fast," I shift my feet, "do you think we should get underground quickly? Before it hits one of us?"

She seems to be frozen, and I notice that the dot – now more of a blob – has changed course slightly – possibly due to the large, black sails that seem to be spread out on either side of it.

"Sophia, move," I warn. She doesn't move. I consider whether to leave her and dive for cover or try to move her.

The thing is very close now. I choose the second option, and fly into her, knocking her out of the way. It crashes to the ground behind me, and I let out a bellow of pain as my tail is forced into the ground. My tail snaps, and we turn to whatever it was.

We are presented with a hole in the ice, with jagged crystals of ice already threatening to close it. Looking down, I can see a human face twisted in terror, a massive pair of birds' wings, flared and snapped, and a pair of outstretched arms.

"A stone angel," whispers Sophia as the bones of my tail return from below the statue to the rest of my tail, "How did that get up there?"

Another shape thuds into the ice, and I grab her wrist and dash for the hole.

"We can ask Kathleen if we find her," I snap, "quickly." We plunge through the false layer of snow, and into the tunnel.

There are occasional small twinges of pain, but nothing I can't live with, and Sophia screams every time something peers out at us from a turning. I leave her to sort herself out as I roll off into the second turning on the left, and stand up.

Half a dozen werewolves or humans are staring at me, so I snarl loudly at them, and they, along with everyone else within fifty yards, flee. I hurry towards the back of the city, seeing Sophia out of the corner of my eye as she wobbles pathetically through the entrance.

"Oh dear," says a voice as I reach the ship, "Kathleen? We have a problem."

"What sort of problem?" Kathleen appears at the door, "I've got a pair of twins being born here – what is that?"

"It's me, Jack," I try to grin. Kathleen's face falls.

"That is a problem. Libby, call me if she starts to have trouble." Kathleen hurries down the steps, "What's wrong with him, Antoinette?"

"He really has the worst luck of all," Antoinette sighs, landing next to Kathleen, "The chances of this happening are about one in a trillion billion."

"What is happening?" I demand.

"There is a very malignant spirit approaching," Antoinette sighs, "You are susceptible to being possessed – susceptible enough for your body to start changing to make a suitable vessel for this malignant spirit to live in."

"What sort of malignant spirit?"

"Oh, you really don't need to know," Antoinette smiles gently, "don't want to know, really."

Sophia collapses at the steps, and rolls onto her back.

"Water," she gasps.

"Come in, Jack," Kathleen calls over her shoulder, disappearing into the ship. I fold my wings tight against my back and hurry up the steps, trying hard not to stand on my tail.

"Jack, this is Charlotte, Charlotte, Jack," Kathleen comments as we pass a Libby holding a baby for a woman half unconscious as she gives birth to another.

"Shouldn't she be anaesthetised or something?" Sophia puffs. Kathleen ignores her, and opens up the room I slept in.

"Can you sit down?" Kathleen frowns. I obey, tucking my tail underneath me, "Now, Antoinette, what do I have to do to reverse this process?"

Antoinette stares at her.

"You think I know? You think I've seen something like this happen before?"

"Haven't you?"

"I've only ever seen pictures of –" she glances at me, and hesitates "– of them. Something like this can't have happened since the tenth century after Christ."

"What am I becoming?" I demand.

"What is he becoming?" agrees Kathleen.

Antoinette hesitates.

"I think he might guess if he could see himself." Kathleen opens the cupboard door and turns the mirror to face me.

"I'm not there," I point out.

Kathleen stares.

"Someone spray water on the mirror," Antoinette sighs.

Kathleen waves a hand, and a reflection jumps into view from amongst the scattered droplets. My face seems to be what has changed without my knowledge – two black spikes of bone are sticking out at the back of my jaw, which has broadened considerably, my ears have been replaced with complicated slits in the side of me head, my nose has gone, to be replaced with two skeletal slits, and atop my now bald head, my skull has twisted out of shape to form two long, cow-like horns.

"Oh," is all I can say.

"Don't forget your feet," Antoinette points, and I tug up the scratchy black cloak to see them.

"This is your fault," Kathleen glares at Antoinette, once she has recovered from the sight of the hooves at the ends of my legs, "It was you who broke between the worlds.

"You would have broken all of them into one," Antoinette retorts, "I didn't realise I was carrying the strongest bad luck charm through the doorway. Otherwise I would have left you all to die in there."

"We could have found a black hole and come back through a sensible way!"

"You would have had to wait half a billion years at least!"

"What do we do now, then?" I snap. They take a while to work out that that's what I said, and they turn to me with a sympathetic smile and an irritated scowl.

"We'll work something out," Kathleen promises, stroking my wings gently, "Don't worry."

"There's nothing we can do," Antoinette shrugs, "You're doomed."

"I'll come down to purgatory and find you," Kathleen promises.

"There will be nothing to find."

We both turn back to Antoinette.

"Nothing to find?"

"That's what I said. Your soul will cease to exist."

"You're having a laugh," Kathleen snaps, "that can't happen."

"Well, I suppose I was exaggerating a little. You will cease to exist; your soul will become part of the dark angel which will inhabit your body. You'll not actually notice yourself going, you see, because your personality will simply become that of the dark angel, minus any knowledge, and your face will become its face, and then you will simply be a copy of the first with a solid form, which the first only has to touch to enter."

"How close is it?"

"When it enters the atmosphere, angels will start to fall to earth as stone."

I stare at her.

"Stone?"

"They can't move out of its path or they will fall, and become like it, in incredible torment and rage, but if they do not move out of its path they will turn to stone and be bound to the spirit realm for the rest of eternity."

"What, like you?"

"No, not like me. I was dead, and then I became an angel. They are dead angels."

"The stone angels were already falling."

"Oh dear," Antoinette bites her lip, "Were there kelpies out?"

I stare.

"They exist?"

"Clearly not, then. Good. That gives you about two more hours as Jack before you start to lose yourself."

"Why has God made it that this can happen?" Kathleen demands,

"You mortals," Antoinette laughs bitterly, "After all these years, you still blame God for everything, don't you? God made me get sick, God made my house burn down, God made me fuck a whore and she got pregnant."

"Nice," comments Sophia, wiping the sweat off her face.

"Jack," Kathleen reaches out a hand to me, "What do you want to do now?"

It takes me a while to realise that she means what I want to do before I die.

"Two hours," I consider. It doesn't seem possible. I can't have only two hours left to live. I don't feel like I'm dying.

"There's no way around this, Jack," Antoinette reads my face, "I'm sorry, but in just over two hours, the last vestiges of your personality will be gone forever." I have to say she doesn't sound as sorry as the last time it was her fault something possessed me.

I say nothing. I can't believe that after all the times people have tried to kill me and failed, some stupid cursed angel is going to manage.

"I could heal you," Kathleen offers.

"There's no point," Antoinette laughs harshly, "there's nothing to heal."

I stand up, and look outside.

"No time to see Cat, I suppose?"

"No," Kathleen shakes her head, "By the time she was defrosted, you'd be gone."

We stand in silence for a moment, and Antoinette turns away and walks out of the door.

"Charlotte's sleeping," Libby pokes her head through the same door, shudders, and retreats.

"You're not supposed to do this, Jack," Kathleen lets go of my hand to close the door. We sit back down.

"I don't seem to have much choice in the matter." I consider as she takes my clawed fingers in her soft white hands.

"No, but," Kathleen looks as shocked as I feel about my fate, "But I'll be the last one left."

"I'm sure Elizabeth's still alive."

Kathleen smiles.

"And Caitlin."

"Maybe Elizabeth remembers me," I shrug.

"How could she not?" Kathleen turns and smiles, "You weren't exactly having the best time of your life then, were you?"

Elizabeth is an immortal, like Kathleen, whose worst memories become solid beings. Caitlin was the memory of her murdered daughter, which Kathleen healed.

"You wouldn't be alone then," I laugh. The knowledge that every moment that passes is a moment closer to my end doesn't seem to have had any real effect on me yet.

"It wouldn't be you," Kathleen grips my hand so hard I expect hers to bleed; "There is only one Jack."

She moves a little closer to me, and wraps her arms around my chest. She shifts uncomfortably to avoid the sword, and I move my hands carefully around her.

"What will you do now?" she whispers, and I can hear her crying.

"More things than I could."

"I could stop time," she sits up, "I could stop time forever so that it would never get here. And you'd never die, and –" she breathes in deeply, "Stop!" she commands. A nearby door stops squeaking on its hinges, and the quiet snores from the new mother cease. Antoinette's head pokes through the metal door.

"I'm afraid that this won't work. Heaven and purgatory and angels and demons don't follow time like you do."

Kathleen's shoulders sag, and the snores resume.

"I'm sorry," she whispers once Antoinette's head has vanished. We sit there, silent, for perhaps a quarter of an hour, holding on to our only witnesses to our whole lives.

"There must be something you want to see," Kathleen whispers eventually, "one thing, somewhere."

"One thing?"

"Anything."

I think about this. What do I most want to do before I die – well, one of the things on the list is out because I wouldn't like to die with Kathleen sick of me. Selfishly, I find comfort in the feeling that someone will miss me.

"Could we go to where Jade is buried?" I ask eventually.

Kathleen looks up at me silently, then nods, and I think both of us find our minds on the space next to Jade's grave where I would have been buried, but never will be now. I won't live to die.

We both know exactly where it is – as the ice thickened, we marked it every day with a wooden cross, moving it up so that it was always on top of the ice. It's not far, really.

It takes longer than normal to get out of the tunnel. When we do emerge into the light half an hour later, thick, black clouds are threatening to block out what sun there is. The bubbling pools of hot water are starting to join together, and shadows are moving below the surface.

"Kelpies," Kathleen points, and a horse's head, black with silver rings around its eyes, lifts out of the steam.

"It's beautiful," I whisper, as the creature comes towards us.

"Careful, Jack," Kathleen whispers, "They're demons."

"So am I," I point out, as the creature stops in front of me, "Anyway, what's it going to do, kill me?"

Kathleen opens her mouth to protest as I climb onto the creature's back and seize the bulrush mane, and I half expect it to plunge back into its pond and devour me – or at least try. It doesn't seem to have any such intention, instead walking quietly alongside Kathleen.

"It's working out how to get us both," Kathleen grumbles as the creature sniffs her.

"It could just be making sure I stay intact for when the dark angel arrives," I point out, "Its master won't be very pleased if its vessel has been eaten." I glance around, "It would be better if there were two."

Another creature, this time with a red ring around its eyes, appears, and goes down onto its knees in front of Kathleen. Nervously, she climbs on top of it, and wraps her hands into its bulrush mane as it stands up. The two creatures start to trot, and then canter, and then we're there.

They vanish from beneath us, and their shadows move away to a respectful distance – possibly because of the cross.

"Hello, Jade," I whisper, sitting down in the snow. I don't know what to say to her – silly really, as she isn't even here, but I feel that somehow, somewhere, she can hear me here.

Kathleen untangles Jade's silver crucifix from the top of the cross, and kisses it before kneeling next to me.

"Here," she holds it out to me, "You should keep this."

I hold out my blackened palm, and the little silver chain drops into it.

There is a quiet hiss, and I let out an involuntary bellow of pain. The crucifix hits the ice, and Kathleen snatches my wounded hand.

"I'm sorry," she whispers, and the cross-shaped hole closes.

"I should have expected it," I whisper, and look helplessly at the crucifix on the ice. Kathleen's free hand reaches down and picks it up, before draping it back over the cross.

And there we sit, for an hour or more, silent. As I start to drift off into sleep, Kathleen looks up at my face.

"Jack?" she whispers, and I stare back at her.

"Of course," I reply.

"Your face," she pushes herself into my wing, "It isn't yours anymore."

I consider this for a moment.

"How much time do I have?"

"None at all," there is a click as an already frozen tear hits the ice, "you've had two hours and ten minutes."

I swallow.

"I still feel like me."

"You don't look like it anymore," she whispers.

There is silence, not as long this time, or as comfortable. I start to imagine it within me, the loss of my thoughts, and finding someone else's there instead. Soon I don't know if I am me anymore. I don't know if I really am still here, or if my thoughts don't recognise that they are changing.

And then I realise, slowly, sickeningly, that I don't remember my name.

"Who am I?" I ask Kathleen carefully.

"Jack," she whispers, "You're Jack."

"Jack," I say slowly. It sounds funny to say it. "Jack."

She looks up at me, and I know she is Kathleen, and I know she is good, but I don't know where we are.

"What is this place?" I ask her.

"This is where we left Jade."

"Jade?"

Kathleen is crying now, but I don't understand why.

"Let's take you home, Jack."

"Where is home?"

Kathleen shivers.

"Don't bring the kelpies, Jack. We'll walk."

"Why not fly?" I don't understand why she wants to walk – flying is so much faster. I flick my tail into a tree and it vanishes in a puff of smoke. I smile in satisfaction.

"Why did you do that, Jack?"

Her questions are starting to irritate me. Who is Jack, anyway?"

"Because I can," I snap, and this time, when her eyes puff up, I'm glad. I don't know why I wasn't last time. She looks stupid when she cries.

"Let's just go home," she whispers eventually.

Why? Why even have a home? And why does she want to take me to her home?

Something stirs in my groin. I think I'll humour her for now.

Water is coming out of her eyes fast now. It's fun to flick the little ice-drops with my tail as they fall. We stop, and the woman peers into a hole in our path. A stone angel lies at the bottom of it. I laugh.

"Stop it," she rounds on me, "Stop it, Jack! This isn't funny, and it isn't you!"

I shrug.

"People change. It happens all the time." I slap the statue with my tail and it shatters.

The woman stares at me.

"I'm sorry, Jack," she whispers, and squeezes my hand, "It's not your fault."

She falls silent, and then we reach a hidden tunnel.

"Is this home?"

"This is home," she nods, and we start to walk down the tunnel. Some people are walking towards us, but when I try and turn them to ash, nothing happens. I shrug, and walk on.

We reach a place full of people, but they aren't there. Only an angel – hideous and shimmering. I glare at her for a while, and she glares back before cursing me. Perhaps not as grotesque as I thought, then.

And then there is a machine. At first I think perhaps it is made to kill, but then I see that the two woman and two small humans are asleep, not dead. Still, the labour and pain that must have gone into the machine are enough to make it worthwhile.

"You've hardly any time left at all," the angel tells the woman. The woman pushes open a door, and I see a bed. At last.

She sits me down on the bed, and sits next to me.

"Thirty seconds," She squeezes my hands, "I'll miss you, Jack."

"Kathleen," the angel calls, and tumbles out of the way as a darker spirit pushes past. "Kathleen, it's too late. You must get out of there, quickly!"

"I'm sorry that you had to hear it now," the water is pouring off her face, "But –" the dark spirit is close enough to smell. It is the rest of me. The missing part that let the angel not turn to stone.

I am behind the woman, reaching out for me.

"I love you, Jack," the woman cries, and then her face is against mine, her mouth against mine, ignoring my tusks, and I am stepping into me, completing me, and then –

Darkness.

I open my eyes to a bright, cold light, and taste the salty tears on my – my – face. She – I can't remember her name – is holding me, crying, sobbing into my chest. I can't remember who I am, either, but this feels right.

"Don't cry," I whisper, and she raises her head slowly.

"Jack," she sniffs.

"Kathleen," I realise.

"I'm sorry," she stands up, and starts pushing herself away from me, "I thought I'd lost you, I didn't know you were –"

"I love you," I interrupt, and suddenly every memory I have ever had comes flooding into my mind, and I stand up to be closer to Kathleen.

"I love you, Kathleen Anchor," I breathe, "I love you." I hesitate, "I think I've always loved you."

And suddenly the past sixty-eight thousand, six hundred and ninety- six years make sense. Our world may be in ruins, there may be an angel kneeling outside the door eavesdropping on every word we say, there may even be another dark angel coming to try again, but nothing matters.

Nothing at all, except my pillar, my rock, my Anchor, my Kathleen.

Epilogue

The Earth lies in tatters. Hundreds of stone statues littered the ice, and hundreds more angels were kneeling around them, not crying, but sad.

As for the human army, they are no more. We have not killed them, but after learning that Kerrow had betrayed them, most of them betrayed her right back.

I'm sorry to say that Kerrow wasn't the only reason for this. Several humans were killed by one of the other scars left by the war. The kelpies, which still seem to obey me, have not vanished as the dark angels were banished to a new universe, and have dragged, among others, a girl named Polly to her death in their boiling depths. They do, fortunately, seem disinterested in everything but adult humans

We cannot save the humans by sending them to Europa – everything except communications has been destroyed, and it will be several centuries before a receptor station can be built on Venus or Mars.

I don't really know why I've told you all this. I'm sure there was a reason, but now it feels like I've told everything there is to tell, and my life has no governing moral. It only has Kathleen – now, nine and a half months after she saved me, with our baby ready to be born. And this, no matter what happens afterwards, is my happy ending.

Goodbye.

Aleksander Granger

I would like to thank:

One biology teacher for boring my socks off,
Another for stealing my chocolate,
And a third for generally making me feel sick.
The fourth, and final, biology teacher is thanked for helping me to survive the other three.

I would also like to thank:

Jessica Irwin for her help with editing, Mikaela Jones, Ashley Lane and Katie Jones (not, so far as I know, related to Mikaela) for her encouragement, and Fatima Vally for providing the inspiration for several of the original, unpublished characters, as well as the original inspiration for Kathleen.

Also Richard "Sniffles" Nicholson, Jordan Abbot and Elise VanCise for their suggestions, which I think I have followed as closely as possible.

On a slightly more personal note, I would like to thank all the people who have made me who I am for making me who I am. If you hadn't screwed me up so completely, I wouldn't be who I am currently, I would be someone else who I currently am not.

I won't name and shame you yet.

Yet.

I would also like to thank anyone who actually bought this, and anyone who actually read through to the end without burning it. I would recommend a psychiatrist, but I don't know any.

Finally, I would like to thank Mrs L Seshmani and Miss J. Aitken for their unfaltering efforts to educate me. They may have failed, but they came the closest anyone could possibly come to succeeding. Thank you.

This page is me. Uncensored, unedited, me.

Woohoo!

I have finished this edition.

I have actually finished this book. Properly and finally. Not just a draft.

This IS the book. Finished.

This book is finished. As in done. Nothing more for me to add.

It feels good. It's the first properly finished book.

As for Jack and Kathleen, they've had their happy ending.

Do you ever feel a bitter emptiness at the end of something like this?

Don't worry. I asked myself enough questions to write more about them. Well, around them, at least.

But you don't have to worry. As Jack said, nothing that happens afterwards can break what they have had. It is a happy ending, and it can only be a happy ending now.

And for everyone else, you're not Jack. Not this Jack, anyway. You don't have the worst luck in the universe. Bad things have happened to you, bad things will happen to you in the future, but the only thing that really matters is the good things.

I feel all preachy and Bohemian.

Goodnight.

www.ingramcontent.com/pod-product-compliance
Lightning Source LLC
Chambersburg PA
CBHW020438180626
46812CB00003B/1290